Engine Nine

by

Bradley W. Wright

Justin Vincent Series, Book 3

This is a work of fiction. Names, characters, places, and incidents are either the product of the author's imagination or are used fictitiously, and any resemblance to actual persons living or dead, business establishments, events, or locales, is entirely coincidental.

Engine Nine

Contact Information: info@thewildrosepress.com

Cover Art by *Jennifer Greeff*

The Wild Rose Press, Inc.
PO Box 708
Adams Basin, NY 14410-0708
Visit us at www.thewildrosepress.com

Publishing History
First Edition, 2023
Trade Paperback ISBN 978-1-5092-4661-8
Digital ISBN 978-1-5092-4662-5

Justin Vincent Series, Book 3
Published in the United States of America

"Are there others here?" I asked, shaken, trying not to show it. "Like us? Chosen, I guess. Although I don't really know what that means. Fonseco keeps telling me I'm here for some purpose. He took me to see Eleanor Jane Sibyl today and she said something about all nine. Three threes…"

Oak and Malena looked at me blankly.

"It's a great honor to meet her," Oak said after a moment. "You and I and Malena, we're the only ones here. Three of us chosen ones. We'll learn about our mission soon. We have great work to do. Elder Fonseco told me too. He said we will have the most important role in the jubilee. Our actions will help move us into the next era of mankind."

"When is it happening?" I asked. "The jubilee celebration."

"Solstice Eve. Only a few days to go." Oak smiled and nodded.

Finally, after a couple of hours of wine and food and conversation, they left.

I sat on the couch, thinking through what I had learned. It was December 16th according to my watch. Only five days until whatever they were planning was going to take place. ICBMs? A screaming across the sky? World War III? What role were the chosen ones supposed to play? Would Eleanor Jane Sibyl be standing on a stage, face raised to the sky triumphantly as the ground rumbled and the rockets lifted off? Were these maniacs even capable of what they were planning? It was, in fact, rocket science—legendarily difficult to get right.

I needed to get out and find a way to warn someone in authority.

Chapter 1

Acapulco Gold
9/30 - 10/17: Acapulco and Culver City

A moth brushed my ear, bumping me with surprising mass, then faded away into the night.

"That moth was the size of a small dog."

Ashna shifted next to me. "Something's going to wander by and eat us before this asshole finally goes to bed, she whispered. "What do they have out here? Jaguars?"

"I'd worry more about the mosquitos. And the spiders. Let me see the binoculars."

From our perch on the hillside I could survey the sprawling grounds of Wayne Abbot's Acapulco compound—bounded by a high stone wall and surrounded on all sides by a dense tumult of tropical foliage. I had snuck in the previous night and cased the grounds so I knew the wall was easy to get over but it did look imposing from the outside. The house and landscaping could be described as rat pack modern, or maybe mid-century tropic. Multi-level terraces dotted with water features, trailing green vines, and creepers rose up to the main building—a two story block of glass and concrete, still and dark. A couple of single-story wings, their slab-like roofs overhanging glass volumes, jutted out at right angles framing the obligatory Olympic

1

size pool which stretched out behind the house. Dim underwater lights gave the rectangle of water a blue-green glow. If I let my eyes unfocus it looked like an elongated, apple flavored Jolly Rancher. Gentle ripples spread across the pool's surface provoked by Mr. Wayne Abbot, the master of the estate himself, who sat on the edge, feet in the water, clutching a nearly empty rocks glass.

A frail old man in a long white tunic and pants approached. He carried a full glass on a silver tray. Negasi Solomon was the man's name, Abbot's long-time servant. According to Wikipedia, Abbot had hired him when filming on location in Ethiopia thirty years ago and had been employing him ever since. Without looking up, Abbot held out his empty. Solomon took it, pressed the new one into Abbot's palm, and headed back into the house.

Still lean and strong despite his age, Abbot looked like he could swim a few laps if he wanted to. Instead he was getting drunk—something he did every night if the pattern I had observed over the last few days was any indication. He had been a big star in the sixties with a string of tough guy cop movies. Back then, he was married to my client Linda Darien. Her third marriage, his second. Casting back, I pictured Linda seated on Julian Wolhardt's living room sofa. Wolhardt was a film composer. Ashna and I had done a job for him and he had introduced me to Linda who also needed a job done.

She looked small and fragile that day, asking me for help but still possessing the ineffable aura of celebrity that is so hard to describe. The constant awareness of the self as an object of others' attention? An outward projection of a carefully honed, workshopped, and market-tested personality?

"What's missing?" I asked her.

"Something very important to me," she answered, gazing out into Wolhardt's immaculate back yard. "My Oscar."

"The statue itself?" I didn't know she had won an Oscar but I wasn't surprised. In her heyday, she was a big name in Hollywood—a serious actress who starred in dramas and big budget period films with casts of thousands.

"Yes, the statue. It was stolen from my home two weeks ago to the day."

"I'm sorry to hear that. I don't know if I can help though. It's not the sort of thing I would normally take on. Have you filed a police report?"

"Yes, of course. The police came and took a report. They can't help me though. I'm very certain I know who stole it. There are two people in particular who would have gone to the trouble. You know, of course, that the statues are not worth much?"

"I guess not if they're stolen. I've heard of a few fetching decent auction prices but those would be legitimate sales."

"Precisely."

"Why do you say the police can't help?"

"If my suspicion is correct, it was stolen by one of my ex-husbands. I have several but only two of them are suspects in my opinion. Both were incredibly jealous that my career was more illustrious than theirs. They both saw my Oscar as a symbol of that."

"Do you have any proof of this?"

"Just my intuition. The burglar took only the Oscar. Nothing else was touched. I have a fair amount of art and jewelry. There's an Albrecht Durer woodcut right above the mantle where I kept the Oscar. A thief would have taken it all. It was someone who knew about the Oscar, was only interested in taking that one thing, and was not taking it for any monetary value." She sat back, hands folded in her lap, gazing at me defiantly. It was an actor's gaze. She might have been Cleopatra or Catherine the Great surveying the ranks of an invading army.

"Do you have a security system?"

"Yes. And it worked exactly as it is supposed to. However, the man monitoring the system at the security company headquarters took a conveniently timed trip to the restroom at precisely the moment of the break in. He claimed he had stomach trouble and was in the bathroom for ten minutes. I think he was paid off by someone to delay alerting the police until it was too late."

"Sounds like a professional job."

"I've switched companies of course."

"Which of your ex-husbands do you suspect Ms. Darien?"

"Wayne or Fernando. It has to be one of them."

Julian Wolhardt shook his head. "Linda, we've been friends for a long time. I know both of them. Both are utter assholes. But, I can't see how it would be Fernando. He at least has principles."

"You may be right, Julian." She placed a hand on Wolhardt's arm.

I had a check from Wolhardt in my shirt pocket. My payment for completing the job for him. A large sum. Half of it would go to Ashna but it was still a lot of money. More than that, though, I was tired. I was still recovering from the job both physically and mentally. Questioning what I had seen in the chapel of the old

Powick Asylum. Questioning my choices, my life.

"Where does this Wayne live and who is he?" I asked out of politeness, trying to keep my lack of enthusiasm from showing. I was ninety percent sure I didn't want the job.

"Wayne?" Linda Darien looked taken aback. "Surely you've heard of Wayne Abbot? He has a sort of compound outside of Acapulco. He bought it back in the sixties when it was still the fashionable place to be. Now it's overrun by drug gangs but Wayne is holding on. He always did. Stubborn. He barely leaves the compound from what I've heard."

"I can't believe you convinced me to take this stupid job," I said without moving the binoculars away from Abbot.

"It's Linda Dairen, dude! You don't say no to someone like her. Think about how many jobs could come from doing this one. Besides, she was my first crush. In Joan of Arc. The armor. The sword. The suffering."

"Your brain does not work normally. You realize that, right?"

"You're one to talk."

"Anyway, I don't like it. Too much like a smash and grab."

Ashna had done the leg work on the job. Or, in her case, the finger work. She had managed to access Wayne Abbot's phone history and found several calls to and from a number in LA around the time of the theft. The number turned out to have been assigned to a burner phone. That was enough to convince her Abbot was our suspect. He had hired someone in LA to steal the Oscar.

"This is not going to be a smash and grab…" Ashna

fell silent for a moment as a spectral bird call echoed like a distant siren through the damp, warm air. "Not if my laser works. Why won't this asshole go to bed?"

I checked my watch. "It's on the early side. He stayed out until eleven forty-seven last night."

Ten minutes later, Abbot finally tossed off the dregs in his glass, rose unsteadily, and lumbered into the house. We had watched him for four nights running. Every evening, he sat by the pool or in front of the TV and drank. He had an enormous capacity. Eventually, though, usually around midnight, he would climb the stairs to his master suite, flop onto his bed and pass out.

I turned the binoculars to the grounds. Abbot had three private security guards, two patrolling the perimeter and one stationed near the gate in a small outbuilding. A local security company supplied the guards who rotated through three shifts. So, nine guards altogether each day. It couldn't be cheap. The overnight shift had just arrived and would stay until seven a.m. when their replacements arrived. A housekeeper and cook worked inside the compound during the day but left at night to go back to their own families. Lastly, there was Abbot's manservant who had brought him the booze. We hadn't seen him do much other than keep Abbot good and drunk. A pretty easy job but not one I would want. He spent most of his time in the main house on the ground floor where he had a small room.

I found one of the guards with the binoculars. He stumbled along just inside the wall on the far side of the compound, looking at his phone screen. The security did not seem particularly worried or attentive. It was undoubtedly a lucrative contract for their employer. A portion of the fee probably went to pay off the local gangs. With the gangs paid off, there was not much for the guards to do. I didn't blame them for taking it easy. It didn't make me less wary of them though. They looked tough and efficient—maybe former gang members themselves, or former military.

I moved the glasses back to the house, focusing on Abbot's master suite which stretched around one corner of the second floor along with its cantilevered private balcony. In all of our surveillance we had never seen Abbot use the balcony. The sliding doors remained closed and probably locked. Those doors were my best route in. I turned the little wheel on the binoculars and focused on the dim interior of the suite. It was still there, the statue—a dull gold glint in the darkness, standing on the mantle of a brick fireplace at the far end of the room. Linda Darien knew her ex-husband well.

The house had a good security system. Everything was alarmed—out of date but effective magnetic contacts that would alert the guards if any window or door was opened without disabling that node of the system. We needed to disable the alarm on Abbot's sliding doors before I went in for the statue. The system could be controlled by phones and smart speakers located around the house. Using a long-distance mic, we had listened to Solomon as he went about locking up for the night once his employer finally went to bed. Bypassing magnetic sensors was something I had done before but it was tricky and never foolproof. Simply turning the alarm off via the controls was a much better option if we could achieve it. Ashna, who I had never previously known to fail, had so far been unable to hack the system but she had a cool idea that would save us a lot of trouble if it worked. That was why we were sitting on the side of a hill under a canopy of camo netting with a laser on a tripod hooked up to a laptop. It wasn't easy to pack in and set up but if it worked, all the effort would be amply rewarded.

Soft ceiling lights glowed to life and Abbot came lumbering into the room. Through the big sliding doors, I saw him collapse onto the bed, sprawling with one arm pinned under his body. He had to be really out of it.

"Isn't he going to brush his teeth?"

"Dentures."

"What?" Ashna slapped my shoulder.

"Yeah. He has full dentures. Top and bottom. Liked to eat candy. Starlight mints. Always had a bowl of them in his trailer when he was filming. Didn't like to brush. It's all there in his Wikipedia article."

"Aren't you supposed to take them out at night and like, put them in a glass on your bedside table. I feel like that's what people do."

"No idea. He's not doing anything until morning though. Look at him." I handed Ashna the binoculars.

"Bird's asleep, too."

"The servant put it to bed two hours ago." Abbot had an Amazon parrot. At night, it stayed in a big cage in his bedroom with a cloth draped over it. During the day, it rode around on his shoulder and pooped on the floor.

"Yeah. I think it's time. You ready?"

"Yes."

"Okay. So the trick here was discovered by a cybersecurity guy I've met a couple of times. Takeshi Sugawara. Smart dude. Turns out if you point a laser at a microphone and change the intensity at a precise frequency, the light perturbs the microphone's membrane at that same frequency. We can use that trick to essentially give voice commands to a smart speaker via a beam of light. So, that speaker on Abbot's dresser is our target. We're going to tell it to disable the alarm on the balcony door."

"Got it."

"I just need to get it aimed right." Ashna fiddled with the little wheels on the tripod mount, changing the angle by degrees, using a rifle site attached to the laser. "Okay, I think I've got it. Do you see the dot on the speaker?"

"Yeah. Little red dot right on the mic grill."

"Good. I'm going to send the command."

I kept the binoculars trained on the speaker. It had an LED that turned blue when listening and then flashed purple to green when a command had been heard and understood. I was watching for the color change that would tell us Ashna's trick had worked. Ashna tapped at the keyboard of her laptop.

"Sending."

"Copy that." I saw the LED turn blue, then a moment later purple/green—the signal we were hoping for.

"Anything?"

"Unbelievable. I think you did it!"

"Hardly unbelievable. The opposite in fact. It's science."

I watched Abbot for another minute. The speaker would have replied aloud to the command but he didn't seem to have heard it. His back rose and fell slowly, rhythmically.

"Okay. I'm going in."

"Don't get yourself killed Justin. I'll pack up while you get the statue."

"I'll do my best," I said, squinting at the house while pulling on a backpack full of the gear I would need. I could feel her gaze on me. "What?" I asked, turning. Dappled moonlight shifted across her face as a breath of wind rustled the netting above us.

"I'm serious. You scared me last time. No blows to the head this time."

"I know. I'll be careful," I said, picking up my pack and pulling it on. "If you see anything weird, cut their satellite connection. We don't want them calling for backup." I had found the main cable from the compound's satellite internet connection during my earlier reconnaissance and installed a remote-controlled switch of my own design—basically just a little battery powered solenoid-actuated guillotine with a radio receiver—that could cut it in an instant. Ashna had the remote.

"Got it," Ashna said, nodding.

The hills surrounding Acapulco are mainly savanna or scrubland with patches of low tropical forest. Our hillside was forested with gourd trees and palms that rustled in a light breeze off the ocean. A thick layer of leaves blanketed the forest floor with grasses, wild marigolds, and other viny plants poking up through the mulch in clumps. Strewn along the hillside, almost like steppingstones, were half buried boulders and exposed rock faces. I kept to the stones, moving silently down the slope. A gecko darted around a tree trunk. Far off, I heard a parrot squawk. We had arrived in Acapulco just at the end of the rainy season but there had been a brief shower earlier in the day. Musty, warm air rose from the leaves and dirt, smelling of rot.

The stone wall surrounding the compound rose ten

feet above the forest floor. The night before, I had made use of a banyan tree obligingly butting up against the wall. I headed that way, found the tree again, and pulled myself up. Crouching on a branch, hidden in the foliage, I watched the grounds.

I would need to time things just right. The two guards on patrol walked the perimeter opposite each other. Each guard took about sixteen minutes to complete a circuit. So, one would pass my position every eight minutes. I wanted to wait for the next guard to pass, hold until he was well away, then drop down and make my way across to Abbot's balcony before the next guard arrived. Lights shone here and there on the foliage and fountains but between them lay deep patches of shadow I could use as cover. I wasn't worried about being spotted as long as I was careful. On my reconnaissance visit the previous evening I had managed to creep around the place for twenty minutes without being detected.

I leaned back, resting against a bend in the branch and watched, trying to make myself one with the tree. I beathed in the rich aroma of jungle, the tropical flowers that grew in lush profusion around Abbot's house, and the slight nose-sting of chlorine from the pool. I heard a TV show, actors speaking dramatic Spanish. Probably the guard in the gate house or Abbot's manservant. A crunching of gravel, distant then closer. The guard passing by. His face, lit by his phone's screen, looked spectral, surreal. I had shifted into the flow state. After all the planning, when the action starts, everything goes hyperreal. Attuned to a thousand inputs, processing and synthesizing, I build a real time model in my mind that can run scenarios and predict outcomes, allowing me to act instantly when the unexpected occurs.

I watched his back recede until he rounded a bend in the path. Silently, I lowered myself to the top of the wall, hung, and dropped, my landing muffled by the thick turf. Forty feet away, a blank concrete wall rose up to Abbot's balcony. I darted through the plantings, up onto a terrace, across a lawn cropped like a putting green, and crouched low behind a tall clump of pampas grass. The balcony was right above my head, twelve feet up, with a tubular steel railing. I withdrew a small, collapsible grappling hook attached to a length of aramid rope from my pack. The hook was strong and lightweight and coated with a layer of EVA foam to keep it from clanging when it hit metal. My first toss was good. The device caught on Abbot's railing, biting in. I climbed the rope, wrapped fingers around the cool steel, and climbed over, pulling the rope up and shoving it back into my pack.

I watched, flattened out on the floor of the balcony, waiting for the next guard to pass below. One minute, two. Finally, he came strolling along. I smelled his cigarette first, then saw the orange glow of the tip, then his face. He passed by without a glance in my direction.

I stood then, crouching, and went to the sliding door. The alarm was off but the door was probably locked. Abbot still lay in the same position. I used a little flashlight to examine the inside door handle through the glass. As I had suspected, it had a rocker switch on the handle that engaged the lock—standard for the time period the house was built. I took a two-part telescoping baton from my pack, opened them both and screwed them together. Sliding doors like Abbot's were generally big enough that you could flex the whole door to create a gap where the door frame met the fixed window frame. I pulled, slipped the baton through the gap, and carefully inched it along until the tip was against the button. Steady pressure flipped the rocker, disengaging the lock. Again, I crouched low and flattened myself on the balcony.

A couple of minutes later, the first guard passed again, still watching a video on his phone. His outline faded into the night and I stood. The door slid open easily, soft on its tracks.

Abbot's master suite smelled like whiskey, sweat, and bird. I wanted to leave the door open but I also didn't want to attract attention so I slid it closed and turned to face the room. Walls painted in a brown so dark they were nearly black. Leather club chairs. Terra cotta tile with Navajo rugs. Brass lamps. A room Hemingway would have approved–maybe even an interior designer's faithful recreation of his bedroom in Cuba.

I tiptoed to the far side where the Oscar stood on the mantle. Strange that he would keep it right there, in plain sight of anyone who visited his room. Maybe no one ever did though, aside from his servant and the cleaning lady. Why steal an Oscar from your ex-wife if you are not going to stare at it and gloat? I wrapped it in a soft cloth I had brought and put in my pack. Abbot still snored softly. Heading back toward the door, I skirted the foot of the bed, making the widest possible circle, passing close to the birdcage. Something rustled inside. A mumbling bird voice. I froze.

"Negasi," the bird mumble-croaked. "Night night. Negasi."

My heartbeat quickened. Why was the bird saying Abbot's manservant's name? Then I heard footsteps from outside the room, approaching. I froze and cast my eyes about the room, looking for a hiding place. The walk-in closet seemed my best bet. I ducked in, pulling the door almost closed.

A moment later, the bedroom door swished open and a low light flicked on in the room. Negasi Solomon passed by—just a white blur through the crack.

"Night night. Negasi," The bird said again. There was a rustle of fabric and I heard Solomon whispering to the bird and shushing it.

"Bitch's Oscar!" The bird shrieked. "Bitch's Oscar!"

"Shhh. You'll wake Mr. Abbot. What about it?" There was a pause. "Where is it?"

"Bitch's Oscar," the bird mumbled.

"Oh, dear. Not good," Solomon said. Sound of a phone being lifted from its cradle. Then rapid Spanish. I caught a few words—Oscar, perdido, ladrón. The phone slammed down and Solomon's footsteps hurried from the room. I opened the closet door a bit wider and looked out. Abbot was still snoring. I squeezed through the opening but just as I stepped out, Abbot shifted and raised his head. He stared at me blearily, eyes unfocused.

"Who the hell are you?" He slurred, heaving himself up, took a step toward me and threw a wild punch. I ducked it easily, stepped in, and hit him hard on the temple. I knew I was risking a broken hand but there was no time to waste. Abbot slumped back onto the bed like a rag doll and lolled there, mouth open.

Flood lights blinked on, one by one, spotlighting the grounds outside. The guards would be on high alert now. I took a deep breath and considered for a moment, allowing my eyes to unfocus while I calmed myself and planned. Going back over the wall would be dangerous. Ashna should have cut the internet when the flood lights turned on. There was no cell service and no other way to call anyone outside the compound. That meant they would send a guard down the hill for backup. They would want to search the grounds and surrounding area. Parked in the garage was a jeep the guards used. I needed to get to it before they left.

Mind made up, I strode from the room. Outside a dark corridor stretched out, crossing the full length of the wing. At the far end, stairs leading down, doors on either side. I hurried past. Solomon would be back soon. I raced down the steps and into a massive living room with low, modern sofas and chairs and floors of coffee colored tropical hardwood. Long shadows stretched toward the center of the room, cast by the light pouring in from outside. I heard Solomon's voice. Another voice. I darted through and into a kitchen, found a pantry and slipped in, door pulled closed. Footsteps clomped up stairs. They would see that Abbot had been knocked out. A door off the kitchen led to another wing where Solomon's room was located and probably laundry and storage and other utilities.

In the hallway I pulled open a door. Supply closet. I grabbed a blanket from a shelf, continued. At the end, a door into the garage where the Jeep was kept along with Abbot's Range Rover and the gardeners' tools. The roll up doors stood open, grounds lit brightly beyond. I pulled open the Jeep's back hatch. A mess of bags, oil cans, fast food debris, and Mexican football periodicals littered the cargo space. I wrapped up in the blanket and dove into the mess, pulling the blanket on top of me, leaving an arm free to pull the hatch closed.

One minute, two. I waited. Stifling, hot air bunched around me. Sweat ran into my eyes. Finally, I heard muffled voices. A door slammed. Someone climbed into the driver seat and started the engine. We were moving slowly. I heard the gate open. Mariachi music came on the radio. The Jeep's worn-out shocks bounced as we trundled over the wooden bridge that connected the driveway to the main road. Just a little longer. The driver couldn't go too fast on the bumpy road. I waited until we were well away from the compound then opened the back hatch, holding it to keep it from flying open. The driver had the windows open, the music loud. I dropped out, shoving the hatch closed with all my strength as I fell.

Cushioned by the blanket, I hit the dirt road with a jarring smack and rolled a few times, ending up in a ditch full of vines and creepers. I lay still while the sound of the jeep's engine droned away into the night, wet ground soaking up through my blanket. Weirdly, I had a strong urge to close my eyes and take a nap. I fought the urge successfully, struggled free of the damp blanket, and limped into the trees.

Skirting the outer edge of the hillside, I stayed well away from the house and grounds–a slower but safer escape. Ashna was not pleased when I finally scrambled back into our hideout on the hillside.

"Jesus Justin. What the fuck? What happened?"

"I'll tell you while we walk. C'mon, we need to get clear of this area."

We had come in overland. On the far side of the mountain ridge from Abbot's compound the Jardín Botánico de Acapulco sprawled across many acres of hillside. Our rented car waited near the entrance, on an overgrown side road leading to a dead end. A long walk in the dark dominated our near future plans—plenty of time to give Ashna a blow by blow.

"Can you zip this for me?" I asked, I had loaded a few things into my backpack.

"What happened to your hand?"

"Let's just say Abbot has a hard skull."

Chapter 2

A Phone Call
11/20: San Francisco

Gulls flying low, feathers fluttering in the chill wind. Waves sloshing algae-covered pilings. The smell of ocean somehow clean and cloying all in one. I watched a commercial fisher heading out toward the mouth of the bay, hazy Alcatraz, and the Marin Headlands silver gray in the distance.

Ishmael's cure for a damp, drizzly, November of the soul was to get to sea. Mine was a little less drastic: take a day off from everything and just bike the city, crisscrossing back and forth, rounding the perimeter, up the seven hills and down, stopping here and there for coffee, lunch, or to browse one of my favorite bookshops or galleries. Today was one of those days. Just after ten a.m. and I had already done twelve miles. One of my favorite coffee shops in the city inhabited a section of the building that had once been Fort Mason's gatehouse. I was half afraid to stop, wondering if it would still be in business.

The pandemic had worked a change in the city. A lot of tech jobs went permanent telecommute. A lot of young people left—moved away to less expensive markets where they could afford a house with extra space for a home office. With all the bars and restaurants

18

closed and the homeless taking over the sidewalks and parks, the city had lost its magnetic charm for them. Long established businesses went under, disappearing overnight. Tourism was only just beginning to pick up again.

Luckily, the coffee shop was still there. I took a bite of my warm tarte aux pommes and a sip of coffee, watching the gulls. I was still holding on, too, like some weird mollusk on a rock in the bay, adapted to ride out storms and waves. I had been in a strange mental state for the last few months—discontent, cranky, prone to long bouts of self-isolation. I saw almost no one. Ashna occasionally. Valerie, my on and off lover, was on again. She had dumped her finance bro boyfriend and shown up at my door one night. Our meetings were carnal, wordless, brief—like two wild animals coming together in a clearing in the woods then going their separate ways.

My last two jobs—Julian Wolhardt's stolen notes and Linda Darien's purloined Oscar—each a kind of debacle in its own way, would creep into my thoughts at night. As soon as I collapsed on my bed, certain I was exhausted enough to slide into oblivion, some image would float into consciousness—unhinged Lester Dworkin charging me in a dark basement, Wayne Abbot rising from his drunken stupor and stumbling toward me. I would thrash, unable to sleep, until my cat, Belka, full of animal wisdom, would settle his prodigious bulk on my chest and hold me down, his purr vibrating through me until I drifted off. The cat was the one thing I had taken away from the Julian Wolhardt job that felt right. He didn't seem to mind being cooped up in the weird space I called home. Maybe he had had his fill of territorial disputes and rain and dodging cars. He went up on the roof occasionally but only in warm weather which never lasted long in San Francisco.

One other thing kept me grounded: I had started teaching. It was Ashna's idea. A mutual friend from art school who had a part time gig at California College of the Arts had contacted her. They needed someone to teach an intro class in sculpture. Ashna suggested me— a somewhat successful local sculptor who had a lot of time on his hands and needed something to snap him out of the depressive funk he had descended into. At first, the idea repulsed me. I had no talent for teaching that I knew of. I had no wisdom to share with earnest young art students. They would be bright eyed, living off their parents' largesse, consumed with worry about how their Instagram feed measured up. Some instinct made me take the job. It was only ninety minutes, three days a week—not much of a commitment. To my vast surprise, I found that I enjoyed it. And not only did I enjoy it, it sparked my own creativity. I found myself working again in my own studio, creating with purpose.

My nights were still jagged with intrusive thoughts. I was still sullen and cranky. I still stumbled through my days, half-human. But, I felt like there was a glimmer in the darkness, I just needed to keep my eye on it and follow it and eventually I would emerge into light and life.

I took another bite of my pastry, another sip of my coffee. A gull cried, alighting on a red tiled roof, water sloshed, and an insistent buzzing started up in my chest pocket. I pulled my phone out and glanced at the screen. Just a number. With an area code I didn't recognize. Looking back, I can't explain why I answered that call. I would normally swipe away a call from an unknown number, let them leave me a voice mail if they wanted. Ninety-nine percent of the time it was spam. Some temporary brain malfunction or intuition made me swipe up instead of down. After that, it was too late.

"Hello?"

A pause, then a female voice, husky, hesitant. "Hello. Justin? Justin Vincent?"

"Yes?"

"It's been a long time."

The voice, familiar in the way a relic from childhood is familiar, echoed down the years with a shiver of recognition—the stranger you used to be who contained the seed of who you are, smaller hands in your mind's eye holding the thing your adult hand grasps now, overlayed, superimposed like two films projected on one screen. I paused, a pop of static on the line, a ghost voice in my ear.

"Who is this?" I asked.

"Malena."

I paused, the outside world draining away like water down a funnel. Narrowing my world to just a voice in my ear.

"Malena?" Her face came to me, the last time I had seen it. Seventeen year old me, packing my few belongings in the little room I shared with a rotating crew of foster brothers. Malena stood in the doorway, leaning on the jamb, watching me. She must have been sixteen— a round face, beautiful but not pretty. Straight black hair in a plait down her back. All the girls and women wore long, high-necked prairie dresses. It was one of the rules of the Community—our foster parents' restrictive religion. Her dress that day was light blue. I didn't remember what we said to each other, if anything.

Malena was the only foster sibling who lasted. The others came and went. We were brother and sister, living in the awful place together from when we were toddlers, tied tightly to each other by love and survival. Our plan had been for me to strike out, find a job and a place to live. Then, a year later, she would come join me. I had kept my end of the bargain, hitched my way to San Francisco, got part time work, found a dodgy apartment south of Market, started college. After I left, though, the Community was closed to me, impenetrable from the outside. I never heard from Malena again. I tried calling many times in the first couple of years after I left. I was never allowed to speak to her. I left messages that were probably never delivered.

"Don't you remember me?"

"Of course I do. Of course. It's just been so long. Twenty years? Where are you?"

A pause. "I'm in a safe place. We don't worry about geography. What matters is where your true being is."

"Okay. I get it." We both fell silent, lost for words. What do you say to a long-lost sister? "This is weird. Sorry. I've missed you, you know. All these years. I've always wondered where you were, whether you stayed, why you never came to San Francisco or got in touch."

"None of that matters now."

"Are you still part of the Community?"

"Yes. We're planning a reunion. A celebration. It's going to be glorious. We're reaching out to all our wayward members, asking them to come back." Her voice was dead, like she was reading from a script.

"Malena, is everything okay? You hated the Community as much as I did. Maybe even more. Why are you still there?"

"We were wrong about it Justin. We were just kids. We couldn't understand what it all really meant. How beautiful it is."

"I think I have a pretty good memory of what it was like."

"Memory can be false. The flesh can lie. The spirit never lies. That's what Sister Eleanor says."

Eleanor Jane Sibyl. I hadn't thought about her in ages. She was the leader of the Community. We never saw her. She lived in seclusion somewhere and sent out video tapes to all of the believers. That was before the internet and streaming media. We had to watch her new tape whenever one arrived. The VCR and TV were kept in a locked closet. Our foster parents would get them out, set them up, and then we would be in for an hour of more of Sister Eleanor droning away in what looked like a windowless, wood paneled suburban basement with a piece of gold lace tacked up on the wall behind her. She was small, fine boned, with the whitest skin I had ever seen and black hair severely center parted. Her sermons were meandering and confusing—full of prophecies, references to the unbelievers and their decaying society, the need for absolute purity if we wanted to be taken up and leave earth with the angels at the time of reckoning—delivered with a steady, unblinking gaze, straight at the camera. I never really listened. I couldn't have paid attention if I wanted to. The atmosphere was so stifling it was like a roaring in my ears, drowning out her monotone. My legs twitched, remembering how I always wanted to bolt from the room, hide until it was over.

"I don't know, Malena." It felt bizarre to say her name, to be talking to her at all. But sometimes when things go sideways, all we can do is pretend everything is normal. "Maybe. Did you say there's a reunion coming up?"

"Yes. In three months, all the believers will meet together. We will contact you again with more details. We want you to come, Justin. We need everyone. Even the smallest gear helps the wheel turn and mill the grain that gives us sustenance." The same dead voice, reading the words prepared for her by someone. By Sister Eleanor herself? Or by some other functionary?

"Malena…" I didn't know how to respond.

"Goodbye, Justin. I'll call again soon."

A soft bloop indicated the call was disconnected. I sat there for a while, phone still pressed to my ear, lost in memory. A gull swooped overhead, crying out. I lowered the phone and was about to put it back in my pocket when it buzzed with an incoming text message.

> Dinner tonight?

> Yes. When? Where?

> Your place.

> You're inviting yourself to my place for a dinner that I am expected to prepare?

> Yes. Make something delicious. Savory. Maybe duck?

> You are bold. See you around 7?

> Agreed.

I put the phone away, shaking my head. Ashna and I had been friends for a long time. She was probably the only person who could push me around. If I was going to make duck, I would need to plan my ride to pass through Chinatown on the way home. My coffee dregs were cold. I dumped the cup and the pastry wrapper into a garbage can next to my bench, hopped on my bike and headed out to circumnavigate the Presidio before circling back for a visit to Hing Lung Company, my go-to butcher shop for roasted duck.

Chapter 3

Dark Patterns
11/20-24: San Francisco

Thoughts of the past and of Malena consumed me as I biked the city, shopped, rode home, and started cooking. When I was younger and first away from my foster home, on my own in the city, figuring out how to get by, I would have said I was figuring out who I was if I had thought about it at all. I was pretty convinced back then that I was throwing off all traces of my weird religious upbringing, striking out on my own, building a moral code and a philosophy just as I built my sculptures out of things I found, borrowed, or stole. Thinking about Malena's call though, I remembered other things. The value of hard work. The value of helping others. The value of a bond like I had with Malena and had found later with Ashna. Was my childhood in the Community a deviation from true self? Or did it form my true self? Did I really build myself up from scratch, pulling the pieces together deliberately, or were the seeds already planted?

My thoughts were interrupted just before seven when the doorbell rang. I pushed the button to unlock the door downstairs and went back to dicing red beets for the salad I was making. Ashna banged through a minute later with a pinot in one hand and a Riesling in the other.

"Mr. Lee's still in his office down there working."

"Yeah, he has a big order to get out. Some fashion start-up that's touting made in the U.S. as part of their value proposition." The longtime tenant on the ground floor of my building was a garment sewing business. Mr. Lee was the owner. He often sat in his office, shuffling papers until eight or nine in the evening, listening to baseball on a little AM/FM radio that looked like it dated back to the 1970s. I suspected that he preferred the quiet of his office to his cramped outer sunset house full of kids and extended family.

"Good for him!"

"Mmmhmm," I gave Ashna a one-armed hug, pulling roasted broccolini and cannellini beans out of the oven with the other. "Seems like his business is recovering. I might have to start changing him rent again."

"I would say so. Hey, you've been working," She wandered back into my studio space and circled the piece I'd started a couple of weeks earlier. It was made up of planes of steel, welded into an abstract form like a twisted Joshua tree. "I like it. It's different."

"Thanks. Push some of that stuff out of the way and we can sit at the end," I gestured toward the long table that served as my workbench, office, and eating surface. "You know where the wineglasses are. I think the Riesling will go better with the duck."

Ashna pushed aside a stack of papers, a soldering iron, and a toolbox to make room, then opened the wine while I set out plates.

Over dinner, Ashna told me a long anecdote about her recent trip to New Zealand where she rented a motorcycle and traveled around the country. She seemed happy, energized.

"So what's going on with you Justin? You've been working," she gestured toward the studio. "You're teaching. Feeling any better?"

"A bit."

"Good. You've been one grumpy asshole lately."

"I know." I'd been trying to decide whether or not to tell her about the call from Malena. It was a weird anomaly but it had affected me deeply—like a stone tossed into a puddle sending settled mud swirling. "I got a weird phone call today."

"From who?"

"Malena."

"Malena? Your sister?"

"Foster sister."

Ashna frowned. "Sister. Maybe not by blood but you always said she was as close as a sister. You never heard from her though, did you? After you came here?"

"No, I haven't seen or spoken to her since I left foster care when I was seventeen."

"Weird. What did she say?"

"It was weird. Very weird. She's still in the Community. It was almost like she was reading from a script. She sounded brainwashed. Just reciting the company line. I didn't get anything genuine from her. I'm a little worried I guess. I don't like to think of her still caught up in that. Trapped. She said they're having a reunion. Calling all the wayward sheep back to the fold. Three months from now. More details to come. Then she just hung up."

"Very strange. This has roach motel written all over it if you ask me."

"I have a feeling I know what you mean but please

28

explain anyway."

"Simple. My employer develops enterprise level e-commerce sites, right?"

"I guess so, I've never fully understood what you do. It's all just twiddling ones and zeros as far as I can tell."

"Well, that's part of it. We do a lot of other shady stuff, too. But in e-commerce there's a concept known as dark patterns." Ashna sat back and looked up at the ceiling. "Dark patterns are all the little ways websites trick you into doing what we, the developers, want you to do. Misdirection, bait and switch, confirmshaming. All neat tricks. One of the best is roach motel. You can get in but it's really hard to get out. I wouldn't attend their little reunion if I were you. Roach motel all day long."

"Yeah. I don't have any intention of doing that. But I *would* like to know where Malena is at least. Do you think you could find out from the phone number?"

"Child's play. Give me the number and I'll get you the info by tomorrow."

"Okay, thanks. Now let's talk about something else. Tell me more about this girl you met in New Zealand."

Later, after Ashna left, I went up to the roof and watched the big boats motor up and down the channel to the Port of Oakland for a while. Ashna was right. It was some kind of trap. Probably not a deadly one. But they wanted something. Maybe just a donation or to try to pull me back into the fold by dangling someone I cared about. One way or the other, though, it bugged me that Malena was still there and seemed brainwashed. When we were kids, she had one of the most indomitable spirits I had ever encountered. If they had broken that…the thought made me furious. I had always hated organizations and the way they warped people to create in groups vs. out groups. That was part of why I'd never even considered going straight, getting a regular job, doing what the mainstream of society thought of as normal. I wasn't a joiner. I had found my own way, following overgrown tracks though uncharted terrain rather than turning my brain off and jumping on the mega freeway with everybody else. Malena should have had that opportunity, too. Maybe she wouldn't have taken it in the end. But if it was denied to her, if the Community had kept her against her will, then I knew I would have something to say about it.

Back downstairs, I dug a small box from the back of my closet and brought it to the table. It contained the few things that remained from my childhood. I hadn't brought much with me when I left. It had been years since I opened it and the contents surprised me. A pocketknife with an ivory handle, yellow with age. A belt buckle. A couple of letters Malena had sent when she went away to a Community camp one summer. And a photo. The only picture I had of Malena. A Polaroid, white bordered, colors faded—we stood outside the Community's meeting hall, noon sun on our heads. Teenagers. I could still feel the heat. Shoulder to shoulder, we were the same height, same coloring, same dark hair. We could have been actual siblings. I wore jeans and a flannel button up. She wore the prairie dress. The expression on my face, squinting in the sun, sidelong glance, said it all. Get me out of here. Who took that photo? How did I get it? I had no clue.

I put the photo down and opened my laptop, hesitating for a moment, fingers poised over the keys. In all the years since I had escaped, I hadn't ever researched Sibyl or the Community. I only knew what I had learned from the inside—the practices, the teachings, the rambling, incoherent sermons on tape. A kind of dread and numbness filled my brain whenever I thought about it. Finally, I put my fingers on the keys and typed deliberately, entering the name: Eleanor Jane Sibyl.

The first link in the search results was the Community's official site. I skipped that, assuming I wouldn't get any real info from their own propaganda, and clicked on the second result—a Wikipedia page.

Eleanor Jane Sibyl. Born January 31, 1952 in Kenosha Wisconsin. Married in 1972 to her first husband. One child—a boy named Bill. Divorced only two years later. Traveled out to the West Coast, taking the boy with her, and spent some time in Big Sur. Met her second husband, Mark Sibyl, who was the proprietor of a small press that published books on spirituality and the occult. Together with a few others from Big Sur, they moved to Montana, bought a small ranch, and started a kind of commune called the Community. Around that time, Sibyl began having what she called hierophantic visions. Were they drug induced? Probably. These people were hippies. A photo of the original founders of the commune accompanied the article along with a headshot of Sibyl. She looked just like I remembered. In the group photo she was seated on a branch of a fallen tree in a meadow, wearing a prairie dress like the one I recalled Malena wearing the day I left, black hair long and tied back, thin, almost severely so, eyes focused inward, unseeing. It looked like a scan of an old black and white shot. Most of the detail had degraded with time but the styles and postures still gave away a lot.

Standing next to Sibyl was a tall, gangly dude I took to be her husband Mark. He had wild shoulder-length hair, round glasses, well-worn jeans and a leather vest with no shirt. A boy about three or four years old was crouched in the long grass, poking at something with a stick. Probably Bill. Another couple stood behind the tree, glancing toward the camera as if the photographer had just caught their attention. A third man and a teenage girl were standing on the trunk about ten feet away from where Sibyl sat. The man on the tree was wearing army surplus pants and boots and no shirt. He was muscular with a heavy black beard and a round poof of thick, curly hair. A Jerry Garcia type. The girl held out a hand toward him, tipping sideways, caught forever mid-fall. I looked at the caption. Devlin Fonseco. The girl, Abigail Fonseco. The photo was dated Summer 1976, Community Ranch, Montana. Devlin Fonseco's name was linked, indicating he had his own Wikipedia page. Curious, I clicked through and quickly skimmed his bio. A biology PhD candidate at U.C. Berkeley in the early seventies, he met the Sibyls at Esalen during some kind of mind-bending, drug-fueled retreat. They hit it off and decided to join forces along with Fonseco's wife Gwen and their daughter.

I navigated back and clicked through to an article about the Community itself. Shortly after they moved to the ranch, Mark Sibyl began recording and transcribing his wife's visions. He published them in both book and audio tape formats and used his existing network to push them out to small bookstores. People found the books, read them, and began to show up at the ranch, wanting to join up. The population grew to about twenty hard core believers. They built a bunk house and a meeting hall and started holding retreats. Pretty soon they had a steady income from the sales of books and tapes and the paying customers for the retreats. The Community became weirder and weirder from that point on. Eleanor Jane Sibyl spent more time in her trances. She stayed in one room of the old ranch house, never leaving. She began recording the tapes like the ones I had seen as a child. By then, they had members all over the country–people who had attended the retreats, formed cells, purchased property in the country, and were living off the land according to the tenets they learned in Montana. The Community had become a religion. They used the Christian bible, Sibyl's books, and a mishmash of Buddhist and Hindu texts as well as a smattering of science fiction UFO stuff that equated aliens with angels. The cells turned into congregations and became established. The ethos was back to the land, puritan, anti-government, self-sufficient. It was like the Mormon church plus hippies plus dianetics.

By the late eighties, the Community ranch in Montana had become a compound. A political ideology had grown along with the spiritual. All members were advised to arm themselves and to recognize no worldly authority—only holy law as revealed by the angels who spoke through Sibyl. Inevitably, they also stopped paying their taxes, claiming a religious exemption although the Community was not registered as a church by the IRS. Neighbors started up rumors about child abuse and satanic rituals. Phones were tapped and bank accounts frozen.

On October 3rd, 1989, approximately fifty FBI agents arrived outside the compound. A standoff ensued. A black and white photo accompanied the article, showing several agents in dark jackets with FBI in big block letters on the back. They stood next to a Chevy Suburban, gazing out toward the compound which incorporated the original A frame ranch house along with a plain, U-shaped, two-story building. Big evergreens surrounded the clearing and mountains rose in the distance.

On day three, Mark Sibyl worked out an agreement with the agents, the inhabitants of the ranch put down their weapons, and the FBI was allowed in. Of the twenty-five adults and sixteen children they expected to find inside the compound, they found only nine adults, all men. Eleanor Jane Sibyl, along with all the women and children and some of the men had been whisked away before the raid—warned ahead of time by someone with knowledge of the FBI's plan. The remaining men had never planned to fight. They just held off the FBI long enough for everyone else to be well away—scattered across the country. Among them were Fonseco and the other original founder Samuel Miller.

In the days following the raid, several interesting facts came out. The agents found a full laboratory and medical wing with state-of-the-art equipment, most likely Fonseco's since he was the only scientist in the Community as far as they knew. They also found a printing press, A/V production equipment, a school room, a basement stocked with enough preserved food to keep the inhabitants going for years, and an impressive collection of weapons. As far as the FBI could tell, none of the children from the compound had been issued birth certificates. They had all been born onsite and had never been to outside doctors or enrolled in school. In fact, no records of any kind were found. No financial documents or ledgers, no personnel files, no information about who had lived at the compound or attended retreats. It had all been destroyed or carried off prior to the raid. All the FBI had were the nine men.

Under questioning, the 'silent nine' as they became known by the press, refused to give up any information regarding the whereabouts of the children or other members who had escaped. None of them, including Eleanor Jane Sibyl, were ever found. Her video tapes continued though and the congregations around the country continued to grow, slowly. According to the article, there were now some 10,000 members worldwide.

The nine captured men all served short jail sentences. Upon release, they mostly blended back into society. Mark Sibyl went off grid, presumably joining his wife in anonymous exile. That wood paneled basement I remembered from the tapes had to be somewhere. Minnesota? Florida? Mexico? The children were never found. The official report postulated that they had been absorbed into small Community congregations around the country. After the raid, members of the Community were forced to get proper documentation for their children. Families could have easily taken on a child from the compound and said it was their own.

I pushed the laptop away, stood up, and began clearing the dishes Ashna and I had left on the table. It was a strange but not unexpected history. Lots of freaky cults and religious groups had come out of the tumult of the sixties and seventies—neo-Hindu, pagan, UFO, Theosophical, Occult. Some of them had ended badly like Jim Jones and his Rainbow Family drinking Kool Aid in Guyana, or the Branch Davidians in Waco. Others like Eckankar and the Love Family were still doing their thing fifty years later. Some, such as the pyramid scheme cult known as Scientology, had prospered and grown into powerful organizations with famous members. The Community seemed to have survived the raid that scattered its leadership. Sibyl, now in her seventies, was still pumping out the videos and the books from wherever she held court and the faithful still bought them.

I dropped an ice cube into a rocks glass, sloshed in some Old Overholt, and walked to the big wall of windows at the back of my studio. A cloud like a dirty smudge half-covered the moon. Patches of fog swirled around the rocks at the bay's edge. I thought about Malena, still trapped, spouting Sibyl's empty pablum back at me. I hoped she was all right, that there was still some fight left in her.

Three days later, she called again. Working in my studio, ear protectors on, grinding away at a long curve of steel, I almost missed it. But, turning a corner on the weld, the phone caught my eye, screen lit up with the incoming call. I tore off my mask and gloves and fumbled the phone off the tool cart where it was half-buried under rags and scrap metal. The same number as before. Ashna had traced it for me—some tiny cow town in southern Utah near the Arizona border. I swiped to answer.

"Hello?"

"Justin. It's Malena."

"Malena! I was hoping you'd call again." I dropped all my safety gear on the cart and pulled up a stool.

"I tried. Several times. I thought you didn't want to talk to me."

"No, of course I do," I held the phone away and swiped to see the notifications. Three missed calls. "I was working. Had my ear protectors on."

"Making sculpture?"

"Yes."

"They told me that's what you do now. That you're a successful artist."

"I do all right. Not top tier by any stretch of the imagination." I paused. At a loss for what to say. "What's your life like now? What are you doing?"

"I teach the children. Preschool and elementary. That's not important. Listen, I called because of the reunion. The celebration. It's going to be glorious. We're reaching out to all our wayward members, asking them to come back." Her voice was dead again, scripted like before.

"Is someone forcing you to call me? You know how I felt about the Community when I left. You felt the same way. Why are you still there?"

"Justin, listen." Her voice changed, she began speaking low and fast. "Do you remember when we were kids?"

"Of course…"

"The barn door's open. Understand?"

For a moment I was confused. Then it came back to me. "Yes, I get it. What's going on? I can help. Tell me."

"I wish I could."

I heard loud footsteps and a deep voice, unintelligible. Then the phone was slammed down, the connection broken. I sat for a minute, frozen, remembering. *The barn door's open*. It was a code we had when we were kids. Hearing her say it took me back. It meant our foster father was in a rage again, looking for someone to take it out on. Best to hide until he calmed down. I remembered hiding in the attic mostly. It was freezing up there in the winter, stifling in the summer. We had a kind of fort we had built behind an old desk, lined with musty blankets. We'd lay there, huddled for warmth and read from the encyclopedia—the only books in the house aside from the bible and Eleanor Jane Sibyl's rambling tracts. Was Malena warning me to stay away? I sat on the stool for a long time, remembering. After the remembering, though, came something else. Anger. And determination. Something was going on. Malena was trapped, whether physically or mentally. I needed to go. I would start with the town in Utah and take it from there. Whatever it took, I would find her and get her out.

Chapter 4

Mr. Anonymous
11/25: San Francisco

"I've been thinking. I don't like that they know my phone number. How were they able to find me?"

Ashna leaned back on my couch and looked at the ceiling. "Seriously, Justin? You think it's difficult to find people these days? An unlisted number isn't going to do it."

"I know that but just the fact that they did as much as it took to get past me being unlisted is creepy. It means I have to be careful. So how do I go there without any chance of them finding out who I am?"

"You're really doing this? Saving the damsel in distress?"

"That's not what this is about. She's my sister. I should have tracked her down years ago. If they're brainwashing her, or holding her there against her will, I need to get her out."

"You're just starting to get back to functional. You want to throw that away?"

"I'm not throwing anything away." I said it but I wasn't sure it was true. Sometimes when you've been down in the hole, when you've clawed your way up to the light and you're on the edge, you can't really understand your own motivations. Could it be a desire to sink back down into the familiar darkness? Easier than struggling upward into uncertainty. But it could also be movement forward, grabbing onto something that can help pull you up, continue the momentum. "I don't really know. I'm pretty sure I have to try though."

"Okay." Ashna thought for a moment. "You're asking two different questions really. One, how can I be untraceable? Two, how can I go in with a fake identity and not get found out? I think you have the fake identity already, don't you?"

"Yes. Dustin Cruz. Full set of fake papers, IDs, passport. Everything."

"But Mr. Cruz doesn't have any kind of banking presence, no social media, no criminal record. Not very believable unless you invent the right identity. He'd have to be poor. Someone who does the kinds of jobs that are paid under the table in cash to get by. Maybe seasonal farm work or construction. He's a nomad. He travels by Greyhound or hitchhiking or hopping freight trains."

"I can play that role."

"You have the hands for it. Not really the face but you'll get by."

"Yeah." I looked down at my fingers, strong with thick calluses and variously abraded. "Fairly believable." Steel working was hard on the hands. It didn't matter whether you were building bridges and buildings or making art. Same result.

"Now, if you want to become untraceable, say, if you don't want the Community or anyone else to be able to track you down. That's a more difficult problem. You've seen the illustrations of how objects with mass warp space time right? They usually show it as a plane with a grid drawn on it. A planet or a star makes a depression in the grid warping the grid lines." Ashna held up her hands, demonstrating. "Like if you put a heavy ball on a trampoline."

"Okay, yes." I nodded.

"Think of people the same way. People are the planets and their mass is determined by their information quotient—bank accounts, social media presence, mortgages, car registrations, phone numbers, all that stuff. Entries in databases. That gives you weight. You warp the fabric of information, you're easy to find."

I nodded. "I get that. I probably have less information mass than most people."

"Yeah but you need to do better if you want to be anonymous. First thing you need to do, set up a corporation. An LLC. That's going to be your new identity. You have to do it in a state where corporations aren't required to identify the owner. New Mexico, Wyoming, or Nevada."

"Sounds like you've researched this."

"Oh, I've done more than research it. I can help you. You'll need a new phone number. Registered to the corporation. No geolocation on your phone. You don't have a car so no need to worry about the DMV. No mortgage on this place so that's good but you should transfer ownership to the LLC. Get a PO Box and make it your official address. No mail to this address. Encrypt everything. Laptop, phone. Ready to start?" Ashna was already pulling her laptop from her bag. "What do you want your LLC to be called? And my glass is empty."

We were drinking a Hakushu 12-year Ashna had brought over. I got up and retrieved the bottle. Belka was curled up on the couch next to Ashna, his broad back pressed against her thigh. A big jet flew low over

Oakland in the distance, lights blinking. "Belka Transcontinental, LLC?"

Ashna typed something, hit enter, waited a moment. "Looks like it's available in Wyoming."

Chapter 5

On the Road
12/7: Helem, Utah

Unwashed bodies. Chemical toilet. Cigarette breath. Bus terminal convenience store food. Plus a thousand other aromas that spoke of poverty, transience, aimless freedom, crushing hardship. After almost thirty hours on the bus, I was covered with it. My skin had taken on an extra layer of grime. My eyes had become the eyes of a different person—focused on the horizon, watching but not calculating. I could have flown to Salt Lake City and then taken the bus for the last leg of the trip but my goal was to become Dustin Cruz. There's an old David Byrne song about becoming someone else by following them around the store and buying the same groceries. I became Dustin Cruz through a process that began with a shopping trip to the lower Mission.

My first stop had been Goodwill. Vintage Dickies carpenter pants, work boots, flannel shirts, sheepskin lined denim jacket—haggard clothes, beat down into a faded apotheosis of American workwear.

Next I hit the Army surplus shop down the street where I picked up a duffel bag with the name Kyle H. Johnson stenciled in faded white across green canvas worn down and blackened with years of grime at the seams. I put my Goodwill purchases inside, wondering idly whether Kyle Johnson was still alive somewhere in the heartland of America. Maybe a middle-aged man now, watching his kids play soccer. From the surplus store, I also added a rip stop poncho, a good pocketknife, some wool socks, undershirts, thermal underwear, hat, gloves, a camp stove, and a mess kit.

Outside the sixteenth street Bart station, a woman in a bright Peruvian shawl displayed her wares on a blanket—a selection of ancient cell phones, sunglasses, bracelets. I crouched down, sorted through them, and selected a flip phone.

"Five dollars," she said in a sweet, high voice,

"Charger included?" I asked, taking out my wallet.

She nodded and pulled a cord from a tangled wad. I didn't have any illusions about the phone actually being useful but I wanted to look like it was something I could use if my bag was searched.

A few doors down, I selected a prepaid SIM card from a rack and took it to the counter. The shopgirl raised a well-shaped eyebrow when I laid the old phone down on the counter but went ahead and set it up, handling the phone only with the tips of her creamsicle orange to smurf blue ombre fingernails.

I washed everything, folded, packed and repacked until I was happy with the weight distribution.

Now, nearing Helem, Utah, population 287, I hefted the duffle onto the empty seat next to mine, more than ready to be off the bus. For the last few hours I had watched red rock bluffs and scrubland roll by the window, breathing the thin, cool air that rolled in, momentarily clearing the Greyhound stench whenever the bus stopped in some tiny blip of a town. About five thousand feet above sea level, we crawled through semiarid high desert. I saw creosote, live oak, indigo, prickly pear, and probably a thousand other species of low bushy plants, wildflower, and cactus, a threadbare, fragile quilt of life over the harsh, rocky land, frost in the shadows.

I thought about Dustin Cruz, my alter ego, planning my story and filling in his background. I decided he was from Southern California, an orphan like me, product of the foster care system. He ran away at sixteen and had been on the road ever since. Somewhere along the line he apprenticed as a welder. He could do the less skilled construction jobs like demolition, clean up, and framing. He had been drifting from place to place, restless, without roots, working construction and catering gigs. A friend from a job in Phoenix, Kyle H. Johnson, who had given him the old duffle bag, had texted him a couple of months before and told him he was in Helem. He'd found religion, had joined up with some kind of church, and was inviting Dustin to come check it out. It was more a loose framework than a detailed history but I thought it would be enough. Dustin Cruz would become more real to me the more I interacted with others. I wasn't worried about getting tripped up over inconsistencies in my story. Dustin wasn't the kind of guy who would talk a lot about his past. Anything I did make up would become part of his story and I wouldn't forget it.

The first sign of Helem was a long, low steel building beside the highway, one lone pickup parked next to it, dark afternoon shadows stretching out from both. I checked my watch. Dustin Cruz's watch actually—a cheap Timex digital. 4:32 p.m.. Next, a cluster of similar buildings, maybe warehouses. A red rock bluff rose up behind them, sharply detailed in the golden light. A minute later, the bus was slowing, gearing down. We rolled to a stop outside a squat Quonset hut. Above the door and below the curve of the roof, LINDA'S MARKET in big red block letters.

"Helem," the driver called out. "All off for Helem. Ten-minute stop."

I hefted my bag and shuffled sideways down the narrow aisle. The cold hit me as I stepped onto cracked blacktop. Not freezing but maybe only ten degrees above. It would definitely go well below at night. Three fellow travelers were already off the bus and puffing cigarettes. I ducked through them and headed across the narrow parking strip.

"Leave your bag over there." A cracked, desert voice accompanied by tinkling bells on the door.

I glanced over. The person minding the store—Linda herself?—perched on a high stool behind the counter. Maybe sixty, thin but sturdy, dark hair going gray and deeply tanned, she wore round, wire-rimmed glasses, jeans, and a colorful shawl with a cross hatched Native American pattern. Her skin seemed at once paper thin over strong cheekbones and tough as old leather. I nodded and dropped the duffle beside the door, under a rack of sunglasses. Country music played softly from a boombox behind the counter. I bobbed my head to it and explored. The market had three aisles with a refrigerator case along one side and an open cooler for produce on the other. I browsed for a few minutes. Cereal, chips, soda, cookies, baking supplies. A couple of bus people came in, bought things, and left. Bubbles of cold air accompanied the opening and closing of the door but the shop was warm. I looked up. Thick insulation covered the curve that formed walls and ceiling. Duct work ran across it with vents—everything clean and orderly.

Three high windows on each side allowed the weak winter sun to shine in, adding some natural light. Next to the produce I found some prepared sandwiches. I chose one and an apple, then wandered up toward the counter.

"Do you have coffee?" I asked.

The woman slid off her stool, gesturing silently toward the right side of the U-shaped counter. Two big, insulated coffee dispensers were set out with cups, cream and sugar packets. I filled a cup, added cream and brought it to the front.

"Six fifty-five."

I dug Dustin Cruz's Goodwill wallet out and removed a ten. "Cold out there huh?"

"Usually is. Bus is about to leave," she nodded toward the door, offering my change. "Better hurry."

"I'm getting off," I mumbled, carefully stowing the change. There was a round café table with a couple of chairs next to the counter on the side away from the door. "Mind if I sit and eat?"

"Suit yourself. What it's there for."

"Thanks." I sat and unwrapped my sandwich. The woman went back to her stool. She wasn't looking at a phone, watching TV, or reading a book. Instead, she just stared, eyes unfocused, maybe just thinking or daydreaming. Watching her, I realized how rare that was in my world—someone content to just be. Things were different here. I shifted, the chair legs squeaked, and I heard a low growl from behind me.

"Jake! Go back to sleep. He's a customer." An old brown lab lay curled in a massive dog bed against the wall. He was skin and bones and white at the muzzle. "He's nineteen years old," she turned to me. "Wouldn't bother getting up if a robber came in and cleaned out the

47

cash register."

"I had a dog like him once," I replied. "Or the family I was living with did. Foster family. Okay if I pet him?"

The smallest and briefest of smiles flitted across her solemn features. She nodded, once, giving me permission. I got up and crouched, holding a hand out. Jake sniffed at it then lowered his head onto his paws. I scratched behind his ears and he sighed.

"You have family in town?" the woman said to my back.

I kept petting the dog. "No. A friend I'm looking for. Said he found religion and I should come out, see what it's about, maybe join up and spend some time at this commune."

An icy silence. Then, "The Community, I guess he meant."

"Yeah, that's it. You know about them?" I turned.

"Sure, I know about them. I know all about them. Red Butte Commune's just up the road half a mile." She pointed toward the back of the store. "I'd stay away if I were you though. Nothing there for anyone with a head on his shoulders. Bunch of brainwashed bliss ninnies listening to tapes of some crazy old lady talk about UFOs and angels."

I nodded. "Could be. I'm not much for religion. Need to see my friend though. If it's a bad scene maybe I can get him to leave."

"Good luck with that."

"Know of anywhere I could get a room in town? While I'm here? Sun's almost down. I'll probably wait until tomorrow to go check out the commune."

"Comfort Inn's a mile east on the highway."

"Anything cheaper than that? Maybe don't need a

credit card?"

She looked at me for a couple of seconds, eyes unreadable. "I have a couple of cabins out back. Normally only rent them to tourists during the summer. People passing through going to Lake Powell or Bryce. Twenty dollars a day. Pay in advance. Room'll be stale. Need some airing."

"That would be fine. Thanks. I'll take you up on that."

"You'll have to light the pilot on the water heater."

"I'll manage."

She nodded, sizing me up. "I guess you will."

I finished my sandwich and paid her the twenty. In exchange, she gave me a key on a brown plastic keychain in the shape of a rounded diamond. The number 2 was embossed in the plastic. I hefted my duffle and was reaching for the door when she spoke again.

"They have a dinner every night up at that place. The commune. Everyone's invited. That'd be the time to go. How they recruit people. Not bad food though." She stared into space while she spoke, not looking at me or anything else. Maybe looking inward. Bitterness in her voice.

I nodded. "Thanks. You know what time?"

"Five-thirty, I think."

My cabin was indeed stale. Behind the Quonset, a chain link fence enclosed a lot maybe half an acre in size. A stand of ponderosa pines clustered by the back wall of the shop. Nestled among the trunks, two small log cabins stood, their high peaked roofs covered with dry needles. I climbed two steps to the porch of cabin two and fitted the key into the lock. Inside, it smelled of old wood, dust, mildew, and lemon Pledge. Wood paneling lined every wall. A pink bedspread covered a lumpy looking mattress. I dropped my duffle on it and sat. The springs creaked mightily but the bed frame didn't collapse. It would do. I cracked the bathroom window and the one in the main room to get a cross breeze. Cold air rushed through but the place needed airing. I got the water heater pilot lit and opened the valves so it could fill. I wanted to wash the Greyhound grime off but it would take an hour or more to heat.

While I waited, I emptied my duffle and reached inside. Before leaving, I had asked my downstairs tenant Mr. Lee to have one of his expert sewers create a false bottom in the bag with a hidden zipper on one side. It was lined with a thin layer of foam rubber. Inside were a smart phone, a fair amount of cash, and a few small tools I might need.

I booted the phone, waited for it to find a signal, then opened the maps app. A pin appeared in the middle of nowhere, then zoomed in, showing the highway and a couple of roads running perpendicular to it. One of them ran alongside Linda's Market and continued for a couple of miles up into the red rock before ending abruptly. A scattering of what looked like houses and small businesses clustered around the town center. A little more than half a mile up the road, the rectangle outline of a building appeared, well away from any neighbors. A couple of smaller outbuildings seemed to be part of the complex and a fair amount of land enclosed by a fence. I switched to satellite view–a parking lot containing the weathered roofs of two SUVs and what looked like a school bus, a gray roof with regular blocks of HVAC equipment and skylights, covered pathways to the outbuildings, the outline of what might have been a field with a track around the outside. It was a school building of the type built in the fifties and sixties. The Community must have bought it or leased it from the county.

I had read what history I could find on Helem. A mining boom town in the nineteen forties and fifties, it supplied uranium to the Manhattan Project and the resulting nuclear industry. But the mines tapped out by the early sixties and the town had been dying a slow death ever since. With only 287 residents, most elderly, they likely couldn't support a school of that size anymore.

I ran a search to see what businesses still existed in town—a barber shop, a diner next door to the Comfort Inn called Lucky's Grill and Taproom, a gas station and repair shop, and a hardware store. That was about it aside from Linda's Market. Lucky's would be the best place to gather gossip. I put the phone away, heaved myself up, and headed for the bathroom, hoping the water was warm.

Later, washed and wearing fresh clothes, I stepped out into the cold and started the mile walk to the diner. The sun was down and the temperature had dropped. I shivered and walked fast under a bright three-quarter moon, my breath condensing into clouds and dissipating in my wake. I passed Linda's, the dark barber shop, the empty gas station, a couple of derelict buildings surrounded by chain link that looked like they must have been worker housing from the mid-century mining days—gray rows of squat, unadorned rectangles, clapboard and cinder block, windows broken out, weeds growing from cracks in the surrounding blacktop. After that, a quarter mile of empty highway and desert, deep blue sky full of stars. I felt like if I let up my concentration for a moment the whole earth might tip and fling me into that sky where I would fall forever.

It was a relief to step into Lucky's Grill and leave that emptiness and sky behind, at least for a little while. I rubbed my hands together, looking around. I saw booths upholstered in red Naugahyde, speckled Formica tables and counters scarred with use, and square floor tiles with converging dingy gray grout lines that might have been white a long time ago—a fifties diner but a real one, not an approximation of a half-understood aesthetic. A few booths were occupied by families. Faces turned toward me, bored eyes looked me over and looked away. Twanging country western guitar joined in with the clatter of silverware and blasts of high-pressure dish washing back in the kitchen.

"Sit here or in the bar. You can order food either place." Behind the counter, a woman in red uniform polo shirt and black apron gestured toward a stool. I wandered over, in Dustin Cruz character—a little hesitant.

"I guess I'll go in the bar," I pointed to a doorway leading into a dark adjoining space. "That way?"

"Yep. Tell Jim what you want if you're ordering food." She gave me a curious look and pushed a lock of dark hair back off her forehead, tucking it behind her ear. She might have been in her mid-thirties judging by the beginnings of fine wrinkles around curiously pale brown, almost golden eyes.

"Okay. Thanks." I nodded and strolled back through the seating area, into the dimly lit lounge where I found a coin-op pool table, a few booths, and a nicely crafted wooden bar. A wave of beer smell rolled across me and the bare concrete floor was sticky under my boot soles. I chose a stool at the bar. There were two other patrons, both hunched over beers and staring at a TV, hockey players gliding back and forth on the ice, bouncing off each other and swarming around the puck. They both glanced at me, nodded, then back to the TV. The bartender put down his newspaper, slid off a stool, winced, and approached stiffly with a kind of rolling gait, picking up a menu on his way.

"Ordering food?" He was tall and maybe in his sixties with a cap of white hair and a good-sized gut over his belt buckle.

"Sure, I'll take a look."

"Drink?"

I studied the tap handles. "Pabst, I guess."

He nodded and turned away, looking for a glass. What would Dustin Cruz order, I wondered? Was he a burger and fries kind of guy? He would go for something cheap and filling. The pint of beer clunked down and I looked up.

"Ready?"

"Sure. I'll take the club sandwich."

"Fries?"

"Okay."

Jim the bartender wrote it down slowly on a ticket, then looked toward the doorway back into the restaurant, squinting.

"Want me to run it back over?" I asked.

"If you don't mind, Hip's acting up today."

"No problem." I took the ticket and got up.

When I came back, he was still propped up against the bar, watching the hockey. I sat and sipped my beer. A player smashed an opposing player into the wall. A fight broke out but was quickly broken up by the referees. The station cut to a commercial—footage of a shiny black truck speeding through a red rock canyon.

"Looks like my back yard." Jim said, side eyeing me.

"They shoot a lot of those commercials around here I guess." I replied.

"Sure do." He turned back to me. "Staying next door?"

I hesitated for a second then shook my head. "Up the road. Linda's Market."

"Those cabins? Linda don't usually open those in the winter."

"I guess I convinced her. Just pulled in on the bus earlier."

"You must have asked real polite."

"I did that," I said, looking down.

"Visiting family in town, then?" He was the second person to ask. It must have been about the only reason anyone came to Helem in the winter.

"No. A friend if I can find him. Wrote to me he joined up with some kind of group. They gave him work to do, a place to sleep, food to eat."

"Sounds like that cult in the old school building."

"Up half a mile from Linda's?"

"That's the one. Lots of folks around here not very fond of them. They're fine as far as I can tell. Keep to themselves, mostly."

"They know how to keep their women under control, I'll tell you that much." It was one of the hunched hockey watchers, looking our way. A big guy in a hunting anorak and camo cap. "None of this equal rights bullshit. Cooking, cleaning, watching children, wearing those dresses. They've got that much right anyway."

"You'll have to pardon Tom there. Thinks it's still nineteen fifty." Jim winked at me. "Probably why his wife left him and went to Salt Lake."

Tom went back to the TV, pointedly turning his back to us.

"Well, I guess I'll check it out." I said. "Know anything about them?"

"That's a recruitment center," Jim said. "Maybe they all are. I spent twenty years in the Army so I know recruitment when I see it. Lots of young people come through here in the spring and summer. Mountain bikers, hikers, runners. All going to Zion, Canyonlands. Those people from the commune go sit at the park entrances and hand out flyers and sell homemade honey and jam. A few kids will take them up on the offer, go by the commune for a free dinner. Even fewer decide to stay for a while, maybe join up. The ones with nothing good going on in their lives. Maybe they see something there. Enough to make it worthwhile I guess. That's how you grow a cult. Aside from having babies. They do plenty of that, too." Jim slapped the bar and smiled like he had made a hilarious joke. I smiled, too.

"I'm sure they do. They're not brainwashing people though are they? Making them stay if they want to leave?"

"Not as such. Far as I know anyway. I think the ones who join up really believe all the mumbo jumbo about UFOs and Buddhas and whatnot." Jim broke off, watching the waitress from out front carry my plate in and set it down in front of me. "Thanks Angie. I'll let you eat now."

"Thanks for the info." I nodded "I guess I'll go see about it. Not looking to get recruited."

Jim slapped the counter again. "Good luck finding your friend."

Chapter 6

Suspect Device
12/8: Helem, Utah

Back at my little cabin after another cold walk under the big sky, I got the phone out, logged in to gardenersparadise.com, navigated to the Variegated Foliage forum, and scrolled through several pages of posts until I found the one I was looking for—Variegated Aspidistra.

On March 11th, 2009, BethAnn1962 of Sioux Falls South Dakota uploaded a nice photo of a Dragon's Tongue Aspidistra. Unfortunately, no one ever replied to congratulate her on her gardening prowess. I tapped the Reply button and become the first: "Lovely Aspidistra!" It was a sign for Ashna, to let her know I was still alive. Driving me to the Greyhound station, she had made me promise to keep in touch. I lay back, head on the musty pillow, remembering our conversation.

"Three days with no contact and I'll assume you've been brainwashed."

"Fine, I'll remember to post. They aren't going to brainwash me."

"Not so sure. Your brain is already the consistency of runny oatmeal sloshing around in your skull right now. A good dose of cult propaganda might blast it right out your ears. Your motivation here is fucked. You know that right? You're going because you feel guilty for something that's not your fault."

"No, I'm going because it's the only way to check up on Malena and make sure she's okay."

"That's your rationalization. I'm sure you believe it. But I think you have reasons so deep you can't even begin to understand them. They've been stacking up ever since you were a kid. Cause, effect, cause, effect. Now you think you have to be the knight in armor, riding off to free the maiden from the evil cult. She's an adult. She made her choice."

"Why warn me, then? Why use our old code to tell me to stay away?"

"I don't know. Maybe she just doesn't want you barging in and messing up the life she's managed to make for herself..."

Maybe Ashna was right. Maybe I didn't understand my own motivations. Unable to agree on anything else, we had at least worked out this gardening forum scheme. It was an easy, completely anonymous way for us to communicate. I didn't want anything on the phone tying me to my real identity if someone found it. We both used burner email addresses to create accounts on the obscure forum. She would check it daily. If I didn't post anything for a few days, she would come looking for me. Meanwhile, she was focusing on trying to hack the Community. When I left, she still hadn't determined whether they even had a computer system or central database.

I dropped the phone on the bedside table and closed my eyes. I hadn't really slept on the bus so I should have been tired but sleep did not come easily. My brain buzzed with what I had learned so far while wind sighed and rattled the cabin's windows. I tossed and turned, finally fell asleep, then jolted awake at 4:00 a.m. when a semi passing through town clattered over a bump. I'd been in the middle of a dream. A memory from childhood. In the barn, helping my foster father replace a rotten beam. The wood was silver-gray with age, pitted with holes and channels. I struck it with a hammer and it crumbled, revealing a warren of termites scurrying in their broken tunnels, swarming through the eaten wood, translucent, shiny bodies perversely juxtaposed with the pulped cellulose. I remember being afraid. Anything could set him off but my foster father just hefted it and lumbered outside, tossed it down in the weeds, doused it with gasoline, and lit it on fire. I watched the termites hiss and crackle in the flames. *You watch it. Make sure the fire don't spread.* I remember his voice, thick with disuse. He almost never spoke.

Why was I dreaming about that? I hadn't thought about it for years. My brain warning me? The Community like a hive of mindless bugs? I slept fitfully for another couple of hours but my body was restless. Finally I sat up, dug out the old pair of running shoes I'd packed, sweats, t-shirt, fleece hoodie.

Frost and a light blanket of snow covered the ground. Golden, early twilight bathed the world, sun not yet risen over the bluffs. Pine needles, frozen clumps of sage grass, an old tire in a ditch shaggy with ice crystals—all etched in sharp relief as I huffed in air so cold it burned my lungs. I headed up the road, away from the highway.

I passed a few houses, set well back with chain link fences demarcating their property. A quarter mile from the highway the asphalt ended. I ran on over dirt and loose gravel. I had to be close to the old school. My muscles were finally warming up. One last involuntary shiver ran through me. A path branched off to the left, leading away toward an escarpment maybe four hundred yards across an undeveloped stretch of rock and creosote. I turned and kept running, feet slapping the cold packed dirt.

Down through a dry arroyo, back up, sun cresting distant rimrock and blinding me for a moment with its brilliance. Shadows jumped from bushes and boulders. I reached the face of the escarpment, turned left. Another minute of running, weaving around boulders and cacti. I found a lower, crumbled area where I could scramble up. Atop the cliff I stopped, bending over and breathing hard. Breath caught, I straightened and looked out over the landscape. To my right in the distance, the highway cut through like a ribbon, the sad cluster of buildings that included Linda's Market, a few blocks of houses on either side. To the left, closer, the windows of the old school, now commune, blazed back reflected sunlight. It looked like the athletic field had been tuned into plots for growing food, and another five-acre field beyond that planted in winter rye. At the edge of the field were several stacks of beehive boxes. I remembered old Jim the bartender mentioning that they sold homemade honey. Closer to me, at the junction where desert met the fenced property, a fairly new looking barn squatted, classic red and gambrel roofed with boxed white Xs on the doors. A woman in a long dress, knit hat, and quilted coat emerged from a side door, carrying an aluminum tub under one arm. A dog, lean and buff colored, followed her. In the parking lot out front, an unmarked white cargo truck was parked with the open back facing me. I watched a man in jeans and flannel lower the lift gate. I had to be somewhere between a quarter and a half mile away from the compound but I could hear the motor clearly, whining as the gate dropped. I crouched down, making myself less visible and watched. Another man approached and together they rolled a big wooden crate over and heaved it onto the lift gate.

I watched them load three more before my muscles began to cool and a shiver crawled up my spine. I was ready to head back to my cabin and then find some coffee and breakfast.

Wrapped in a couple of shawls, watching Jake, Linda was outside the back door of the Quonset when I came huffing up. The old dog looked up at me and whined.

"Just get your business done so we can both go inside where it's warm," she said, then glanced up at me. "Chilly morning for a run."

"No argument there," I replied.

"Go by the commune?"

"No. Turned off the road. Found a way up onto a bluff. Good view from up there," I took a deep breath, heart rate slowing. "Saw some rabbits looking for breakfast. Saw a hawk looking for rabbits. Saw some people over at that commune I guess. The old school. Pretty far away but it looked like they were loading up a truck with old ammo crates."

Linda nodded, watching the dog who finally decided to poop. "Mmhmmm."

"What would they be transporting out of there? They're not into guns are they? Like those people in Texas back in the nineties?"

"Not as far as I know," Linda said, bagging the

steaming turd. "They seem peaceful. Coffee's on in the shop if you want to come around."

"I'll do that. Thanks."

Back in the cabin I showered and dressed, wondering why a branch of the Community had chosen this backwater to settle in and speculating about what might be inside those crates. They were undoubtedly military surplus but that didn't mean they had anything nefarious inside. Anyone could buy old ammo crates. They sounded heavy though based on the scraping, bumping sounds they made as they were loaded into the truck. Jars of honey and jam? Maybe, but not likely. The commune would have to be running an industrial operation to produce enough to fill those crates.

The Moscow rules, a set of basic principles developed by spies working in Moscow during the cold war, say that you should always trust your gut. My gut was telling me there was more going on in that old school building than large scale production of sugary toast toppings. I hoped they weren't into drug running or arms dealing or stockpiling weapons for an insurrection. That would make things more difficult if Malena was in there and they didn't want her to leave. The Moscow rules also said to assume nothing. It was all guess work and assumptions. I needed to get inside and check it out.

Five o'clock came soon enough. I stood outside the commune's front gate with the last sliver of the day's sun warming my back and shining on the chain-link fence. Someone had woven strips of colorful plastic in and out of the metal links, painstakingly spelling out *Red Butte Commune* in intarsia letters. Below that, a button was attached to the links with zip ties, the wire braided through and running off back toward the building. I pushed the button and heard nothing. A moment later, a dog barked, muffled.

The building sat back about forty yards from the gate. Casting long blue shadows, the white cargo truck I had observed that morning, the old school bus parked along the fence line in a patch of weeds, a jeep, and a land cruiser were all arrayed between me and the front elevation of the old school which looked like pretty much every other school built in the same era—single story brick, big windows, a covered walkway leading back to glass double doors. Beyond the doors I could see a dimly lit lobby. Heavy curtains hung in the other windows, blocking out any light that might have escaped.

After about a minute, a woman appeared in the lobby, pushed one of the doors open and peered out. She saw me and came tromping across the lot, skirt billowing behind. From a ten-foot distance, she examined me, squinting against the last bit of sun that lit her face up red-gold. Her long blond hair was pulled back in a plait and her face was thin, hard, and beautiful in that molten light.

"Hello," I said, raising a hand. "They told me you hold dinners here, all invited."

"We don't usually have visitors in the middle of winter," she replied, voice clear and low. "Who told you?"

"Linda at the market," I pointed down the road. "I'm looking for a friend who joined your group. He sent me an email last summer, said I should come check it out."

"Name?"

"My friend's name? Kyle. Kyle Johnson."

"Don't remember him. A lot of new people come

through in the spring and summer." She came forward. A chain and combination padlock held the rolling gate closed. Her fingers spun the code out nimbly and she pulled the gate open far enough for me to step through. "What's your name?"

"Dustin. Thanks for letting me in."

"Of course. I'm Anna. We're getting dinner ready now. Like I said, we're not used to having guests in the winter but we always welcome the stranger. This way. Where are you from Dustin?"

"Grew up in California. Southern. I've been all around since then, though." We passed the truck. I looked back, hoping to see the door still open but it was closed up tight. "I never really stay anywhere for long. My friend, Kyle, he said you people have something good going here."

"We think so," Anna said, pulling the glass door open. "We live by simple rules. Our leader, Eleanor Jane Sibyl, Sister Eleanor we call her, she tells us the best way to live."

We walked into the lobby and I stopped for a moment, looking around. It was a large space. A glass case, made for trophies, held a selection of books. I recognized a couple of covers—Sibyl's books. On the one nearest to me Eleanor Jane Sibyl's face was raised, her eyes half closed, mouth open as if inhaling. Soft, hazy light bathed her thin features. She seemed to be floating in a golden sky. The title, in a curvy seventies-era font, said *Whispers of the Sacred*. There were audio and video tapes too, and stacks of brochures, all with the same kind of design, all preserved here in the little shrine meant to house celebrations of adolescent glory on the field and in the gym.

"Those are her words," Anna said behind me.

The polished floor shone bright, reflecting fluorescent lights above, covered with the same 12 x 12 inch vinyl tiles you find in schools everywhere, in shades of ochre to match the hills outside. A receptionist's office with a dark wood counter and metal shutter rolled down took up the far end of the lobby. I imagined the receptionist who might have sat behind the counter as a sort of washed-out Eva Marie Saint type in a sweater set, fingers poised on her manual typewriter. Wide hallways led off in either direction, lined with doors to what must have been administrative offices and classrooms. Large windows on both sides of the reception desk showed a dim courtyard beyond. I heard a giggle and looked to my left. Two children disappeared around a bend in the hallway.

"The children will be excited to have a guest," Anna said. "They get bored in the winter."

"I'm happy to oblige. Always liked kids."

"Come this way. Dinner is in the refectory."

"Refectory?"

"Yes. As you can see, this used to be a school. We prepare food and eat in the building that used to be the gym and cafeteria. We call it the refectory." She led me down the left hallway. We passed doors, all closed, far enough apart that I guessed they led to former classrooms.

"Do you all live in the old classrooms?"

"Married couples, yes. Younger, unmarried members of our congregation sleep in the dormitories, segregated of course."

A door opened up ahead and a man walked out into the corridor—tall and wiry, with long dark hair pulled straight back in a pony tail. He wore jeans and flannel with suspenders like the two I had seen loading the truck. His heavy boots clomped on the floor, echoing down the hall. He glanced back, saw us, and turned. I watched him approach. He moved like a jungle cat on the prowl, not stiff like the farmer or laborer his clothing suggested, muscles rolling with every step, eyes watching with a supercilious distance.

"Noah," Anna said, raising a hand. "We have a visitor for dinner tonight. This is Dustin."

He strode forward and stopped five feet from me, not offering to shake hands. His face was dour, hairline receding though he seemed young. "Welcome," he said, monotone.

"Thanks." I glanced at Anna. We stood in awkward silence for a moment. "I came looking for a friend of mine. Kyle Johnson."

Noah nodded. "Nobody by that name here."

"He emailed me a while back. Might have just passed through."

"Maybe. We have a lot of new members join here. They go on to other congregations mostly. I can check the database for you." His eyes turned cold, suspicious for a moment, then went back to neutral. A bell rang. "Dinner bell. Come eat. It's time. I'll check later." He turned away.

"Noah is our manager," Anna said. He was walking fast, twenty feet ahead of us by then.

"Manager?"

"Yes, every outpost of The Community has a manager who takes care of financials and membership and other details like that so the rest of us don't have to worry about it. Noah is gone a lot, working at

66

headquarters. But when he's here he's our manager."

"Where's headquarters?" I asked. "And how many are there? Outposts I mean," I asked.

"Oh, I'm not sure." She sounded guarded and I realized my question was a bit out of line. I would have to be more careful. "Probably hundreds. Some are like this, communal living. Others are just places where several households of believers live close to each other and meet on Sundays. Like any religion, just people going to church!"

I nodded. That was what it had been like for Malena and I and our foster parents. "So maybe my friend Kyle went to a place like that? Or another commune?"

"Both are possible. Noah will look it up for you."

We reached the end of the hallway and Anna pushed through a glass door, holding it open for me. A breezeway led from there to a big cinderblock building. We hurried across, shivering in the sudden cold, and entered the refectory through another set of double doors. Inside, I stopped, bracing myself. If Malena was there and she recognized me what would she do? Wait until we could talk privately I hoped, examining the room.

It reminded me strongly of the gym and cafeteria in my childhood elementary school but instead of canned vegetables and grade C, overcooked meat, the food smelled delicious. And instead of championship banners and motivational sayings, fabric hangings draped the walls, depicting saints and holy people from every religion. I remembered those banners. Our gathering hall when I was a kid had them too—a weird mashup of medieval European, Russian orthodox, Buddhist and Hindu holy men and a few women too, all staring out with piercing eyes from blue fields of sky with rays bursting around their heads, pouring out in halos of divine light. Between them, an abundance of children's' artwork exploded colorfully from bulletin boards. Above, the high ceiling rose to a peak, supported by big wooden beams. The hardwood floor still showed remnants of painted lines, red and white, denoting basketball and volleyball courts, long planks leading my eye to the far end of the big room where a stage rose up a few feet above the floor level, red proscenium curtain closed and a bulky old CRT television on a rolling cart in front of it. Pillows in sunburst colors scattered across a giant blue carpet formed a rough arc around the TV, like stones in a river.

Filling the other half of the space, nearer to us, the inhabitants of the commune sat at rows of rolling cafeteria tables which, judging by the faded green Formica tops, blasted nearly white in places by time and use, must have come with the building. Altogether, I estimated about forty people—men, women, children of all ages—either seated at the tables or lined up at the window where food was being served.

The women and girls, like Anna, all wore long, high necked prairie dresses and kept their heads covered with bonnets, knit hats, or scarves. I scanned their faces as casually as I could, looking for Malena. The men all wore some variation of what I had observed already—jeans and button up shirts, suspenders, worn work boots. I watched them all for a frozen moment, bent over their bowls. Nobody spoke above a murmur. They were turned inward, insular, acting in harmony like a murmuration of birds. I could easily imagine them raising a barn together or bringing in a harvest, all hands working together. I could just as easily imagine them standing shoulder to shoulder as a witch was burnt at the stake, or crouching behind barricades with rifles, united against the government.

Something bumped my leg. I looked down into pale green-gold eyes. A girl maybe four years old gazed up at me.

"Hi," she said. "I'm Alma."

I crouched down, eye level with her. "Hello. I'm Dustin. Nice to meet you Alma." I offered my hand and she shook it solemnly.

"Would you like some soup?" she asked. "It's chicken and rice with carrots."

"Yes, I'd love some. Thank you."

"Come on, then." She took my hand and dragged me toward the food line. Heads raised and nodded, eyes followed me, tight smiles appeared and faded quickly as I passed by. These were reserved people. Alma seemed to be an outlier.

Anna followed and we joined the end of the line while Alma ran off to sit on her mother's lap—a round, tired looking woman—and glance at me shyly, looking away when I returned her gaze. Other children peeked too, turning and leaning to get looks at me. They must have been very isolated. I wondered if they ever left the commune. I remembered Malena telling me she taught the young children.

At the window, a wide, matronly woman nodded a welcome as she passed me a plate holding a bowl of the soup du jour and a hunk of freshly baked bread with a generous pat of butter melting into it.

Anna led me to a table nearby where we sat with a teenage boy, face florid with acne, a middle-aged man with a barrel chest and thick arms stretching his sleeves, and a stout woman around the same age. I was about to introduce myself when a deep voice rose up from somewhere to my left.

"The wise and holy beings, those who have ascended and those who come to us from far away, masters of the ancient wisdom, great builders, they see us gathered around this table, praising the bounty provided by the earth and the supreme being, master of masters. With our gaze set upon their wisdom and our hearts open to the words spoken through their earthly medium, Eleanor Jane Sibyl, we give thanks for this nourishment."

A murmur flowed like a wave through the room, a symphony of clinks and dings as silverware was raised, and everyone began to eat.

"Welcome to our community," the big guy across the table said, looking up from his bowl. "I'm Luis. This is my wife Maria, and our son Xavier."

"Nice to meet you all." I nodded and smiled. "Thank you for inviting me in. I'm Dustin." I tried, as I had been since arriving in Helem, to give an impression of simpleminded humbleness. I wanted them to see me as non-threatening, beaten down by life, ready to cling to anyone who deigned to say a positive word. No actor, I wasn't much good at being anyone but my irascible, sometimes haughty self so my best bet was to try to be a bit simpler version of me.

"Dustin is looking for a friend," Anna said. "His friend joined us last summer and wrote to Dustin. Told him he should come see about The Community. See if it might be the right place for him."

"I was hoping he might still be here but I guess he

moved on to another location."

"Yes, most of our new members move on from here. Cold here in the winter," Luis said around a bite of bread. "And hard work and quiet. They go on to the congregations farther south, closer to the coasts, where we have younger members, help us get out the good word, find a partner, settle down."

"I don't mind the cold myself," I replied. "Or hard work."

"What kind of work do you do?"

"I'm a welder by trade. Do framing, drywall, concrete, and general carpentry, too."

Luis nodded. "Useful skills." His hand, wrapped around a spoon that looked like a toy in his grip, was weathered and callused from work. "We could use a welder. Needed one just the other day. We've got an old arc welding rig out in the barn but nobody knows how to use it much. Was thinking of sending Xavier here out to a class to learn but the community college is all the way in Kanab. Long drive."

"Well, I'd be happy to help out. Maybe I could teach Xavier the basics." I smiled and nodded to the kid who kept his eyes down, embarrassed or shy. "Welding is easy to learn but hard to master, they say. You only learn by doing it."

"Very kind of you to offer," Anna said, giving me a sidelong glance and a smile.

The boy's mother, Maria, nodded her agreement. "Yes, thank you."

Chapter 7

Inside
12/9-10: Helem, Utah

I woke the next morning in my cozy cabin thinking
of the videotaped sermon I had been subjected to
following dinner the night before. Just like when I was a
kid and they brought out the TV at home or in the
meeting hall on Sundays, there was Eleanor Jane Sibyl,
older now, hair gone gray, face even thinner, still
spouting the same strange mix of aphorisms and obscure
theosophist doctrine peppered with references to alien
visitors, saints, and angels. Even the wood paneled wall
behind her and the subterranean basement lighting were
the same. Surreptitiously, I had observed the people
around me, trying to determine how much of it they
believed. Were they taken in by the nonsense? Or did
they just like communal life? It was hard to tell. Anna,
seated on my right, had listened intently, eyes closed and
head bobbing silently. Noah, on my left, sat stone faced,
eyes never leaving the TV screen.

I hadn't seen Malena. If she had been there, she
wasn't any longer. Unless they had a secret call center
somewhere in the old school where they were keeping
people prisoner and forcing them to call lapsed members
of the flock. That seemed unlikely. More likely was that
she had simply been moved to another location. As far

as I could tell from what I had been able to learn the night before, members were moved between outposts frequently. Even when I was a kid, I remembered people coming and going—especially my foster brothers and sisters but that was usually because they ran away, fed up with life on the farm.

I had agreed to go back, arriving mid-morning to start teaching Xavier how to weld. Meanwhile, Noah would look up my non-existent fiend Kyle Johnson for me. My goal was to ingratiate myself enough to be invited to move into the compound. Once I was in, I would find an opportunity to get into their computer systems and track down Malena, or at least get Ashna the info she needed to hack in. Brother Noah had said there was a database so somewhere in the old school, there was a computer. If it had an internet connection, Ashna could hack it.

The more I turned it over in my mind, the more I felt something was off at Red Butte Commune. I had felt a pervasive unease from the people there, like they were all expectantly waiting for something unpleasant to happen. The thought of going back aroused an atavistic, edge-of-panic aversion deep in my brain—like a mouse crossing an open stretch of ground at twilight dreads the blurred whoosh and snatch of the owl. Behind the taciturn faces of Noah, Luis, and a couple of the other men and women I had met, I sensed zealotry, distrust verging on hatred of the outside world, and a readiness to deal swiftly with anyone or anything that might threaten their quiet life. Anna, in contrast, had seemed trapped and resigned. Xavier, too. He reminded me a little of myself at that age. It would be tricky to pull off but I didn't need to hoodwink them for long. I just needed enough time to find out where Malena was.

"Had dinner up at Red Butte?" Linda asked as I pumped coffee from the airpot. I watched the black liquid whoosh into the cup, then turned and brought it to the counter.

"Yes. Nice people up there. Good food, too."

"They do know how to make a meal. Half of why anyone ever joins up I think."

"Could be."

"Find your friend?"

"No, he moved on, I guess. They're going to look him up for me, see if they can figure out which of their places he went to."

"And did they make you watch one of those videos of the old lady?"

Jake bumped my leg and I leaned down to pet him, nodding. "Yes, I watched it. I can't say I understood any of it."

"Well, be careful. Eleanor Jane Sibyl might seem like an old dingbat nattering about aliens and angels but she's powerful."

I looked up and met Linda's eyes. "Powerful?"

"Yes. There's a reason all those people keep believing in her and giving the Community their money and their lives. She's got some kind of magic. Hypnotism? Mind control? Drugs? I don't know."

"I'll be careful." I nodded, thinking. It wasn't how I would describe her appeal but maybe Linda understood better than I did. Had she spent time there herself? She must have. I didn't want to ask her about it just then though. I wasn't ready for her story, if she was even willing to tell it. "Thanks."

Back in my cabin, my brain returned to the video

from the night before. It was like a loose tooth I couldn't keep from poking. Some clue there? I thought back to the videos from my childhood, too. Sibyl wasn't charismatic in any usual way but, like Linda said, she did have something that pulled all those people in. I got my anonymous phone out and found a video of her on YouTube. She was younger by about ten years, same wall, same gauzy gold lace tacked up behind her. I realized with a start that the videos had originally been shot at the compound in Montana, then continued wherever she had posted up after fleeing from the FBI. Bizarrely, they had meticulously recreated the original setting.

"...my beloved family, realize that there is a time and a place for the interpretation of the writing of the old ones, the masters who bring the light of wisdom to our hearts. There is a time for prophecy spoken out of time and space and communicated to us on light waves beamed back by travelers from the outer realities. There is a time for sheep to speak and the wolves to listen. There is also the time for the one who bears the mantle of Saint Catherine and of Azreal and of Gora Kumbhar, to speak as a prophetess in the wilderness of this degraded nation and to point to the star of wisdom to lift us all into the light of transcendent peace where the evils of Sodom that warp our youth will fall away and the hands and hearts will lift up God-victorious. A new, golden-age of the three flames! The flame I call violet flame. The flame I call sapphire flame. The flame I call ruby flame. The trinity of flames of manifesting and becoming. The flames that propel the trinity, the ancient three on their journey to the stars. To all of you I say that our end is the saturation of earth in the flames of renewal, the ending of the black iron prison, the liberation of…"

I poked the stop button. Her rhetoric boiled over in apocalyptic, messianic waves but her delivery was dry, stilted. Was that its appeal? She seemed to have become more focused and whittled down with age, like she existed solely as a conduit for the words that poured out.

I hid the phone away again in its secret pocket and rose from the bed, clearing my mind. I wasn't trying to solve the mystery of Eleanor Jane Sibyl. My mission was to find Malena and extricate her if she was in danger or held against her will. People did and believed a lot of things I couldn't understand. I had always been a weirdo, out of step with the society around me. My failure to understand the appeal of Eleanor Jane Sibyl was just one more brick in that wall. *Let it go*. Focus on the mission.

****

I arrived at the gate right on time and pressed the button, then waited, loneliness and cold and weak winter sun wrapping me in foreboding fingers. A chill wind blew from the north, rustling the creosote and biting my exposed parts with a fine desert grit.

Xavier came out this time and let me in. He was a quiet kid, looking down and turning away to hide his face in the shearling collar of his jacket.

"Thanks for coming out to get me. Ready to learn some welding today?"

He nodded, unspeaking. We passed by the white truck, still parked there with its mystery cargo. I glanced through the windshield. A door behind the seats gave access from the cabin back into the cargo space. Good to know.

"Listen, kid. I'm not here to hassle you," I said. "If you don't want to learn I won't force you. This just

76

something your dad wants but you don't?"

"No," he croaked, stricken faced. "No, I want to learn."

We strode side by side around the side of the school building. There was a fence closing off the front lot from the main grounds. Xavier lifted a fork latch and pushed the gate open.

"Keeps the dogs out of the front," he mumbled. "They can push through the rolling gate and get out." As if on cue, a big rottweiler mix came bounding up and stopped five feet away, staring at me with wary eyes. "It's okay, Casey. Mr. Cruz is a guest. Now shoo."

The dog turned and walked with us. I smelled a pungent aroma, dark and earthy, wafting on the breeze. "What's that smell?"

"Beets," Xavier answered. "They're canning beets today." He glanced toward the cafeteria and gym building where the kitchen was located. I saw a plume of steam rising from a chimney pipe on the roof.

An axe thunked wood and I spotted two men outside the barn, splitting and stacking, puffs of breath forming little white clouds.

Hands in pockets, Xavier trudged on, leading me to the barn on a well-traveled path around the perimeter of the old athletic field, glancing sidelong every now and then.

"Is there work? Welding?" he asked.

"Work? Sure. You do a training program, get certified. Plenty of work building ships, bridges, offices." I was making it up, never having really thought about it but what I was saying sounded right. I had learned to weld in art school but Dustin Cruz would have apprenticed or done a vocational course. Was Xavier thinking of it as a way out of the commune? Probably, if he had any brains or ambition. It was a stultifying life.

We reached the barn. Next to it was a prefab metal building with big open doors, distinctive colors and forms of farm equipment beyond. I saw a John Deere combine parked just inside. Luis, Xavier's father, wandered out, waving to us.

"You made it. Thanks for coming out. Come look at this. Little crack here on the reel," he pointed to a metal bar that made up part of the front assembly of the combine. "Think you could fix that?"

I examined the crack, running a finger over it. "Xavier can fix it," I answered. "You have any scrap metal? Something we can practice on? Give me half an hour to teach him and he'll be ready."

Two hours later, we sat in the cafeteria eating left-over soup from the night before, warmth slowly seeping back into my fingers and toes. I had been right about Xavier. He was a good student and motivated. Welding could be his ticket out of the commune. His face was flushed and happy, integrating a new skill and talent into his psyche—a chunk of self-confidence. Luis gave him proud father glances, trying to be surreptitious but Xavier saw and took it in. It felt good. Part of what had surprised me about teaching was my investment in my students' learning and growth.

"Nice and warm in here," I said. "How do you heat this old place?"

"Boiler," Luis explained. "The original boiler from 1952 when the place was built. Runs on gas."

Noah strode up with a bowl and joined our table. His face looked windburned, hair tangled over his high, creased forehead. He had spent the morning outside. He gave the impression of a wild animal still but more fox now maybe, or a hawk. I had my share of wild animal, too, and I felt the tension between us. Some unspoken signal passed between Noah and Luis. Luis turned to me.

"How do you like our community here Dustin?"

"It seems like a great place. You run a tight ship. Everything well maintained. Great food. Good people."

"Why don't you come stay with us for a little while? Learn how we do things, find out more about our faith. We welcome people who come to us. You don't seem like you have a destination. Maybe you're seeking what we have to offer."

"I'd like that," I looked down, trying to play it the way Dustin Cruz would, but my mind was racing with suspicion. Why were they suddenly giving me the hard sell on moving in? I'd assumed it would take some work on my part to get an invitation—more than one morning's work anyway. Did Noah suspect me? Was he taking Julius Caesar's advice and keeping his enemy close? "I've just been wandering most of life," I said, keeping my voice steady. "Never found anything to keep me in a place."

"You might find that here," Noah said. "You might not. Worth a try. You know how to work with your hands. You're not one of the soft city people sitting in an office all day, going home to sit some more in front of a TV. Eleanor Jane Sibyl says the working people, those who toil with the strength of their bodies, will be lifted up. The wisdom of the masters is heard when the body is tired and at rest. There is no true rest for those who labor only in the mind. They live inside a machine they can't understand. We stand on the earth. When the fire comes, those who have heard the teaching will create a new order…" He broke off, face consumed with fervor, body tense. With an effort he calmed himself.

"Can't say I understand all of the things she said in that video," I looked at my hands. "But I like how you live here, if that's what she preaches."

"Good," Luis said, grasping my arm. "Good. Come try our way of life."

"Okay. I'll give it a try," I said, meeting their eyes. "And you'll look up my friend on your computer? Try to find where he went?"

"Yes," Noah said. "You come tomorrow morning. We'll get a room set up for you by then. I think Xavier would like to keep learning welding. We all work. We work hard and sleep deep. You'll fit in."

****

I had all afternoon to kill and I'd already eaten lunch so I decided to walk around what was left of Helem. I hadn't walked it in the daylight yet. I knew what was west of Linda's Market–just the old housing I had seen, Lucky's Bar and Grill, and a few warehouses–so I headed east, walking along the highway. The air felt almost warm compared to the chill of the morning. Thin, too. Helem was at 5000 feet. The far side of the highway was just gravel, a fence, and scrub beyond all the way to the bluffs and buttes in the distance. On my side of the street I passed a shuttered hair salon, dead flies belly up on the window sill. A hardware store with an OPEN sign but nobody at the counter and, from what I could see through the window, inventory that hadn't been restocked in twenty years. That could be a good thing. Old tools were qualitatively better than new ones in my experience–higher quality parts, materials, and workmanship. I made a note to stop back by.

After the hardware store I passed another road leading up into the canyons, then came to a little brick building that struck me as municipal–government architecture inscribed in its proportions and materials. I followed the gravel path to the front door and put my face up to the window, hands shading my eyes. Inside I saw a small lobby with two shuttered service windows, a gumball machine, a couple of upholstered chairs in a tiny waiting area. The sign above the door said Helem City Hall.

I tried the door and was surprised to find it open. The air was thirty degrees warmer in the lobby and almost humid. A radiator against the far wall hissed and spat. Bells on the door jingled as it swung closed. The gumballs piled inside the glass globe atop the machine were vibrant on one side, faded nearly colorless by the sun on the other. Not a lot of gumball business in Helem, Utah.

"Coming," someone called from far away in the back of the building, his voice muffled. I waited. A couple of minutes later, the shutters on one of the windows opened and a man peered out, maybe in his seventies, wispy white hair on his liver spotted head.

"Help you with something?"

"Yes, actually," I said, realizing there was something he could help me with. "Do you have any records on the old school building where the commune is now? Leases or ownership deeds? I'm interested in who owns it."

I was taking a chance but I was pretty sure this guy wasn't a friend of the Community. Bureaucrats are rarely friendly with cults. My guess was that nothing I did in Helem City Hall would make it back to anyone at the

Red Butte Commune.

"Sure. I have the records on that but I don't need to dig them out. It's all right here," He tapped his forehead. "Bill Sanderson, by the way." He held a hand out to shake, "Mayor of Helem, not that that's much of an honor."

"Nice to meet you," I stepped forward and shook his hand.

"Now let's see. The old school was sold about thirty years ago. Not enough kids in town. Too expensive to maintain. The kids were bussed to Kanab after that. If you're trying to figure out who owns it though, you're out of luck. Some kind of syndicate, incorporated in the Cayman Islands. Paid by anonymous wire transfer. Blue Light Industries I think the name was. No way to find out anything about who the actual owners are unless you have inside contacts."

"Got it," I nodded stupidly, pretending I didn't really understand anything he'd said. "I was out there looking for a friend. They told me he moved on. Just curious I guess. Thanks for the information."

"You're welcome. Staying up the street at the Comfort Inn?"

"No, one of the cabins behind Linda's."

"Oh," He gave me a surprised look. "She doesn't usually rent those out in the winter."

"I guess she took pity on me. Anyway, thanks again. I'll let you get back to your work."

****

2:00 a.m., crouched behind a rock, shivering, watching the front lot of the commune, I thought through everything I knew, lining up the facts and intuitions and blank spots. My goal was to find Malena but I also didn't want to get killed. I needed to know more about what was going on at Red Butte Commune. I'd been watching for twenty minutes. No movement, no lights. I turned my gaze to the truck with its cargo of unmarked crates. Once I was inside, living in the commune, certain things would be more difficult. Finding out what was inside that truck might be one of them. It would require sneaking through the corridors at night and going out the front without waking anyone. My best chance was now.

The truck had manual door locks—the old style you could pull up if you hooked them just right. I had lock picks, a wire hanger from my cabin I had twisted into just the right shape to squeeze through the door frame and pop the lock open, a rubber door stop I'd seen near the front door in Linda's and pocketed surreptitiously, a little penlight, and a multitool that would hopefully get me into one of the crates once I was in. My biggest worry was the dogs. I had observed three of them the day before. Luis had pointed out their heated shelter just outside the barn. The main reason they kept dogs was to protect the farm equipment from thieves and the livestock from coyotes. It was 22° out according to the old thermometer nailed to the back wall of Linda's market. The dogs would be in their shelter. I just needed to be as quiet as possible.

I rose and crept up to the fence. Going over the top would be noisy but Xavier had said the dogs could push the gate open enough to slip through if they got into the front lot. That meant I could slip through, too. I wedged myself between the rolling gate and a post, pushing with steady pressure, frozen ground numbing my side through my coat and all the layers I was wearing underneath. Slowly, I wriggled forward and squeezed through the gap.

Crouching inside the fence, I listened for any sound of human or animal but heard only wind. All senses heightened now, I smelled chicken stock cooking in the cafeteria, left to simmer overnight, heard the hoot of a great horned owl somewhere far off in the dark. The truck's passenger side door was forty feet away, facing away from the curtained windows of the commune. I crossed to it, careful not to kick any gravel or scrape shoes on the asphalt. With the doorstop wedged between the frame and the door to force it slightly open, I fed the wire down into the truck. The hook was not quite right. I adjusted it with the multitool pliers and tried again. This time it caught. I pulled with steady pressure and the lock popped up. Tools stowed, I lifted the door latch and pulled, wincing in anticipation of a squeaky hinge but it opened silently. I gave thanks to Noah the zealot. He wasn't the type to let any kind of maintenance slide.

Inside the truck, I crouched and pushed the door between the cabin and the cargo area open, shining a weak beam from my penlight into the dark. They had left a narrow aisle down the center with crates stacked two high on either side. The smell of old wood and oil was strong. I crept down the aisle. At the back there was one single height row made up of larger boxes—maybe four feet high. I stooped, sweeping the light across the top of the nearest one. A hefty Phillips-head shone at each corner, nearly buried in the soft wood. I twisted them out with the multitool screwdriver, working slowly and muffling the squeaks and creaks with my coat. It took nearly ten minutes and my fingers were frozen but I got them all out at last, lifted the lid off, and set it aside. Inside, my flashlight beam glinted off machined metal, cone shaped, with streamlined tubes and lines wrapping the curves, all buried in fragrant wood shavings. An engine of some kind? Fuel lines? Red Cyrillic letters and numbers were printed on the side of the cone in a font that might be best described as Soviet sans. I got my phone out and snapped a photo. What it was, I couldn't tell. I would have to look it up. Open another one? The back of my neck was prickling, sweat opening my pores like pinpoints. Intuition was telling me to get out of there. I put the lid back on and replaced the screws, forcing myself to take deep breaths and do it right. Two minutes later I was walking back down the lonely desert road toward town, shivering and thankful for the bright moon above.

In my cabin with the heat cranked up I ran a reverse image search using the photo of the thing in the crate as input. It didn't take long to find. It was part of a Glushko RD-251 rocket engine—Soviet, designed during the cold war to power the R-36 family of intercontinental ballistic missiles. Also later used in Tsyklon space launch vehicles. A later version of the R-36 was known as the SS-18 Satan—the heaviest lift ICBM ever produced. Launched from silos, they had an operational range of up to 16,000 kilometers.

I read through the facts, seeing the words but not really taking them in. What were a bunch of communal farmers in rural Utah doing with cold war-era Russian ICBM engines? Arms dealing? Smuggling? It didn't compute. I felt very alone all of a sudden, sitting in my little cabin surrounded by the vast, empty, wind-swept desert. I wanted to call Ashna and tell her but I knew what she'd say: *Get out of there. Send the photo anonymously to the FBI. Let somebody else handle it.* I wasn't ready to do that quite yet. I was in a unique position to get more information and I wanted to see it through. If the commune was raided I might never find Malena. Their computers would be seized. The rest of the members of the Community would go underground again. I just needed a day or two. I was confident I could get into their systems somehow, probably at night while everyone was sleeping. After that, I could turn them in.

I lay back on the bed, looking again at the photo, those red Cyrillic characters wrapping around curving aluminum, mocking simulacrum of the arc of the rocket, gravity's rainbow as Pynchon called it. Thrust. Apogee. Descent. An entire city obliterated in a flash. A dangerous game for farmers to be playing. Once again, I had stumbled into something bigger and more ominous than I bargained for. This time, I needed to be more careful.

Chapter 8

Curious Data
12/10-11: Helem, Utah

The next morning I packed my duffle bag, locked the cabin up, and walked around to the front entrance of the market. Linda was in place behind the counter, wearing the same Navajo pattern shawl as the first time I met her—little triangles in orange, yellow, and blue joining to create stepped patterns like stars. She tipped her glasses down her nose and looked me over as I dropped my bag by the entrance and straightened up.

"Checking out?" she asked.

"Looks that way," I placed the key on the counter, soft country music twanging away from the radio, barely audible. "I'm grateful you let me use the cabin. They asked me to come stay out at the commune for a bit so I'm thinking I'll take them up on the offer. Young kid there wants to learn how to weld."

"Xavier, I guess?"

"Yeah, that's him. You know them pretty well? They must stop in here sometimes."

"Them? No, never. Grow or raise almost everything they eat out there. Drive into Kanab and shop at Costco for the rest. I spent some time there is all. Got to know them all pretty well."

"Oh, I didn't know you had lived out there. You

used to be a member?"

"Yes." Linda nodded, squinting at me. "Yes. I was young and stupid when I got caught in their trap. Dumb hippie girl. Took me a long time to get out. I was one of the originals out there at the school. It was nothing then. Abandoned for years and full of mice. The church bought it for a song. I lived there for twenty years, helped them turn it into what it is now. For nothing. All that hard work. They never paid me a dime or gave me anything but more work to do and a hard bed to sleep on. Finally I met Stan. He was the sheriff here in Helem, used to come around the commune sometimes to check in and make sure we were doing things by the book, educating the children mainly." Linda shifted on her stool and crossed her arms. "I'm telling you all this for a reason now so listen up. I'm not just some old lady maundering. Stan was old already when he asked me to marry him. A widower. His first wife died of cancer. She was a downwinder. I jumped at the chance to get out. He retired. We bought this place. He died of a stroke two years later and here I am all alone in this godforsaken place. Different kind of trapped now but I wouldn't go back for anything. Those people have good hearts but the Community warps them. Something about Eleanor Jane Sibyl, she gets into people's heads like a worm. Eats the part of their brain that can think for itself, leaves just the part that's content to be led around like a sheep. So, you watch yourself out there. You make sure you question everything they tell you…" She broke off, turning toward the door which had just banged open, bell tinkling. A semi was idling in the lot out front. The driver nodded to us and wandered down an aisle.

"I need some coffee," I said. "Be right back. I want

to ask you a question about the commune if I can?"

I poured coffee and sipped it, petting Jake for a minute while the trucker paid for his chips and soda. When he was gone I wandered back over to the counter.

"I want to make a confession."

Linda looked at me over her glasses again, nodding. "Yes?"

"I'm not who I'm pretending to be. My real name's Justin, not Dustin. I grew up in a foster family. They were members of the Community. I don't need any warnings about the Community, Believe me. I know all about them. I had a foster sister growing up. We were close. I haven't seen her or talked to her since I left that place when I was seventeen. She was supposed to leave, too, and come join me once I was settled but she never did. She called me out of the blue a couple of weeks ago. She said the Community was having a reunion, inviting everybody, including lapsed members, to come together. It was like she was being forced to call, reading a script. But then she warned me, using a kind of secret code from when we were kids. I got the message: stay away. That made me worried. I traced the call to here so I came out but she's not there anymore. I need to find out where they sent her. I need to get her out." I stopped speaking. Shafts of morning sun angled through the high windows on the east facing side of the shop. One cast a sunspot near my feet, dust motes circling slowly, turning the old floor boards into molten gold. I looked up and met Linda's eyes. "Her name is Malena. Did you know her? Was she there when you were?"

"Malena?" Linda was gazing at me steadily, adjusting to a new way of seeing me. Her eye twitched. "No. I don't remember her. I left in twenty fifteen. She might have come there after. They cut me off. I haven't been there since the day I left or even seen anyone from the Red Butte Commune except through the window when they drive by. I miss the kids. I used to teach them. I taught Xavier. He was good at math, hated spelling."

"Malena said she was teaching the kids, when she called me. Maybe that's why they brought her there, after you left."

"Could be. I can't imagine how you'll find her though, if they sent her away again. That Noah is a snake. Watch out for him. He won't tell you anything."

"I have…certain skills. I think I can get the information. Do you know where they keep their computer? They must have one out there. Noah said there's a database."

"Oh, I think there was one in the old reception office off the lobby. Ancient looking thing. That was years ago though. Maybe they have a newer one now. You won't hurt anyone there will you?"

"No. I don't work that way. I just want to find out where they sent her, then I'll disappear. Thanks for all your help. I really appreciate it."

"Well, I judge people by their faces. You have an honest face. I could tell right off you were a good person, a little lost, adrift. I grew up on the Navajo reservation, not far from here. My granny would have called you *hajei doo bina'adloo'góó*. That means honest hearted. So, that's why I let you stay. Be careful at Red Butte. If you find her, let me know. I'd like to know that someone else made it out, too."

I made the hike to Red Butte Commune once more with my duffle slung across my back this time. Maria, Xavier's mom, came to the gate to let me in. She was a short, plump woman with a broad face that beamed a steady joy out into the world—one of those saint-like people who remained calm and content in almost any situation.

"Hello. Welcome. I'm going to show you your room. I'm glad you decided to come stay."

"Thanks. My own room?" I glanced at the truck as we passed it, thinking about the strange cargo inside.

"Oh, we have a couple of rooms for guests, just temporary. Then if you decide to stay on, you'll get a permanent room. The boys and young men stay in the bunk house." She gave me a sidelong glance as if seeking my opinion on whether I was a young man.

"Wherever you have room is fine with me," I mumbled.

She led me through the lobby and down the corridor that branched off to the right. Looking at an aerial photo on Google maps, I had worked out that the old school was a rectangle with a small courtyard off the lobby. Former classrooms ringed the periphery. In the center, I guessed, was where the library had been. We turned left, walked the full length of the building, then turned left again, passing a door to the outside. Maria stopped and opened a door facing toward the inside of the rectangle.

"This was the librarian's office," she said as I followed her into a tiny space and then through another door. "We divided it into three small guest rooms."

The room, maybe eight by ten feet, had a mattress on a low wooden frame hand built out of two by fours, plywood walls painted white, and a small rag rug on the floor. A thick, rusty red blanket, folded immaculately, occupied the foot of the bed. There were no windows but there was an old, steel framed skylight in the high ceiling.

"This looks wonderful Thanks."

"I'll let you settle in," Maria said, backing out of the room. "Lunch in an hour. After that, I think Luis needs some help out in the barn. He's putting new belts and chains on the combine today."

Before dinner, Noah found me walking up from the barn with Luis and gestured brusquely, indicating I should follow him. We marched in silence past the chicken coop and around the main building, one of the dogs keeping pace with us, then entered via a side door and headed down a short corridor to the empty lobby. Our footsteps echoed as we crossed to the registration office. Noah pulled a big ring of keys from his pocket and opened the door, flipping on an overhead light. Inside, a tableau from another era greeted us.

A long, built-in desk of dark wood stretched wall to wall below the counter and roll down shutter that closed the space off from the lobby. A Steelcase chair was pulled up in front of an IBM Selectric typewriter and a rolodex in matching avocado green. Just as Linda had said, Red Butte's one bit of digital technology—a bulky beige PC that appeared to be approximately twenty years old—occupied the far corner of the desk. It was old enough to have a CRT monitor and a floppy disk drive. Noah dropped into the chair, scooted it over, and slapped the enter key a few times. Nothing happened. He sighed and pressed the main power button. The fan spun up and whined like a jet engine. I expected a Windows 95 logo. Instead, green monospaced text jerked across the screen. The computer appeared to be running some Unix variant, maybe Linux.

"Takes forever to boot," Noah mumbled. "I usually

leave it on but we get power surges pretty often."

After a couple of minutes of fan whine and hard drive grinding, the ancient machine offered a login prompt. I watched him type his username, nfisher, at the prompt. A new prompt asked for a password.

"Turn around for a minute," Noah commanded.

While I gazed out into the lobby, I heard him tap something out, keys clacking. He cursed under his breath. Tried again. Cursed again. Very softly, I heard the rolodex move. He was looking for a card but trying to do it quietly so I wouldn't hear. More clacking and a beep. He was in. I turned around as he typed a command: commdat. A text based interface appeared, some kind of custom database software. I watched as he navigated via key strokes to a search field. He was a slow, halting typist, hunting and pecking.

"What was your friend's name again?"

"Johnson." I answered. "Kyle."

He poked at the keyboard. The hard drive made a stuttering, crunching noise. No results found.

"Looks like he's not in our database." Noah turned around, gazing up at me with an intense stare.

"He must not have stayed, then," I said. "He was never much for settling down."

"Does that mean you'll be moving on too?" His jaw muscles bulged like tree roots. His suspicion was palpable. I could feel the tension between us like an electromagnetic field. He had to be the one behind the truck full of rocket parts and was probably not happy about having a random stranger around who showed up in the middle of winter, alone, looking for someone who might not even exist. I didn't blame him for being suspicious. Providing hospitality and converting people was so deep in the DNA of the Community though, there was no way he could refuse me openly without offending the other residents and risking his position. He was a predator trapped, hemmed in. A trapped predator responds unpredictably, fights desperately. I needed to be ready when he made his move.

"Not sure," I said, putting on my best humble simpleton act. "I guess I'll stay at least until Xavier learns a bit more. He's got a good aptitude but he needs more teaching."

Noah stood. The chair rolled back and banged into a filing cabinet with a loud crack. I counted one second, two. This was a good opportunity. Nobody around. Knock me down, strangle me, hide my body in the truck. *Oh, he decided to leave when he found out his friend was never here. Took his things and walked off down the road.* I could read the whole thought process in his eyes. Either he had no poker face or he didn't care if I knew what he was thinking. He was trying to decide whether or not he could take me, sizing me up. He was twenty or thirty pounds heavier, taller, strong and fast with a longer reach. Still, he wasn't sure. Another second passed. His face calmed, the tension relaxed. He had decided to wait, plan, deal with me on his own schedule.

"Let's go get dinner," he said, pushing past me, hard shoulder against mine, putting me on notice.

I was bone weary by the end of the day, lying on the lumpy mattress in my little room and thinking while pretending to read a brand new copy of Eleanor Jane Sibyl's latest book titled The Odyssey of the Self. Maria had pressed it into my hands after dinner, nodded silently and walked off. On the surface, if you subtracted the weird religious beliefs and the misogyny, the place was almost idyllic—a return to a simpler and more wholesome way of life. Still, something needled me about it. The residents were too familiar with someone who was essentially a stranger. Admittedly, if there was a bell curve of comfort with strangers, I would fall somewhere on the lower left edge. Still, the way they seemed to accept me without question, allow me into their community, feed me, house me, all sent a creepy chill down my spine. The kind of creepiness you feel when a salesman asks for your name and then uses it in every sentence. *Now Justin, I know you're going to love this feature. You see, Justin, the value of this product...* It was all a little Glengarry Glen Ross. Did they want people to convert that badly? Especially someone like fictional Dustin Cruz? With nothing to offer but labor? Maybe it was the difference between being a true believer and a person of no faith like me. As a person devoid of religious fervor, understanding people who possessed it was a blind spot. I needed to tread carefully, especially with Noah. He would make his move within the next few days, I was sure of it. Were the rocket parts his own side venture? Or was it something Eleanor Jane Sibyl and the other leaders of the Community knew about? Where were they taking them? Who was the buyer?

I wanted to get the phone out, leave a post for Ashna on the gardening forum, and do some research but I was worried they were watching me somehow. It was probably paranoia but I imagined hidden cameras tracking my every move.

Outside in the hallway I heard giggling and running feet, then an adult voice, admonishing. What if I had grown up in a place like Red Butte Commune with my own parents, whoever they were, instead of as a barely acknowledged foster child on a family farm? How would I feel about the Community now? No way to know. The answer didn't matter. My plan was to wait for everyone to go to bed, then sneak out of my room and break into the reception office. I set the book down and played with the unfamiliar interface of my Dustin Cruz watch for a minute, figuring out how to set an alarm, then closed my eyes and flopped down, falling asleep in a matter of moments.

The insistent beeping woke me several hours later from a dream in which my task was to repair a piece of farm equipment. Somehow, I discovered that the bulk of the machine was below ground in a hidden room. I prowled the dim subterranean space, tracing coils, gauges, instrument panels, and fuel lines with my fingers while a horrific sense grew in me that the machine went on forever, filling room after silent room. Sitting up and rubbing my eyes, I congratulated my unconscious mind for coming up with this truly deep and original symbolic representation of my current situation. Perched on the edge of the mattress, I let my fear dissipate into the dark, then did five minutes of deep breathing and stretching, preparing my mind for the task ahead.

A heavy silence filled my ears in the empty corridors, like being buried in sand. Inky shadows. Starlight from exterior doors reflected on shiny linoleum. I crept past each door, breath held. In the lobby, I crouched, pulled pick and tension wrench from my pocket, and worked the lock of the office door—a vintage, solid brass Kwikset that had to be original to the building. It turned reluctantly after a minute, gummy with age, and the door creaked open.

Inside, I sat on the old Steelcase chair, remembering the solid crash of metal on metal when Noah had stood abruptly to face me, pushing it backward. The monitor flickered to life, responding to a key tap, green prompt blinking. I typed the username I had watched him use:

> nfisher

Now I needed the password. I knew it was in the rolodex somewhere. Card by card, I scanned through, keeping one ear cocked toward the open door, listening for any sound of footsteps from the lobby. I went through all the cards, squinting in the dim light from the screen. Nothing. Flipping back, I started over a second time, straining my eyes. I almost missed it again, faint pencil on a time yellowed card.

> ejs13152

The computer grunted, hard drive spinning up, and the prompt changed. Eleanor Jane Sibyl. Born January 31, 1952. I was in. And I was even more convinced Noah was a true zealot—using his prophet's initials and birthdate as his password.

I was at a standard BASH prompt now. Before trying anything else, I leaned over the monitor and inspected the back of the computer. An ethernet cable snaked from a port on the rear down through a hole drilled in the desk. I got down underneath and used my little penlight to trace the cable to a box mounted low on the wall. A T1 modem? I inspected it more closely—beige plastic covered with a thick layer of dust. It looked old enough to be a T1. I got out from under the desk and sat back down in front of the computer. Remembering the lesson Ashna had given me once ("The ten most important commands Justin! You need to know them. Some day you're going to find yourself in front of a computer and I won't be there to help you.") I carefully typed in *curl ifconfig.co* and hit enter. A moment later, an address appeared on the next line down and the prompt sprang back to life below it. I dug through desk drawers until I found a pen, took an empty card from the rolodex, and wrote down the IP address. If I was remembering right, that would be the WAN interface address, the one Ashna could use to hack into the network and then this computer.

With the card tucked into my pocket, I turned my attention to the database. One of the other things Ashna had taught me was that you can use the up arrow to scroll through the history of commands run in a BASH shell. I hit it twice and there was the one Noah had run to open the database: commdat. The program opened. I navigated it the way I had seen Noah do it, with the tab and arrow keys, until I got to the search field. Holding my breath, I typed in Malena's last name Campbell and hit return. I had no idea where she had gotten that name, or where I had gotten mine–the one I had before Vincent. Vincent was my choice–a legal change I made after leaving the Community. Twelve results. Malena was the fourth.

I tabbed down to her name and hit enter. A detail screen opened. First name, last name, DOB—I scanned for any clue to her whereabouts. Near the bottom was a field labeled CommLoc. Community Location? Next to that, it said CR3. I went back and searched for Noah Fisher. His location was listed as US37. I searched for Smith and sampled a few. Locations were all US except one that said MX5. So, it looked like the first two letters were country and the number was for a facility or commune in that country. I went back to Malena's record. So what was CR? I could only think of Costa Rica. But what would she be doing there? Below the CommLoc field was a button I hadn't noticed on the other records I had viewed. It was labeled TRIAD. I tabbed down to it and hit enter. A message box overlaid the center of the screen: TRIAD Access Protected. Authenticate to Continue. A password field below that. If I tried it and got it wrong would someone be notified? I shrugged and entered Noah's password but was met with an incorrect password error. There was a cancel button. I hit it and Malena's record came back.

Costa Rica? And what was TRIAD? I navigated back to the main menu and was about to close the database but decided to search for my own name just out of curiosity. They had my cell number but not my address. There was a notes field with two entries corresponding to the dates Malena had called me. The notes were terse: 'Called. Informed of reunion. Details to come. MS.' Under CommLoc it said none. Below that, the same button I had seen on Malena's record: TRIAD. I stared at it for a moment, uncomprehending. Why on my record and Malena's but not Noah's or the other random records I had checked? I looked at my watch. Too long. I needed to get back to my room.

With a few taps, I was out of the database. I cleared the BASH history. There was some way to clear only the last command but I couldn't remember it so I just nuked it all. The chance of Noah noticing was low. Monitor off, I replaced everything I had touched, and tiptoed back to the door. Silence and shadows reigned in the lobby. I slipped into them, pulled the office door closed, and crept back down the hallway toward my room.

Chapter 9

An Inauspicious Accident
12/11: Helem, Utah

I got back to my room without running into anyone, closed the door and exhaled. But, just as I began to relax, I became aware of a soft, almost imperceptible sound of someone crying nearby. A woman. Curious, I went back out into the little hallway. It seemed to be coming from one of the other makeshift guest rooms. Who would be in there? And why? I pressed my ear to the wood. Definite sobbing, muffled. Not abject or in pain. Just sadness. I knocked lightly. The sound stopped but no answer came. I turned the knob and opened the door. Someone was on the bed. The room had a skylight like mine. She sat up quickly and I saw her face in the moonlight from above.

"Anna? Are you okay?"

"Yes, fine. Sorry." She wiped at her eyes with the hem of her dress.

"Why are you here?"

"Shhh." She put a finger to her lips and looked toward the door. "Close it," she whispered.

I closed the door and sat on the foot of the bed. "What's going on."

She took a ragged breath, then turned to me, composed. "Sorry. I came by. To see you. But you weren't in your room so I sat in here to wait. Thought you just went to the bathroom or something."

"Why were you crying?"

"Someone…told me to come see you. But I was scared."

"I don't understand. Why would someone tell you to come see me in the middle of the night?"

She looked at me sideways, not meeting my eyes. The silver light lay across the planes of her face. She raised a thin hand and brushed back a loose lock of hair. "Noah," she said at last. "He doesn't trust you. He wanted me to seduce you, get you to confide in me. He doesn't understand anything."

I nodded, thinking. "Were you and Noah involved? Together?"

"We used to be. We were married. Not legally. Nobody's legally married here. Just in the eyes of the Community, not the law."

"What happened?"

"Eleanor Jane Sibyl happened," she whispered, bitter. "He only thinks about her and the fight to get her teachings out to the world. He thinks she's some kind of divine prophet."

"And you don't?"

"I don't know. Not anymore. Maybe I never did."

"Why stay?"

"Nowhere else to go." She turned and looked at me, eyes liquid. "I've been in the Community since I was eighteen. I'm thirty-four now. That's almost half my life. No work experience. No college. What would I do?"

"How did you end up here?"

"Same as most. Left home when I was sixteen. I was following the hippie circuit. Phish shows, Grateful Dead reunion shows. Selling bracelets and tie dye out of my car in the parking lots. Went to a show at Red Rocks, then headed down through Utah, going to L.A. My car broke down in St. George. I had a ninety-five VW Golf. Yellow. It was a cute car." Her eyes turned distant, remembering. "I met some people from here. They were selling stuff, handing out flyers. I ended up coming back with them and I've been here ever since."

I nodded, turned my attention to my hands. "Common story I guess. What's up with Noah though? It doesn't seem like something that goes along with the beliefs of this place. Sending you to seduce me."

She laughed at that. "He'll ask people to do anything. He only cares about the destination, not how we get there."

"What will you tell him?"

"That you're not a spy. You're not are you?"

"No. Just a lost soul I guess." I felt bad lying to her but I didn't have a choice.

"I'm not actually going to try to seduce you. Not that I'm so averse. It's been a long time."

"That's okay. I don't know what Noah asked you to find out but I'll tell you anything you want to know."

"Are you actually looking for your friend?"

"Yes. Can I show you something?"

I took her to my room and showed her the duffle bag with Kyle Johnson's name on it.

"He left it with me last time I saw him. He got it in the military and carried it around forever. Said he was just going on a quick trip but he never came back. Then I got an email from him telling me he was here. I guess he just passed through. Noah couldn't find him on the computer." It seemed to convince her, even though

102

anyone can walk into a surplus store and buy an old duffle bag.

"Listen," she said. "Noah's going to be suspicious if I go back to my room right now. He'll find out somehow. Can I sleep here? With our clothes on?"

"Yes, of course."

Anna was gone by the time I woke. Rose tinged dawn lit the sky in the square of glass above and, next to me, a warm impression where she had been. Things just kept getting weirder. I'd been expecting garden variety cult behavior but what I had found was something more sinister. I sat up and rubbed my eyes. I needed to communicate with Ashna, send her the information I had. I didn't like using my phone inside the commune but I would have to risk it.

The phone booted and found a weak cellular signal. I navigated to the gardening forum and found the Dragon's Tongue Aspidistra. How to get Ashna the information in a manner she would understand but would not trigger whoever monitored the forum to delete it as spam? I thought for a minute, then started typing.

Wonderful! Back in 73 I planted an Aspidistra like this. But then in 91 we had a heat wave and it died…

I continued, working the last two 8 bit octets of the IP address into the rest of the comment and bolding them. The last sentence was the hardest. I had to mention TRIAD in a way that would alert her to look for it. Finally, I wrote:

I could never find that variety again until a nice young man at the garden store looked it up for me in his database. It's from TRIAD farms.

It would have to do. I was confident she would

understand. Phone back in its hidden pocket, I got up and headed off for a shower before breakfast. The day before, Luis had shown me the former locker rooms in the gym, repurposed now as communal bath houses.

As I was exiting the building, a woman fell into step beside me. I glanced over, surprised. Had she been waiting for me? I recognized her as one of the community members I had seen around but had not yet met. Luis had pointed everyone out to me, telling me their names. If my memory was right, her name was Beth. She didn't look like a Beth though. More like a Clarissa. Or a Monique.

"Dustin, I need to have a word with you." She squinted in the harsh sunlight, just a hint of crow's feet at the corners of her pale green eyes. My height, slim and vigorous looking with red hair pulled back from her face.

"Okay…Beth?"

"Yes, Beth. In here." She wrapped strong fingers around my arm and pulled me through a door which clanged shut behind us.

"What is this?"

"Storage closet. Used to be for athletic equipment when this place was a school. See the racks." She pointed to a wooden rack sized for basketballs. The only light came from a single low wattage bulb above our heads. Cans of beans, corn, and tomatoes in cardboard boxes were stacked on shelves against the back wall.

"What's going on? Why did you pull me in here?"

"What are you doing here?" Her voice was clipped, authoritative, unlike the retiring demeanor of the other women I had met at Red Butte.

"Not sure what you mean. I came looking for a friend…"

"Bullshit." She cut me off, cold anger in her eyes. "Listen. I know how to read people. You're no hayseed drifter. You're playing a part, taking in the gullible cult members. I can see it in every aspect of your being. The way you move, talk, notice things, size people up. You're a pro. I don't know what kind or from what agency but you need to back off. This is my investigation. I got here first."

My mind was racing but I tried to keep my face calm. "I'm not from any agency. What are you? FBI?"

"You know better than to ask me that. I'm not asking where you're from. I'm just warning you. Get out. Tell your handlers this is already under control. Whatever your angle is, you're not needed here. I don't know where the crosstalk happened but somebody missed a beat, didn't check in or follow protocol. You shouldn't be here. If you interfere in any way with my investigation or do something stupid and blow your cover this is all going to explode. Two years of research and undercover work shot. You have no idea how dangerous this organization is. Remove yourself and let us handle it properly."

The door banged open again and she was gone. I stood for a moment in the dim, silent room, trying to assimilate this new information. So they were under investigation—some kind of massive, years long infiltration operation. It was the FBI that had busted them before, back in the eighties. I needed to get the information I was after and get out. I didn't want to be around when Beth and her friends brought everything crashing down. After a while I shrugged, opened the door a crack and peered through. No one around. I slipped out and continued on toward the showers.

On the way, I ran into Glenn Morgan, a lean, weathered guy in his fifties with long gray hair and a full beard. He managed the commune's beehives. I got the feeling he liked bees better than people and I couldn't really blame him. His grandson Christian was with him—a talkative six year old with red cheeks and thick, bowl cut blond hair. Christian held an encyclopedic knowledge of chickens in his young head and related nearly all of it to me as we worked our way from locker room to shower to sauna.

The bath house, like most things at Red Butte Commune, was not luxurious. Its locker room origins were obvious—concrete floors, hard benches, and industrial grade shower stalls. The sauna was a surprise though. It was new looking, cedar lined, and large enough for ten. A heater topped with a pile of igneous rocks stood in the corner.

"Great sauna," I commented to Glenn.

"Yes, just finished last year." He was leaning back, eyes closed, elbows on the stepped seat behind him. "Sister Eleanor says the heat is good for purifying and removing toxins."

"You all do seem to take good care of this place."

"We do our best."

"Have you been here long?"

"Since the Community bought this place. That was nineteen ninety. I was twenty two years old. "

I did some quick mental math. That had to be just after the FBI raid on the compound in Montana. Was he one of the original members? Maybe one of the children born at the compound?

"Why did they choose this place? I mean, it's a great place. Don't get me wrong. But Helem's a little out of the way."

"It was Devlin Fonseco's school," he said, reaching for a ladle hung on the wall and scooping water from a wooden bucket. The rocks sizzled and a cloud of steam rose up. "One of the founding members. He grew up here. Went to school in this building. His father worked for the mining corporation doing something. They dug uranium for the government. So those fools could make bombs."

"What bombs?" Christian asked, looking up.

"Never you mind," Glenn said, placing a hand on Christian's head.

"So does Mr. Fonseco still live here, then? One of the actual founders?" I thought of the photo I'd seen. Fonseco standing on the tree like a young Jerry Garcia, his daughter caught in that forever fall.

"Sure he comes through. Spends all day locked up in his laboratory when he's here though. Even sleeps in there. He's away now. Getting ready for the reunion."

"Reunion?"

"Yes. Founders of the Community, select members, all meeting up to celebrate the fiftieth anniversary."

"It's been around that long?" I asked, wiping sweat from my forehead.

"Counting from when Eleanor Jane Sibyl's son was born. That was when she had her first vision that told her to go west, found a new mission, teach people the truth, how to purify themselves and prepare for the ascension."

"What happened to her son? Is he part of the leadership?"

"No," Glenn shook his head sadly. "Died. Died in Frisco years ago. They say it was a drug overdose."

I took that in for a moment. Maybe the source of

Sibyl's animosity toward youth culture? "Where are they doing the reunion?" I asked. "Are you going?"

Glenn shook his head solemnly. "We don't know yet who will be called. Don't know where either. They'll tell us when it's time to leave. They say there are great works to be built, a new center for our people. Many of us have gone already. Maybe this one will see it someday." He squeezed Christian's shoulder and the boy squirmed.

"So most people will stay here at Red Butte Commune?"

He nodded. "We'll celebrate in every home of the faithful. They're going to stream it live for everyone. Christian here will be able to see it. Eleanor Jane Sibyl herself will speak live to all her flock."

"Sounds like a great event. Are you excited?" I asked, looking over at Christian.

"We get out of school that day," he answered, guarded.

"Don't you like school?"

"Not since Ms. Malena left," he said, then glanced sharply at his grandfather, expecting a rebuke. I kept my composure and the rebuke came quickly.

"Now you watch your tongue. Ms. Malena was a great teacher but Ms. Susan is fine, too."

"She makes us do spelling tests every day!" Christian complained but I was barely listening. I knew Malena had been there but this evidence of her life and her impact shook me anyway. It made my purpose loom up again, pressing down on me with its urgency.

"I'm going to head on out now," I said, standing. "You all enjoy the rest of your sauna."

That afternoon I worked with Xavier, showing him how to control the length of the arc and the angle of the electrode. He was improving quickly. I watched through the shaded lens of my helmet as he drew an inch long practice weld along a ninety degree join of two pieces of scrap. He pulled the electrode away and we raised our visors, watching the metal cool.

"Your arc was a little long on that one. You see the spatter there?" I pointed.

"Too long," he agreed, nodding.

I heard a sound behind me and turned. Noah was standing in the open doorway of the storage building with another, younger man. I had met him the night before at dinner. I racked my brain. Paul? Pete? Something with a P. I thought he was one of the two I'd seen loading the truck out front when I was up on the ridge. I had been pretty far away though so I couldn't tell for sure.

"Dustin, can we borrow you for a bit? We're setting up a satellite dish on the roof of the main building. We might need to make a mount for it."

"Okay," I said, removing raw hide welding gloves and helmet. "Xavier, that's probably enough for today. Nice work."

"Thanks." He looked at his feet. I reached out and gave his shoulder a squeeze, then turned and followed Noah and friend.

"What's the satellite dish for?" I asked. They were walking in front of me, shoulder to shoulder as we passed through the doorway into weak sunlight. Something was up. I could tell from the tension in their backs. I flexed my fingers. Two against one. Were they going to lead me off somewhere deserted?

"Broadcast from Eleanor Jane Sibyl," Noah said, turning his head. "We have an event coming up. Big celebration." He turned toward Pete/Paul. "We need to get that box from the barn."

"Oh, yeah."

They both switched direction and headed toward the barn. I followed, dropping back a few feet. The big doors were open. I smelled straw and cow shit. Inside they turned left. I followed, wary. Three more steps and Noah stopped abruptly, turned toward me looking up.

"Look out!" He darted forward as I glanced up, following his gaze. Something was falling, black shadow blocking out light from a window high up in the hay loft. Numbing pain exploded from a point just below my ear. My vision went black. Brachial stun, I thought, falling. It was a Krav Maga move I knew about but had never tried—good for knocking out an opponent if you could catch them by surprise and hit them just right. Did Noah hit me? Or Pete/Paul? Something landed on my back, pushing me down. Consciousness drained away, carrying me into darkness.

My first thought when I woke was surprise that I was still alive. Going down, I hadn't expected to come back up. I nearly sprang out of the bed but a hand pressed to my chest held me down. Following the line from fingers to wrist and on up, I came to Anna's face, her eyes wide.

"Calm down. Lay back. You need to rest."

"What happened?"

"A tarp fell on you."

"A tarp?" I tried to sit up again but she was stronger than she looked. I remembered the flat of someone's hand striking my neck. It wasn't just a tarp that knocked me out.

"Sure. A big vinyl tarp we had up in the hay loft.

They're recycled from billboards. We use them for a lot of stuff around here. Must weigh about a hundred pounds or more. You're lucky you're not dead."

I took a deep breath and looked around. Formica counters. Wooden cabinets. I was laid out on an exam table like they have in doctor's offices. The cracked red Naugahyde pressed cool against my back. My body felt numb and my brain was foggy.

"Nurse's office?"

"Yes, back when this was a school. We use it as our infirmary."

My left arm ached right at the inside of the elbow joint. I flexed it, examining the skin. It seemed like I'd been poked. "Did somebody draw my blood for something? Did paramedics come out?"

"Not that I know of. They just brought you up here from the barn and then called me to come sit with you. I don't think Noah would have called an ambulance. We don't really invite the outside world in unless we have to."

"Yeah, I guess not." I rubbed my arm, thinking. Something weird was happening and I was caught up in it. That tarp falling on my head was obviously not an accident and Noah didn't seem concerned whether or not I thought it was. The charade seemed to be for the other residents of Red Butte Commune. He didn't want them to know anything was up. So why the needle wound? Had he drawn my blood? If so, what did he want it for? It struck me suddenly that he might have searched my room and gone through my bag while I was out of commission. I sat up and Anna didn't try to hold me down this time.

"How long have I been unconscious?"

"About an hour I guess."

"They must have given me something. It's not normal to be knocked out for that long." I raked my hair back with my fingers, cold sweat on my forehead. "They gave me a sedative. Has to be."

"That doesn't seem right," Anna said, speaking slowly and not meeting my eyes. "They wouldn't do that."

"I think I want to go to my room and lay down for a while. Is that all right?"

"Sure. I'll help you."

We hobbled down the hallway together. My watch said 4:03. At the door, Anna let go of me.

"Want me to come in?"

"No, that's okay. I'll see you at dinner."

"All right. Get some rest." Her eyes crinkled at the corners showing concern, worry. Something else, too. Suspicion? She was wondering why they drugged me. Wondering if I was a threat.

"I will. Thanks."

My bag had definitely been searched. I kept it tidy and everything was out of place. I opened the hidden pocket and found everything still there. Did they miss it, I wondered? Or find everything but decide to leave it? Nothing about the situation made sense to me.

I sat down on the bed and thought through the Moscow Rules. The rules existed to guide people in exactly my situation. Number 10: Keep your options open. Number 8: Do not harass the opposition. Okay. I would play it low key and see what happened. Noah clearly didn't want to kill me or I would be dead already. He didn't believe I was Dustin Cruz. But I was pretty sure he didn't know my true identity yet. I kept coming back to the needle though. Was it just from whatever sedative they gave me? Or did they take a blood draw? That morning Glenn had told me there was a laboratory in the building where Devlin Fonseco worked when he was in residence. I didn't imagine they would have the capacity or requisite knowledge to sequence DNA though. And even if they did, how would that help them? They couldn't have any of my DNA to match, saved from when I was growing up. I never once went to a doctor until I left the Community and went to San Francisco as far as I could remember. My first ever trip to a doctor had been near the beginning of my second year in college when I developed a case of walking pneumonia.

I lay back on the bed but couldn't relax. High above me, a turkey vulture floated, magnificent feathers spreading out and embracing thin air. Another appeared, wheeling around the first. I watched them until the air currents carried them away from the patch of sky framed by the skylight. Dinner was going to be interesting.

Chapter 10

Undersea Community
12/11-12: Helem, Utah

Entering the cafeteria, I immediately noticed a change in the atmosphere. The room buzzed. People were excited. It didn't take me long to see why either. Devlin Fonseco had arrived. Nearly fifty years older than in the photo I'd seen, he still had the same look. He'd gone from young Jerry Garcia to old, grizzled Jerry—beard and hair white but undiminished in thickness, still powerful looking but stouter, same round, wireframe glasses. He wore a blue and white striped Baja hoodie, jeans, work boots scuffed and worn at the toes.

"Justin. How are you doing?" A hand on my shoulder. Luis eyeing me with concern.

"I'm okay. Just a bump on the head. Nothing major."

"Oh, good. I'm glad. We were worried about you."

"Who's that?" I nodded toward Fonseco.

"That's Devlin Fonseco. He's one of the original three founders of the Community. He stays here sometimes. Moves around. It's always a celebration when he arrives for one of his visits."

"We're having pie tonight!" It was Alma again, looking up at me with her owl eyes. "Because Mr. Fonseco is here."

"Wonderful," I said, patting her head. "I love pie. What kind?"

"Apple!"

She ran off and I walked with Luis to the food line. Caroline, the alpha matron of the commune, was serving again. She gave us each a big chunk of ham, roasted potatoes, and green beans.

Fonseco had joined the line behind us. Luis nodded to him as we passed. At the table Xaiver gave me a worried look.

"Are you okay, Mr. Cruz?"

"Yes, fine. Thanks for asking but it was just a minor thing. Got knocked out for a few minutes. Those tarps are heavy!"

Xavier nodded, looking down at his food. Maria patted my arm. At the next table, I saw Beth the secret agent seated with some other women. She ignored me pointedly. Beyond her, I could see Noah's back a couple of tables away. He sat with Paul/Pete. Both were waiting to eat, not talking. As I watched him he turned and glanced back, eyes bouncing off me and going to Fonseco, back to his food. Interesting. Fonseco was a perplexing addition to the equation. I turned to see where he was and found that he was headed straight for me. With a grunt, he lowered himself into the seat next to Xavier, setting his plate down.

"Good evening everyone. How are you tonight? Luis and family, looking well." He had a kind of patrician air despite his hippie look, speech stilted and a little artificial. Past acne had left pits and welts on his face, just visible at the edges of thick white beard.

"We're great, thanks. Nice to see you here again," Luis said.

Fonseco craned his neck and looked around. "Ah, I think everyone is seated now. Shall I say grace?" The room quieted and he began. "The wise and holy beings, those who have ascended and those who come to us from far away, masters of the ancient wisdom, great builders, they see us gathered around this table, praising the bounty provided by the earth and the supreme being, master of masters. With our gaze set upon their wisdom and our hearts open to the words spoken through their earthly medium, Eleanor Jane Sibyl, we give thanks for this nourishment."

It was the same litany I had heard every evening before dinner. I wondered if there would be a video to watch after. We hadn't watched any videos since my first dinner at the commune. It was apparently not a regular occurrence, but they might put on a show for Fonseco. As he finished speaking, there was a murmur from the assembled community and a clanking of silverware and plates. I picked up my own knife and fork.

"You must be Dustin," Fonseco said, offering a hand across the table.

I reached out and shook his hand. "Yes, that's me. Glad to meet you. Luis here told me you were one of the original founders of the Community."

"Yes, correct. Along with Mark and Eleanor. That was many years ago but it seems like yesterday. But how are you Dustin? I heard you had an accident today." He was eying me with a weird combination of curiosity and wariness.

"Oh, I'm fine. Nothing to worry about."

"Good, good. I hope you're enjoying your stay so far. We love to welcome newcomers. Now, let's eat before our food gets cold."

They did pull out the TV after dinner but I escaped by complaining of a headache. I wanted quiet and solitude to think things over. Back in my little cell-like room, I sat on the mattress, got out a little notebook and pencil, and wrote down all the clues and questions I had uncovered so far, then tried to pull it together into some kind of sensible narrative. Thirty years ago, the old school in Helem was purchased by a shadowy organization and Red Butte Commune was started. Malena stayed in the Community after I left. Somehow, she ended up at Red Butte as a teacher. That had been after Linda left in 2015. Devlin Fonseco was also a part-time resident of Red Butte and had a laboratory somewhere in the building. The 50th anniversary of the Community was approaching and some sort of event was planned to commemorate it. I didn't know where or exactly when the event would happen.

Malena had been forced to call me and invite me to come back for the reunion but was moved out of Red Butte shortly after, possibly to Costa Rica. Was Eleanor Jane Sibyl in Costa Rica too? Was that where she fled to after the FBI raid on the ranch? Maybe that was the location of the anniversary event and that was why Malena had been moved. Or were they worried I would figure out the source of the call and come looking? Was that why Noah mistrusted me? And how did the truck full of Russian rocket parts figure in? There were too many missing pieces. To top it off, the Community was under investigation and an undercover federal agent had told me get out. What was my next move? Glenn had told me Fonseco stayed in his laboratory when he was at Red Butte. Maybe there were clues there. A notebook or a laptop I could search. Anything. One big problem: I didn't know which room it was. It had to be one of the old classrooms. Probably the science room since that would have lab tables, sinks, ventilation.

I looked up at the skylight. It was hinged on one side, latched on the other. If I could get to the top of the wall that separated my room from the next, I could open it and climb out onto the roof. Between the top of the wall and the ceiling was a gap of about three feet. I had an hour at least before they would be done watching the video. I stood and pushed on the wall. The two by four and plywood construction was rough but sturdy. I gathered a few tools from my duffel's secret pocket then closed it and covered it with clothing. They couldn't have found the pocket. They would have taken my tools and phone and cash.

Standing on the mattress, I was able to jump high enough to just get my fingers over the top edge. I hung for a moment, then pulled and swung a leg up, nearly overbalanced and plummeted into the next room but steadied myself with a hand on the ceiling. The skylight was close now. How long since it had been opened?

I reached out and pulled the handle. It moved with a groan of old, oxidized metal. With my shoulder, I applied steady pressure to the frame. It rose slowly, bits of rusty paint falling from the hinge. The move was awkward, but I managed to lean over and get my shoulder through the opening, feet still on the top edge of the wall, then place hands on either side and push up.

Out on the roof a cold breeze chilled my face. The moon hadn't risen yet but just by starlight I could see the big square the building made around the central courtyard. The roof sloped down from the edges toward the center. I wondered idly how often it rained in Helem as I crept from skylight to skylight, looking down. Most of the classrooms were subdivided and converted to family apartments for the married couples and their children too young for the dormitories. I saw beds covered in homemade quilts, antique dressers, cribs, closets. I was about to give up hope when, looking down through the second to last skylight, glowing points of light met my gaze, green and red and amber. As my eyes adjusted, I made out the sleek shapes of scientific equipment and the glint of LEDs reflected off rounded Pyrex surfaces.

I drew a long, thin loop of flexible wire from my pocket. Holding it stretched the width of the skylight, I worked it under the seal, pushed in to create a bow which I flipped over the handle, then drew the left side slowly over until it was looped around. A hard jerk of the wire pulled the handle to the open position and I was able to lift the skylight up. From inside, a whoosh of warm air lifted out. Below the skylight was a lab table. If I hung and dropped it would be about a four foot fall. I needed to close the skylight behind me though. There was a wooden lip inside. Cautiously, I lowered myself into the opening, then, grasping the handle in one hand and curling the fingers of my other hand over the wood, I dropped down, pulling the skylight closed. My fingers began to slip. With a jerk of my body, I shoved the handle sideways, latching it, then let go, twisting and landing with one foot on the edge but the other firmly in the center of the table.

I crouched, listening to the echoes of my landing die away, replaced by a smooth hum of electronic equipment and, somewhere, a faucet dripping. One wall, from counter height up, was all windows overlooking fields and barns and outbuildings blanketed with sparkling frost. I could see lights in the gym. I imagined the faces of the congregation, gathered around, listening to Eleanor Jane Sibyl. For a moment, a weird visual anomaly took over my brain and everything looked wavy and hazy like the commune had been submerged in a still ocean. I blinked, trying to clear my head. Delayed reaction from the drugs they gave me? Or the knock on the head? I needed to stop bumbling and move fast.

Below the windows, a startling array of equipment was set out on lab tables and counters that followed the periphery of the room. With my flashlight on low, I crept around, checking the unfamiliar brand names and making guesses about what the machines might be used for. There were microscopes, racks of glassware, a giant machine full of little test tubes and a centipede-like swing arm that could target each. One machine in particular, the source of the hum, drew my attention. It was about the size and shape of an old-fashioned cash register with a six by six inch backlit display where the number keys would have been. A rapidly updating readout showed the output of some process going on inside—temperature measurements mixed with cryptic messages. A plate near the base said LifeCor 46C PCR Thermal Cycler. I wrote it down in my notebook and continued around.

One corner of the former classroom was enclosed, making a small bedroom with the same kind of two by four and plywood construction they had used to build my little guest room. I went in. A big rucksack had been dropped on the queen size bed and a blue velour bathrobe hung on the back of the door. I opened the various pockets and felt around inside the pack, finding nothing but clothing, toiletries, and a book titled *Age of Illusion: Fall of the American Empire*. I recognized the title, and the author–a professor of economics well-known as a right-wing conspiracy theorist, misogynist, and anti-vaxxer. His detractors called him the dumb man's smart man. A little light reading for Devlin Fonseco.

Back out in the lab, I saw the rounded planes of a Steelcase desk near what would have been the front of the classroom. On its surface, a sleek, modern laptop stood open, screen dark, several file folders fanned out next to it. I tapped the space bar and the laptop screen lit up, showing a password prompt. If I had more time, and Fonseco didn't have his files encrypted, I could probably get into them. I'd done it once before with tech support from Ashna and mostly remembered the steps. A glance at my watch told me not to bother. Instead, I checked the file folders.

They were like the ones you see at a dentist's office—color coded and alphabetized. Glancing back, I saw that behind the desk a door stood half open, several tall file cabinets in the shadows beyond. I inspected the labels: S. Miller, J. Martin, M. Campbell, E. Baker—a meaningless collection of Anglo-Saxon names. Each folder also had a curious design on the front—a circle bounded by an equilateral triangle. Inside S. Miller's file a printout from the database system I had hacked into the night before was the top sheet of a thick sheaf of papers. DOB: 6/12/1988. Close to mine. Full name: Sarah Jane Miller. I turned the page to what looked like a medical chart but a sound, subconsciously detected, froze me in place. I looked up and turned my head, listening. Footsteps approaching? I closed the file and stepped back. A key scraping in the lock. I took another step back, ducking into the closet and pulling the door closed, cold metal file cabinet against my back.

A click and light flowed under the gap between door and shiny linoleum floor. I moved back farther into shadows.

"…don't like it. At all." Fonseco's voice.

"…a threat…know soon enough." I was pretty sure it was Noah's voice responding. The words were difficult to make out. They must have left early. Or it was a short video.

"We'll have to initiate…" Fonseco speaking again. Several sentences followed that I couldn't make out. Then, "Damn fool idea with that tarp."

There was a pause. "We did the best we could. Had to improvise."

Fonseco began talking again in a lower voice. I crept up to the door but wasn't able to make anything out.

"All right. We'll see by morning," Noah said.

"Yes, about three hours left for this to finish the analysis. Come by before breakfast."

"Okay. See you in the morning." Noah's footsteps crossed the room. The door opened, closed.

I had to get out. Fonseco might open the closet at any moment if he needed to access files or even if he just noticed the door he had left open was now closed. I looked around and took stock. Maybe six feet wide by eight deep, the closet was mostly devoted to the file cabinets, all lined up on one side. On the other side were a sink and counter and Formica-fronted cabinets. A narrow aisle ran down the middle. Near the ceiling at the back was a grate set into the wall—probably HVAC. I couldn't hear anything from outside the closet except the hum of the machine running. What was Fonseco doing?

Carefully, I put one foot on the counter and bracing myself with my arms on the backmost file cabinet, pushed up until I could get a foot on its edge. Straddled there, I peered through the louvers of the grate, shining my flashlight beam inside. Beyond I saw about six inches of empty conduit, then another grate, maybe leading into an identical closet in the room next door. The duct ended just below. Above, it joined a larger duct that had to lead back to HVAC systems somewhere in the building.

The grate appeared to be held in only with tension clips but it was firmly attached to the wall by many coats of paint. I drew the point of my pocketknife along the edges, cutting though decades of paint and grateful for having sharpened it before I left for Utah, then exerted steady outward pressure on the grate until it popped loose. The opening was just large enough to crawl into but I needed to remove the neighboring grate before I could try. I pushed on it hard, straining and trying not to slip from my perch. It wouldn't budge. Taking a chance that the closed door and the loud machine in the laboratory would muffle the sound enough, I pulled the cuff of my shirt down over my knuckles and punched the bottom right corner. It gave a bit. I punched again and it popped halfway open. Carefully, I pushed it the rest of the way out and pulled it back through the opening, setting it on top of the other one, atop the filing cabinet within easy reach if I made it through.

As I squirmed through, I tried not to think about the dark, silent interior world between walls. That space always made me uneasy—better left alone and undisturbed. Spiderland and dustland. Mouse and silverfish domain.

Flashlight held in my mouth I looked down into the

connecting closet. Directly below the opening was a dresser. I slid down into a handstand on top of it, freeing my legs from the hole, then lowered slowly to one shoulder and managed a sort of flopping roll onto the floor. I breathed deeply for a second, then hopped back up and replaced the grates. Fonseco's closet was dark and empty. I could still hear the humming of the machine out in the lab and now, faintly, Fonseco typing furiously on the laptop. He might notice the grate had been pried open if he was observant. I thought about the files on his desk, visualizing the labels. J. Martin. M. Campbell. The image swam in my head and then my stomach felt like it was dropping to the floor. Justin Martin. Malena Campbell. How could I have been so stupid? Brain fog from the drugs they gave me? One of those files was mine, one of them Malena's.

In a daze, I stepped down from the dresser and pushed past hanging dresses and flannel shirts smelling of dryer sheets. The room beyond was empty, windows mostly covered by curtains. I went out into the corridor, closing the door softly. Why did Fonseco have a file on me? And Malena? Why were they on his desk? The coincidence was too great. I shivered, an icy chill running down my spine. I felt an urge to flee—go to my room, grab what I needed, run for Linda's market, get the first bus out of Helem. They knew who I was. They had to. Or maybe they just suspected.

Back in my room, I got the phone out and ran a search for LifeCor 46C PCR Thermal Cycler. It was a DNA sequencer. The day's events became clear. They suspected me. They thought I might be Justin Martin, Malena's old foster brother. So they manufactured an accident. Noah hit me with a brachial stun just to make

124

sure I would be unconscious long enough for them to drug me with plausible deniability. They carried me to the infirmary and took my blood. Now, they were analyzing my DNA. But why bother? And how did they have a sample to analyze against? As my heart rate slowed and I thought through it carefully, I realized I must be important to them somehow. Otherwise they would have just gotten rid of me. That brachial stun wasn't a technique hayseed hippie commune farmers knew. Noah had to be a trained fighter. Maybe an ex-Marine or Special Forces. Fonseco had been mad about the tarp thing. Worried that I might have been seriously injured. So, they needed me for some reason. I could use that knowledge to my advantage. Rather than run, I would play it out and use my leverage. What was it though? Why did they need me?

Chapter 11

A Plane Ride with Strangers
12/12-13: Helem, Utah and in the air

I tried to sleep but my mind was alive with tangled possibilities twisting, branching, rejoining. After an hour or so I fell into a fitful doze but was awakened soon after by a soft knock on my door.

"Yes?"

"It's Anna. Can I come in?"

"Sure." I didn't want a visitor but Dustin Cruz would not have said no.

"Hi. Just coming to check on you." She slipped in and closed the door. "How's your head?"

"Fine. No lasting damage." I looked up, trying to read her face. Uneasy? Scared? "Did Noah send you again?"

"No." She hesitated. I couldn't read her expression in the dark. "This time I came because I wanted to."

"Good. That's okay."

She lifted her dress over her head. Moonlight from above shone down on her pale shoulders, limning her features. I pulled the blankets back and made space for her in the bed.

Anna slipped out some time in the night and I woke alone, snapping awake abruptly from a deep sleep. I lay for a few minutes, thinking over my situation again and coming back around to the same conclusion I had reached the night before. I would play my hand and see what happened. They might know my identity but that didn't mean they knew every card I was holding. I had to stay clear of Beth the federal agent though and get away as soon as I found out where Malena was.

At breakfast I looked for Agent Beth but didn't see her. I caught Anna's eye. She gave a little head shake so I veered away and sat with Luis and Xavier. We ate silently. They weren't morning talkers and neither was I. I liked them better for it.

I dropped my dishes off at the serving window, thanked a young woman with a red-cheeked baby on her hip whose name was Brigit if I could trust my memory, and, sunk in my own thoughts, began walking toward the bath house. Noah and Paul/Pete were waiting for me outside the cafeteria doors.

Noah stepped into my path, thumbs tucked into his belt, head cocked.

"Need your help today, Dustin."

"I was just on my way to have a shower."

"That's fine. Meet us out front in an hour. Paul and I are driving some stuff over to Kanab. Need some help unloading."

"Okay." I nodded, noting Paul's name although I was sure I would forget it again.

The air was cold on my still damp hair when I pushed through the front doors. Noah, Paul, and Devlin Fonseco stood by the cargo truck in a huddle. They broke apart and watched me approach, puffs of condensing breath drifting upward and dissipating.

"You ever drive a big truck?" Noah was holding a key out toward me.

"I can probably manage."

"We don't have driver's licenses here so we don't drive on the government man's roads if we can help it."

"The government man." I squinted at him for a moment. I couldn't help it. I wanted him to know how stupid that sounded. I wasn't a big fan of the U.S. government with all their corruption, infighting, and ineptitude. But I also wasn't under any illusions about how great it would be to have no government, or people like Fonseco and Noah in charge. "I get it. I can drive."

I walked around, climbed in and started the truck, cranking the heat up. Noah and Paul climbed in and sat on milk crates in the space between the seats and the access door to the cargo area. Fonseco sat in the passenger seat. There was a tension in the air. It felt like being next to a steel cable stretched to its breaking point—so close you can almost see the stress fields rippling. Nobody spoke. I turned a wide circle, engine loud in the silence, and pulled up to the gate. Fonseco climbed out and opened it.

I found myself wondering how Dustin Cruz would react in this situation, then reminded myself they knew who I was. I didn't need to pretend to be someone else anymore.

"What's in the truck?" I asked. "You all seem pretty tense."

"Just some cargo," Fonseco replied softly, barely audible over the engine. "Nothing interesting. Turn right here."

Linda's Market was coming up on the left, frost on the curved roof sparkling in the morning sun.

"That's not the way to Kanab."

"Shut up and drive." Noah said, close to my

shoulder.

We traveled about a mile on the highway before Fonseco gestured to the right and I bumped the truck off onto a dirt road, heading straight into the desolate wilderness. The road ran through flat desert for a quarter mile then curved up onto a bluff. We had to be close to the spot where, only a few days before, I had stopped during my run and gotten my first glimpse of the commune. That was also when I first saw the truck I was driving now. Noah and Paul had been loading it. I didn't like the fact that we were driving out into no man's land. I wasn't eager to face those three with no one else around. My brain rifled through strategies furiously. I could point the truck toward the edge of the bluff, then bail out. Or, just run it into a big rock. Noah and Paul weren't buckled in. Maybe I could send them through the windshield and only have Fonseco to worry about. Before I could decide, the road curved down again and the truck was bouncing so much it was all I could do to keep it under control. At the bottom, on flat ground again, I looked up and saw what seemed to be an airstrip. Beyond a row of fifty gallon drums, an antique propeller plane squatted at one end of the runway—dull gray metal, maybe sixty feet long. Desert camo netting draped over it to hide it from above.

"What the actual fuck?" I asked, braking and juddering to a stop near the plane.

"Nice driving, artist boy." I turned, looking over my shoulder. Noah scowled at me. "Now we're going to see if you can do some honest work." He pulled open the access door. I could see the crates in the back, nylon straps cinched up and holding them secure to the sides of the truck. "These need to go on that plane. We're the labor."

The plane had a cargo bay near the rear of the fuselage with big double doors. Noah loaded the crates onto a dolly and deposited them on the lift gate of the truck, then Pete and I would carry them over and lift them into the plane. The interior was just an empty cylinder with a couple of jump seats near the cockpit. We lined the crates up, keeping the weight balanced, straining to lift the heaviest of them.

Around mid-morning, the jeep from the commune pulled up. Pete, Noah, and I were taking a short break, sitting on a crate and staring off in different directions. At fifty yards, I couldn't see who was driving through the glare on the windshield. Fonseco spoke to the driver for a minute, then pulled several backpacks and duffle bags from the back, dropping them on the ground. The jeep engine whined and it took off back up the road. One of the duffle bags looked a lot like mine.

My hands were cramped, frozen, and barely functional by the time we finished. I dropped to the lift gate of the empty truck, flexing and straightening my fingers, trying to get the blood flowing into them and release the cramps. Noah sat down on the lift gate, too.

"I guess we're all getting into that plane and going somewhere," I said, staring off into the desert.

"Not Pete. You, me, Fonseco."

"Who's flying it?"

"Fonseco. He's a good pilot."

"Good enough to evade radar?"

"Fly 'em low, well outside the normal routes. He's done it plenty. What makes you think we need to be on the down low?"

"This isn't exactly an official airstrip. I don't know

much about planes but I do know the private ones are required to have a radio call sign in big letters on the side. I don't see any on this one. My guess, there's contraband in those crates. You're smuggling it somewhere. Where is it? Where are we going?"

"Can't tell you that. Maybe Fonseco will once we're in the air."

"What if I don't want to go?"

" 'Fraid that's not an option."

"Thought so,"

"There's water and sandwiches in the truck," Noah made a tic-like gesture with his chin. "You should eat now. Long flight. Could be bumpy."

We bumped down the dirt airstrip at an alarming speed, engines roaring. The runway seemed too short, I couldn't see how we were going to get airborne before the end but the old plane and the old man flying it had a few tricks. Just as I was about to throw my hands up to cover my eyes, I felt the lift kick in and we swooped upward, horizon replaced with nothing but blue sky through the windshield. I sat in the co-pilot seat next to Fonseco. Noah strapped into one of the jump seats. We had secured the cargo well with ratcheting nylon straps and nets. They weren't taking any chances of it sliding around if we hit turbulence.

Fonseco and I wore headsets. He was flipping switches and checking gauges, leveling off, running low like Noah had said.

"What kind of plane is this?" I asked, my voice picked up by my mic and crackling in my headphones.

"DC-3," Fonseco answered, keeping busy with the controls. "Built in nineteen forty three. Pratt and Whitney twin wasp engines. Solid plane. Good speed,

Good cargo capacity. Good range. Able to take off from a short runway as you saw. We'll have to stop in Mexico to refuel. Fill it up and we'll have just enough to get us there."

"Get us where?"

He glanced over at me, eyes shrewd, judging. "You'll find out."

"Why are you taking me there, wherever it is?"

"You'll find that out too, in due course."

"I thought you were a scientist. When did you start flying planes?"

"Scientist?" Another glance in my direction, eyes crinkled this time with something like humor or disdain or both. "I guess I am, yes. But only in the service of something greater. Flying? When did I ever not fly? My father was a pilot. Navy. World War Two. Hobbyist after he left the military, when he wasn't working. I grew up in airplanes right around here." He pointed down. "Learned to fly by the time I was eleven. I wasn't a normal kid."

We were cruising over and through the desert now. Fonseco banked the plane, angling between two immense outcroppings, sedimentary layers throwing sharp shadows in the midday sun, saguaro and ironwood dots of green in the dull red landscape below.

"Not normal?" I asked, hoping to learn anything that might be useful. I didn't know what I was hoping for. The drive to the airstrip, loading the place, and now flying over the red rock canyons—it all seemed like a weird dream, like I hadn't fully woken up yet. They had me off balance. But I knew Fonseco's ego would keep him going as long as I gave the right grunts and *yeahs* and *oh, reallys*.

"No, not normal. I didn't speak a word until I was almost five years old you know. I learned to read first. Airplane manuals. I was obsessed. I probably started talking so I could ask questions about airplanes. Later I expanded my interests. Chemistry and biology. I spent seven years in the decadent cesspool of UC Berkeley. Undergrad. Grad school. I didn't realize it at the time of course. I was a kid, excited by the drugs and the music and the utopian ideas. I didn't know yet that America was a rotting corpse that couldn't be reformed. It was rotten then and it's only gotten worse. Kevorkian had it right you know. Sometimes when the disease has progressed to a certain point, you have to help the patient die." He glanced over at me nervously. "But I'm getting ahead of myself."

A chill crept up my arms. I thought about the cargo behind me—soviet ICBM parts—and here I was with a man who thought society needed to be put to death like a diseased patient who could not be saved. What were they planning?

"Why did you come to us, Justin?" He paused, side eyeing me. "Surprised? Yes, of course I know your real name. We checked your DNA, of course. That's what the little 'accident' Noah arranged was about."

"How did you have a sample to compare against?"

"Ah, good question." The plane dropped several feet and I felt that freefalling, stomach left behind sensation. "I'm afraid I'm not ready to answer that yet. But why come back? You left the Community as soon as you could. You get a call from your long-lost sister and come running back. Why? And why undercover?"

"What happened to Gwen and Abigail?"

He was silent for a moment, eyes hidden behind

mirrored aviators. "Gone. Like flotsam from a shipwreck when we were raided. They went back to straight life. Like flies to the rotting corpse. Gwen never really understood. I haven't seen either of them since that day when they all left. We knew the FBI was coming of course. But you didn't answer my question."

"I guess I'm not as cavalier about writing people off as you are."

"She made her choice," he snapped. "Your sister. You'll see her soon enough. Her and all the others. It's going to be glorious."

Fonseco was sullen and uncommunicative for the rest of the flight. When I got tired of watching barren land and water scroll by, I got up and stretched out on top of two crates. It was not the most comfortable bed but I fell asleep for a couple of hours. Just as the sun was dipping below the horizon, Fonseco brought the plane down, bumping along a cracked and overgrown landing strip in the middle of the jungle.

Outside, it was hot and the air shimmered with the intense humidity of the tropics. Stepping out of the plane felt like sliding into a warm bath.

"Where are we?" I asked Noah.

"None of your business," he answered. "Stay where I can see you."

Fonseco walked off toward an unfinished cinder block building. A small man stood in the doorway. They spoke rapid Spanish, too fast for me to understand. We had to be somewhere in Southern Mexico by my estimation, maybe Yucatan. Frog croaks blended into a symphony of creaks and groans. I felt something hop across the toe of my boot and looked down. The little frogs were everywhere, crouching on the runway, sitting in shallow puddles. I walked to the edge of the blacktop near the building, careful not to step on any amphibians, and relieved myself on the bole of a royal palm.

Against the side of the building was a large metal cabinet showing signs of rust. The doors hung open and I saw the glint of tools inside. I glanced over my shoulder. Noah was inspecting something on the plane. I grabbed a Stanley knife, a length of spring steel ribbon, a small spool of wire, jammed them all into my pockets, turned and headed back across the runway.

Some money changed hands, a tank was rolled out, and the plane was refueled. As the small man from the building rolled the empty tank away, Fonseco and another guy I hadn't see before stepped out of the cinder block shack. The unfamiliar man, bald and florid, wearing a wilted seersucker suit over a guayabera, fanned his face with a piece of cardboard. Fonseco must have arranged to pick him up here.

"I hope this plane has AC," he complained in a French accent as he passed without a glance in my direction.

"Of course not, Dr. Vernier. It's an antique," Fonseco replied.

Doctor? What kind, I wondered. Medical? I followed them onto the plane and Noah came after, closing the doors. Dr. Vernier strapped into one of the passenger seats so I resumed my seat next to Fonseco.

"Not an official airstrip, I guess," I commented once we were back in the air.

Fonseco nodded. "Private. The land belongs to an old friend. Someone who supports our mission."

"Why are we still flying south? Where you taking me? And who's our new friend?" I had a pretty good idea of where we were going but I didn't want Fonseco to know I'd been sneaking around and breaking into his database.

"All will become clear in due time, Justin."

We flew for several more hours. Despite the noise and the shuddering of the plane, I drifted off a few times. Just after 5:00 a.m. I felt the plane bank into a descent and opened my eyes. Fonseco, who had been flying with only one short break for nearly fourteen hours, looked haggard but alert. Out the windshield I saw a dark sky full of stars, a darker horizon of rolling hills broken by a jutting volcanic peak, and, below that, two lines of dim lights, presumably outlining an airstrip ahead. Fonseco brought us down, dead center between those lines, the sturdy craft bumping along, slowing, coming to a stop.

Noah had the cargo doors open by the time Fonseco, Vernier, and I had unbuckled our harnesses and stumbled to the back. The air outside hung motionless, cool and damp and smelling of earth and vegetation. I hopped down onto blacktop, followed by Vernier, who lowered himself down gingerly like a man with bad knees, then Fonseco. Nearby, two people emerged from a bunker-like, one story concrete building, silhouetted by a light mounted above the door, long shadows reaching out toward us as they marched forward. A man and a woman, young, small and lean, of about equal height, both dressed in a kind of paramilitary outfit—dark t-shirts tucked into cargo pants—and carrying automatic weapons slung over their shoulders.

"Take Mr. Martin to building one please…"

"It's Vincent, not Martin," I said, cutting Fonseco off.

"Martin is the name we gave you, Justin. It's the

name you will use while you are here with us. As Noah indicated to you earlier, we don't have government issued ID and we don't care what yours says. We know your true name." He turned to the guards. "Take him now. Give him some food."

They patted me down and found the Stanley knife, my pocket knife, and the wire but not the spring steel which I had worked into the waistband of my pants surreptitiously during the long flight. Noah examined the items they had confiscated, shook his head dismissively and motioned for them to take me away. Leaving the landing strip, they led me along a path that curved down the hillside and entered a stand of trees.

It was dark in the forest and cooler. After about ten minutes, we came out on a clearing. Directly ahead stood a big two story Spanish style ranch house, red tiled roof damply reflecting moonlight, wraparound porch, dark windows. A couple of other concrete structures lurked nearby—blocky and brutal like something you would find on a military base. Pathways laid with white gravel and bordered by low shrubberies curved between the buildings. I realized after a moment why the scene looked familiar. They had recreated more or less the original ranch setup in Montana—same U shaped, three-story building behind the house, similar outbuildings—the placement and size of everything was eerily reminiscent of the old photos I had found online from the time of the FBI raid.

"What is this place?" I asked.

"We call it the ranch," the woman said.

"How big is it?"

"Many many acres. Very large."

They led me to one of the concrete outbuildings—

two stories with small, evenly spaced windows. Their faces were impassive, shiny with the perpetual perspiration of the tropics. The woman opened an exterior door, unlocking it with a key from her belt, then led the way down a windowless corridor lit by buzzing overhead lights. She stopped at an interior door, unlocked it, and gestured for me to enter.

"Please go in. We will bring you something to eat."

I didn't seem to have much choice. The room was about twelve by twelve. A cot took up one corner, a toilet and sink the other. Aside from that, bare concrete. One window opened on a view of the ranch house, screened and crossed by thick rebar. It was a prison cell. A small lizard clung to the wall near the window. As I entered, it darted out through a little hole in the corner of the screen, just big enough for its lithe body to squeeze through.

"This doesn't look like the room I saw on the website. It was supposed to be a luxury suite with a view of the pool."

The woman stood in the doorway, the man behind her. They didn't smile. They looked like dangerous children.

"We will return with food."

"Can you being me something else to wear? It's a bit warmer here than it was in Utah."

The door closed with a solid thunk. Seated on the cot, legs crossed, I waited for my new lizard friend to creep back in and keep me company.

Chapter 12

Conversations
12/13-15: Costa Rica, Alajuela Province

Over the next three days I did almost start to see that lizard as my only friend. They tried to break me down. It began with sleep deprivation and forced labor.

The two guards returned about twenty minutes later with clothes for me to change into—a pair of the same fatigues they wore, underwear, socks, and a t-shirt. The pants were made of a very light but tough fabric, obviously designed for warm climates, with a plethora of cargo pockets. It was a relief to change out of my Dustin Cruz clothes and drop the last bit of pretend. When I was dressed, they returned with plates of food and we all sat cross-legged on the floor of my cell to eat. They had left their automatic weapons somewhere but I didn't doubt for a minute they were tough fighters.

"I'm Brother Saul," the young man said. "And this is Sister Serah. Elder Fonseco has put us in charge of taking care of you today." He had the accent of a native Spanish speaker but his English was fluent.

"Brother and sister? They don't use honorifics like that back at the commune."

"This is a holy place," Sister Serah said, catching my eyes with hers. Irises of such a dark brown they appeared almost black bored into mine. "Those who are called to work here are a special family so we recognize each other in this way."

My plate was heaped with eggs, fried plantain, beans and rice, and avocado. We were all silent for a bit, focusing on the food. The sun, just risen above the tree line and the ranch house, cast orange-gold light on my guards' faces.

"You eat well here."

"Yes," Brother Saul answered. "We have heavy work to do so we fuel our bodies well."

"Am I going to get my duffle bag back?"

"Eventually."

"What do you do here? What's the heavy work?"

"Building the temples. You'll see. Finish eating and we'll take you."

Outside, people were emerging from the ranch house and the bunk house behind it, men and women, all dressed for work in jeans and boots and t-shirts. They were a multicultural lot, with skin tones from fair to dark, all lean and strong and mostly young although I saw a few greybeards. They reminded me of the itinerant outdoor life people I met sometimes in San Francisco, passing through, crashing on a friend's couch, on their way from leading white water rafting trips or rock climbing camps to a seasonal job teaching snowboarding at a ski resort. They had to be the chosen ones from the Community's network of farms and communes, brought together in this place for the jubilee anniversary of Eleanor Jane Sibyl's reign over their religious order. I wondered if Glenn Morgan, the beekeeper at Red Butte had made the cut. I didn't see him in the crowd. We joined the straggling line on a well-worn path leading back up the hill in the direction of the landing strip. Far up, a jumbo jet cut across the sky, engines droning and leaving a contrail of billowing white vapor.

Among the trees we had passed through on our way down from the plane, I studied the forest, trying to gather clues to help me figure out where exactly I was. It seemed like we had to be high up. Off the path, around the massive boles and roots of the trees, a riot of ferns, orchids, and bromeliads grew. A hummingbird darted among them, looking for its morning nectar. A howl erupted above and I looked up to see dark shapes moving in the canopy.

"Howler monkeys," Brother Saul said.

The path turned and a smaller trail continued uphill—probably the way to the airstrip. We walked another quarter mile before emerging from the trees into a massive clearing on a natural plateau. I stopped, taking in the scene. Brother Saul and Sister Serah came to halt on either side of me. In the distance, the unmistakable peak of the Volcán Arenal rose up, symmetrical and blue with atmospheric optics. Costa Rican cloud forest, then—probably mid-way between the coasts and in the north. Below us, in the center of the clearing, squatted a Mayan-style stepped pyramid with a broad stairway running to the flat top where an anachronistic circular structure had been placed. The pyramid was petite by Mesoamerican standards—maybe only seventy feet wide at the base, narrowing to thirty at the top. The weirdest part about it was how clean and new it looked. Also, one corner, the one nearest to where we stood, was unfinished. I watched as the crew of workers wandered down, opened a shed, and started carting out tools and wheelbarrows. A row of something like kilns sprawled along the tree line nearby.

"Wait," I said, confused. "Are you building this pyramid?"

"Yes. It's our new temple. Temple number three."

"Number three? Of how many?"

"Three."

"So, the last one?"

"We're building them all at once. We just give them numbers to make it easier to assign work crews. We're assigned to this one today."

TRIAD. A visual memory of the computer screen in the little office back at Red Butte Commune came to me. I remembered the CR in Malena's record which I had interpreted as Costa Rica, and, at the bottom of the record, a button labeled TRIAD. It couldn't be a coincidence.

"We build them just like the ancient sages did," Sister Serah said. "They built with wisdom and faith. Limestone quarried from the earth, quicklime baked in the kiln, slaked with sand and water to make mortar."

"I don't think the ancients had one of those." I pointed to a crane poking up on the far side of the building.

"We can't spend fifty years building like they did," Brother Saul said wistfully. "Although I would gladly give my life to this work. We must finish in time for the celebration. Now, Elder Fonseco told us you are a sculptor. So, we'll have you work with Brother Samuel. He's our master carver."

By the end of the day, I had surpassed the master. In my own estimation anyway. Brother Samuel was a taciturn guy, short and broad, maybe in his forties. He had a pile of cut blocks ready, each one a rough rectangle about half a meter on its longest side. They must have weighed 150 pounds. We wrestled one up onto a low workbench and he set about showing me how to use the various chisels, then a rasp, and finally sandpaper and files in a variety of shapes and sizes to smooth and finish. In the tool shed he pointed out where everything was kept. After that, I was on my own. It was hot work and painstaking. My low back and arms ached by the time we broke for lunch. From the back of a jeep, the day's kitchen crew (I gathered it was a rotating duty) served tamales and bottles of cold water. After that, we went back to work and didn't quit until late afternoon. Samuel and I lifted my last block down and added it to the pile of finished stones. It was perfect.

"Nice one," He said, eyeing me sideways. "Sculptor huh?"

Putting the tools away, carefully stowing them where Brother Samuel had shown me, I was alone for a moment in the shed. I glanced around, taking stock. An oxy-acetylene torch rig hung on the wall. Various shovels and picks. Straps for carrying heavy loads. A shelf of chisels and other small tools. One of the small files called out to me. A half round. Not very useful for shaping stone. It probably wouldn't be missed. I pocketed it and finished replacing the chisels.

Exhausted, everyone trudged together along the path. As we walked, I thought about what I had learned so far. They were building pyramids. Three of them. Presumably for some purpose related to the big event coming up. Brother Saul had said they needed to be finished in time for the celebration. I had also noticed two interesting bits of information. First, a guard was on duty at the top of the pyramid the whole time we were working. Second, at the base of the pyramid on three sides were vents of some kind, framed with concrete instead of limestone, with vertical sections of rebar set in close enough together to keep a person out. Together, those facts told me the pyramids were not just decorative. There was something inside. I hadn't been able to get close enough for a good look but I had seen a flat vertical face about halfway up the steps that could conceal a door.

As we walked, clouds rolled in and a brief rainstorm pelted down, drumming on the leaves around us, soaking my clothes, running down my face in rivulets. After the rain, tiny black flies came, biting. I slapped at them and kept stumbling along.

We emerged from the forest and Brother Saul took my arm at the elbow, steering me toward the concrete building, splitting off from the other workers. As we passed the ranch house, a passenger van pulled up, outfitted for bad roads with high suspension and big tires. A group of people climbed out, stretching and yawning–same genre as the other Community members I had spent the day with. Noah emerged from the house and sauntered out to meet them, pointedly ignoring me.

"More guests?" I asked.

"Yes, that should be the last group. They've been arriving all week," Brother Saul answered.

He led me back into the concrete building and shut me in my cell. I lay down on the cot, completely depleted. I had been awake for thirty-six hours at that point, not counting my fitful naps on the plane. My eyes felt seared, my brain foggy. I was just starting to drift off when the cell door opened, my brother/sister team back with dinner.

They had to poke me and call my name to keep me

awake enough to eat. After, they led me to a bathroom with a concrete floor, a buzzing light surrounded by dancing moths, a shower head that shot needling jets of tepid water. I must have undressed but I didn't remember doing it. Someone turned the shower off and threw me a towel. Sister Serah, leaned against the opposite wall, eyes averted. Reality was coming in frozen still images, one superimposed on the next every few seconds or maybe minutes.

Back in my room, alone, I lay on the cot, thinking: *I've been drugged. They gave me something. In the food? In the water?* What was it? MDMA? It felt like MDMA. I had a very high tolerance to that drug, as I had discovered at a rave one time in college. Still, it was affecting me. Adding to the speediness, every time I began to fall asleep, a loud beeping, alternating root and third, sounded outside my cell, echoing down the corridor.

"Hey! Hello?" Pounding on the door in the middle of the night. "Someone turn that beeping off."

"Justin. Calm down." Brother Saul outside the door. "I'll try to find it and shut it off. Go to sleep."

It didn't stop though. All night, every time consciousness finally drained away, the last grain of sand slipping through the bottleneck and numbing darkness spreading like static through my body, it would come again—beep BLEEP beep BLEEP—and I would start awake, my head aching and body slicked with sweat. Each time, I would look out the window, through the bars, and try to remember all over again where I was and why.

Days two and three were replays of day one. The evening of the third day, a couple of hours after dinner,

Fonseco came to my cell. He dropped my duffle bag next to the cot, unfolded a stool, and sat down. Brother Saul followed him into the room and closed and locked the door. The key hole was on the inside of the door, as if they had just taken out the knob set and turned it around when they made the room into a prison cell. Brother Saul and Sister Serah had a key on a carabiner which they kept clipped to their belts. They locked the door every time they came in. On the outside, it had a thumb turn so they could easily lock and unlock it without the key. How to get that key? How to escape into the night? I had been thinking about it for three days. Were they afraid I would bolt for the door and get out? I was hardly in shape to outrun them.

Fonseco cleared his throat and the sound echoed around the room, brittle at first, going flat and sludgy in the damp air. All my senses were simultaneously deadened and aggravated by sleep deprivation. I flexed my hands, curling my stiff and calloused fingers, sore from the stone work.

"Brother Samuel tells me you are a great help in his work."

"He needs the help."

"Yes, unfortunately, he does."

"Why are you keeping me locked up?"

"I apologize for that Justin. We can't let you run off into the jungle though. It's a long way to civilization from here and there are many dangers."

"You didn't answer my question." I felt feverish. An involuntary shiver rattled my teeth. "Why are you drugging me? And not letting me sleep?"

"Ah, Justin." Fonseco had a mango in his hand. He held it up and began to peel it, slowly, with a pocketknife, letting the strips fall to the floor. "You see this fruit? Where is the center?"

"I don't know what you mean."

"If I remove the peel, what is left is the center isn't it?"

"Maybe."

"But if I then eat the fruit," he broke off and began devouring the mango. It was very ripe and the juice dripped from his fingers onto the pile of peelings. Finally he extracted the pit from his mouth and licked each finger. "Is the center the seed? And if I cut the seed you see it is just a husk. Inside is what? The real seed? And if I cut that? And keep cutting? Down to the DNA?" He was dicing up the pit on the floor. Inside was a gummy white substance. "Layers. Layers covering what is real. You asked why we are keeping you like this. I am trying to help you peel back layers and rediscover your true self. Your DNA, if you will. We break you down to rebuild what was lost."

"I know who I am."

"Are you what you see in the mirror?"

"I'm not what the Community tried to make me be."

"Even a mirror can't show you your self if you refuse to look. I'm helping you look."

"I don't want to look." I closed my eyes. Another shiver passed through me. I took a ragged breath, opened my eyes and found Fonseco's face right up in mine. He was kneeling next to the cot.

"Do you know what time is, Justin? Do you think we choose what is brought to us? Where we go? Who we become? Time is a weather system moving us along a trajectory beyond our control. Other things, other people are picked up by the storm. They pass by. We catch them.

We travel with them for a time. They blow away. Those who know the secret accept what comes, knowing they didn't choose it. Those who do not know the secret say 'Oh, yes, I wanted this. I sought this out. I'm the master of my own fate.' Only when we realize we are not the master, that we are leaves in the wind, do we know our true path. You didn't choose to come back to us now, at this juncture. The wind brought you to us. You're here for a purpose. A great purpose. I'm here to help. To guide. Don't be afraid of what you will find." He got up slowly and looked down at me. "Sleep. More work to be done tomorrow."

"You know they won't let me sleep," I croaked.

Fonseco stopped in the doorway, Brother Saul beside him, holding the door open. "Of course they will. Don't be silly."

The door closed with a dull thunk. I sat up, stared dazedly at the mango peel and cut up pit he had left behind for a moment, then pulled my duffle bag over and unzipped it. They had found the secret compartment. Everything was gone except the money. Leaving the cash felt like a deliberate insult. I lay back and held still for a few minutes, tense, mind engaged in a kind of battle. Part of me wanted to believe Fonseco. Another part of my brain knew I was drugged and sleep deprived and they were using classic psychological torture techniques to destroy my self-image and will power so they could replace it with blind acceptance of their ideology. That cold, rational part of my brain could see what was happening but it couldn't stop the other part, the wounded animal part, from wanting to do whatever it took to stop the abuse, to give in and say what they wanted to hear and maybe come to believe it.

I thrashed onto my side and something sharp poked me in the hip. Rolling back over, I felt in my pocket. The small file I had stolen from the tool shed.

Now, I drew it out of my pocket and ran a finger over it. I still had the piece of spring steel ribbon I'd found at the landing strip in Mexico. I sat up, reached under the cot mattress, and found the bit of steel still in its hiding place. I had made lock picks before from street sweeper bristles found in gutters. This was very similar. Professional picks were made from the same stuff. I bent it straight. It was about twenty inches long. By bending back and forth, I broke it into two pieces, then broke one of those in half—one longer section which would become the tension wrench, one short which would be the pick. Looking up as I worked, I saw my lizard friend clinging to the wall by the window. Did they have ratcheting tendons like birds of prey? Or did they have to exert constant grip force to stay on the wall? My mind wandered for a minute, brain scarcely functional from lack of sleep and whatever pharmaceutical they were drugging me with. With an effort of will, I brought it back.

"You're going to be my talisman," I whispered to the lizard. "You will remind me who I am and why I'm here, no matter how much they try to brainwash me. I'm putting my faith in you." *I really am starting to go crazy, talking to lizards. That would be an effect of the ecstasy*, the rational part of my brain chimed in—increased empathy and feelings of oneness with other people and animals.

An hour and two beeping alarm cycles later, my picks were ready. I had bent the longer piece into an L with a twist at the elbow. The shorter one I had filed down to a hooked point. While I worked, between bouts of shaking from the drugs and blank periods of spaciness, I decided on a course of action. My instinct was to run but I knew that wouldn't work. I was there to get Malena out. To do that I needed information. First, I needed to find out what was at the center of the pyramid I was helping to build. An armed guard stood on the steps near the top at all times during the day, keeping the worker bees away from the round temple at the top. Sometimes it was Saul or Serah, sometimes other guards. According to Brother Saul, there were three pyramids. The other two had to be complete or close to it. I hadn't seen any large groups of workers heading off in other directions. What was their purpose? What were they hiding? I still hadn't seen any trace of Malena. Was there another building somewhere? Was she being held in the main house?

A solid wood door with a small, reinforced window closed my cell off from the dimly lit hallway beyond. I peered through. Out in the corridor I saw nothing but empty gray concrete wall and floor for ten feet in either direction. Beyond that, my field of view was blocked. If my guards were watching, they would notice my exit. If they did, I would just claim the door wasn't locked. I was in no shape to fight them. Just in case I made it out successfully, I balled up clothing from my duffle and arranged it under my sheet to hopefully fool anyone who glanced in from the hallway. Fake Justin dummy complete, I started working on the lock. It took about five minutes with my shaky fingers but the tumblers lined up and the lock turned at last. I crouched there for a moment, fear eating me from inside. Then, a deep breath, an exhale. I eased the door open a crack and slipped out.

Chapter 13

City of Gold and Lead
12/15: Costa Rica, Alajuela Province

Outside, placed out of sight from the door's narrow window, I found a Bluetooth speaker—presumably the source of the alarms that had been keeping me awake. I considered stomping on it. Or throwing it against the wall. My willpower was at low ebb but I resisted mightily and quelled the urge. Brother Saul and Sister Serah had to be close by, probably asleep with ear plugs in—no sense in waking them up. To my left, I could see the exit door twenty feet away. To the right, the corridor ended in a T. I crept down and peered around the corner. More closed doors like mine, a yellow bucket with a mop handle sticking out leaned against a wall, and, far away, a window beyond which dark forms of trees gathered.

I turned back and went to the exit. The steel exterior door opened silently and I hurried across the little landing outside, avoiding the pool of light cast by a lamp above. Remembering that the door required a key, I caught it just before it swung all the way back, jammed the latch with a small twig I found on the ground, and eased it closed. Down two steps, then I hit the ground, moving quickly into the shadow of the building. It felt good to be outside. My head cleared a little in the night air. Still, I had been awake for too long. My eyes were having trouble staying focused. My body felt heavy, muscles not responding normally.

Curious, I crept around the perimeter, peering into windows, placing my feet carefully in the damp earth, stepping over shrubs. Most of the rooms were dark, set up as storage or offices. It took me a moment to recognize the next room as my own cell with the fake Justin under the covers. Farther down, I found two more cells similar to mine. In one, Sister Serah snoozed, curled into a ball on the cot. In the other, Brother Saul was seated on his cot, bent over a book, pages tilted toward a little lamp on his bedside table. I ducked down when I saw him. These were obviously not their regular quarters. They had been detailed to keep me under observation and had taken whatever beds were available. Continuing around, I passed a dark office where a bulbous desk phone might have sat untouched since the eighties. The other side of the building housed the industrial kitchen where all the communal meals were prepared and a double garage.

A gravel road emerged from a stand of trees a hundred yards away, made a long curve, passed by the closed garage doors, and ended at a circular drive in front of the ranch house. Across the road, the path leading to the pyramid construction site and the airstrip cut straight up a gentle slope and into the forest. I didn't see anyone patrolling or any lights on in the bunkhouse or main house. My only option was to hurry across if I wanted to get to the building site. I guessed it would take about ten seconds to cross the open area. I would have to take my chances and hope no one was watching.

Running, trying to keep my feet light, I nearly tripped over a stone but recovered and made it into the deep shadows among the trees. I paused there for a moment, breathing hard, while I surveyed the grounds, watching for movement. A shiver ran through me, rattling my teeth. The drugs they had given me were still doing things to my heart rate and synapses, altering my visual acuity. The doors of perception were open and I was seeing with exceptional clarity. A tree branch fifty yards away was as clear and detailed as if I held it in my hand. I could see the warp and weft of curtains waving softly in an open window of the ranch house. Physical exertion and danger had flipped my focus from hazy and unreliable to sharp and intense. It was an illusion, of course, caused by the drugs and misfiring of my sleep-deprived brain, but it gave me confidence. Nothing stirred below. I was sure of it.

Looking down on the building where they had imprisoned me, rage built slowly, tightening my chest, and a line from Sherlock Holmes came to me: *We have our web to weave while theirs is already woven.* In nearly every case, there is a moment when Holmes turns from careful fact gathering and deduction to sudden, decisive action. I was almost ready to make my Holmesian move. The Community had woven its web. I hadn't even begun yet. I was one person up against a hundred but there was a certain strength in going second. I had enough information to begin to see where they had left openings, their blind spots, the limits imposed by their ideology. I just needed to fit a few more pieces together to see the whole system. I would find Malena and get her out one way or another. If I had to pull the whole thing down in the process, that was fine with me. I turned then and hurried up the forest path, determined not to think about jaguars and giant spiders.

Coming out of the trees, I found the pyramid bathed in moonlight. With my altered perception, it looked like a black velvet painting. There should have been a priest king standing atop it, frozen mid-swing, just before he brought his dagger down to complete a sacrifice. I stood at the edge of the trees for several minutes, watching. If there was a guard, they had to be hidden inside the rotunda at the top. I waited some more. A sloth eased its way through the canopy off to my right, munching leaves. Something rustled through the undergrowth behind me. Still no sign of human occupation.

I strode forward across the meadow onto the bare earth surrounding the stone structure. At the bottom step I paused again, looking up. Maybe only half the size of the largest ancient Central American pyramids, still it was a massive accomplishment. If nothing else, the Community knew how to run a project and get things done.

The steps rose, awkwardly spaced and steep. I climbed with hands and feet, feeling the cool stone, stopping every few steps and resting my forehead against it. Halfway up, as I had guessed, a low door penetrated the structure. They had faced it with stone to match the pyramid, but a circular perforation showed steel behind and a key hole. I would come back to that but first I wanted to see what was at the top.

Continuing up, I came to the plateau at the apex and crossed in two strides to the rotunda that looked more like a mini-Stonehenge than anything Central American in origin. The stone columns were capped by plinths but the center was open to the sky and contained nothing but a recessed floor of metal plate. I could tell it was not very thick. It bore my weight without warping but my footsteps echoed through what had to be a vast vertical space below. Feeling along lines radiating from a central point, I discovered the metal floor was not solid but made of six wedges that together formed the circle. They had to be welded together on the underside unless they were held up by some structure. Maybe a structure that could be removed to allow them to open like the petals of a flower? I paced it off and determined the diameter to be approximately sixteen feet. So, the pyramid contained a cylindrical volume at its center covered by a metal pizza. Why? It's a wonder I didn't figure it out then and there but my brain was not at full capacity. I needed more data.

Back down at the door, I got my new pick set out and worked the lock. It was a good knob set but I was an expert. Years of experience told my fingers what to do without much help from my blasted neocortex. The lock clicked open and I pulled on a handle set into the stone. The door swung out with a thin whine of metal hinges approaching their weight limit. Beyond, a dim passage led straight into the heart of the pyramid.

Cool, dry air carrying a slightly acrid smell billowed out. Pipes and electrical conduit ran along the ceiling. Caged fluorescent lights tied into the conduit led my eye down the passage, casting just enough illumination to see by. Cautiously, I entered and pulled the heavy door closed. Dull silence, broken only by a low hum I could feel through my boots as much as hear, replaced the chittering and rustling of the jungle outside. I started down the hall, trailing fingers along rough cinderblock as I went, shivering as my sweat cooled and dried in the parched air.

To my left, a stairway led down, turned ninety degrees, continued into the depths. Ahead, the corridor kept on straight into the heart of the pyramid. I chose straight. Twenty feet in I came to another door, solid steel. I turned the knob slowly and eased it open a crack. Beyond I saw a short hallway that opened into a control room of some sort. To the left, a corridor branched off and ended in steps leading up out of sight. Beyond, on the left and right, small glassed-in areas divided the space. One looked like a kitchen—bare bones with concrete counter, stainless sink, microwave. The other contained two workstations facing each other, each with a large computer monitor, keyboard and mouse, coffee cups, and stacks of papers. Both were uninhabited. I wanted to explore those but first I was drawn toward the control room. I could only see a small portion from where I stood. I listened for a moment, trying to detect any slight sound—a cough, a creaking chair, keyboard taps. I heard nothing except the incessant hum. Slipping through, I crept to the open doorway.

Two chairs faced banks of monitors, dials, button panels, and glowing LED indicators. It looked like the kind of control room you would see in an industrial factory, power plant, or, I realized seeing what was displayed on the monitors, a missile silo.

The monitor nearest to me showed a grid of four grainy, monochromatic video feeds. The feeds appeared to come from four cameras placed at various angles inside what had to be the cylindrical volume at the heart of the pyramid. Inside that cement cylinder stood a rocket. A really big rocket. My skin prickled with an atavistic fear response. The shape of the missile said weapon. It said death. It said destruction. I knew the silo was about sixteen feet in diameter and the missile I was looking at didn't have more than three feet of clearance on either side. The silo had to be deeper than the height of the pyramid.

I dropped into the closest chair and stared at the video feed, mind blank with horror. It all came in a rush, a wave of connections snapping together like magnets—the rocket parts. TRIAD. Fonseco's doomsday talk. The upcoming celebration. Three pyramids in the Costa Rican cloud forest. A temple complex. Each pyramid housing its own vintage Russian R-36 ICBM. The SS-18 Satan had been NATO's reporting name for the missile, I remembered from my research. They considered it to be a first strike weapon with a massive range and fearsome destructive capacity. I remembered the maximum range was 16,000 kilometers—nearly halfway around the earth. Far enough to strike China or Russia from Costa Rica? I wasn't sure of the distances but my guess was yes, plenty enough range to get to Russia and probably China as well. Were they trying to start World War Three? Nuclear annihilation? A response strike from Russia followed by the U.S. firing its missiles?

I stood and stumbled back down the corridor, into the office I had passed. The desks were just plywood on sawhorses, the chairs molded plastic. I sat in the nearest. A tap on the keyboard woke the computer up. A technical manual showing an electrical circuit design was open. I didn't recognize the desktop environment. Probably some version of Linux. I did recognize the Firefox logo. I double clicked it, holding my breath, hoping for an internet connection. An hourglass icon appeared, then the browser window. I typed in gardenersparadise.com and it loaded nearly instantly. Not just a connection, a fast connection. Of course they would be wired. With the celebration coming up they would need it for the live stream. Probably a satellite connection.

On the variegated aspidistra page I scrolled to the last comment. It wasn't the one I had left with the IP address and mention of TRIAD. The screen name on it was crazyforcacti and it just said 'such fascinating mammals, aspidistra.' Ashna's weird sense of humor. At least I knew she had received my message. I clicked to open a new comment box and began typing.

>*Few people realize that a variety of variegated aspidistra has been known to grow in the cloud forests of Costa Rica. Native to Russia, it prefers clearings and the centers of ancient ceremonial sites where it grows immensely tall. Interestingly, it is only found in threes or triads. The botanical classification is R-36. If allowed to proliferate, it can have massive destructive power. The Community of aspidistra enthusiasts, however, is well aware of this dangerous flora.*<

I sat back and read it over. I was having a hard time focusing. My mind kept wandering off, eyes heavy. I read it once more, forcing myself to track each word. Ashna would understand, I decided. I clicked the button to post the comment then closed the tab and deleted the last hour's browsing history. They probably had some other way of tracking internet traffic on their network but hopefully a visit to a gardening forum wouldn't set off any alarms.

On my way out, I glanced down the hall to the control room with its glowing LEDs and screens. Could they really start World War Three? Were they crazy enough to try? Maybe and definitely. I would have to do what I could to stop them. Hopefully Ashna would get my message and go to work from her end if she hadn't started already. She was probably already deep into their databases and systems based on the information from my previous post if I knew her at all.

Outside, the humid air settled over me. I descended the stone stairs and headed off toward the path. Walking, feet dragging, my goal was just to get back to my room and sleep the rest of the night after disabling the alarm outside my door. If I had a hope of foiling their plans and finding Malena, I still believed it would be best to do it from within. If they had noticed my absence, I would just pretend they left the door unlocked and I decided to go for a walk. After about twenty minutes of walking though, I started to feel like I should have made it back to the ranch complex even at my slow pace. Had I made a wrong turn in the dark? I'd noticed smaller paths leading off from the main on previous trips back and forth to the pyramid. I stopped and stood still for a moment, disoriented. The forest seemed closer, the path narrower than I remembered. With a shrug, I started moving again. I would keep going and see where I ended up.

Another ten minutes of walking brought me to a wall. It rose up toward the night sky shining with stars, maybe twice my height. I placed my hand on it. Rough concrete still holding warmth from the sun. To my right and left the wall continued, curving. The outer margin of the forest followed, cleared back ten feet from the edge to make a wide pathway. The shallow arc of the curve pointed to a large space contained inside the wall if it continued and formed a circle. I turned right and walked, tall grass wet with dew brushing my knees. About a hundred feet on I came to a door. There was no handle, lock, or hinge exposed from the outside. Just a blank door that had to open inward. It did present an opportunity though. There was a kind of frame around the door cast into the concrete. I reached and tested it with my fingers, finding it was just deep enough for me to grasp. Halfway between the top of the frame and the upper edge of the wall was a square indentation housing a spotlight. I considered for a moment. If I fell, I would land in soft grass. Worth a try.

Wrapping fingers around the frame, I jerked up and used the friction of a foot on the door to push high enough to get a hand into the square opening above. I raised my other foot, got the toe of my boot on the frame, then pushed and pulled, throwing myself up and casting a hand up to grasp the top edge of the wall. At the last moment, an image of broken glass topping the wall flashed through my head and I balked. My fingers slipped off and I plummeted down, landing on my back in the wet grass with a dull thunk. I lay there for a moment, breathing slowly. One more try. I knew now that there was no broken glass, just smooth cement.

My second attempt was a success. I threw a leg over and got myself into a prone position on top of the wall. Looking down, eyes struggling to focus, I felt a disorienting sensation of flying back in time to the hillside in Acapulco above Wayne Abbot's compound. An eerily similar landscape of lush plantings, pathways, palms, and glowing pool lay spread out inside the wall. Instead of one house and a couple of outbuildings though, a complex of structures lay below me.

The area contained by the circular wall seemed to be divided in two with a wall down the center. On my side of the divide, two large buildings rose up in the center of the grounds, their style like a greatest hits of brutalist seventies community college architecture—vertical ridge textured concrete, large flush windows, cantilevered decks and recessed planters trailing vines. Filling the space between them, paths curved, crossing koi ponds with arching bridges, and intersected around susurrating fountains. Beyond, in the open area, an athletic field and an Olympic size pool reflecting the stars above. Closer, I counted twelve small, single-story villa-like structures arranged in a semi-circle. Square and taller on what I assumed was the front side, creating a sloping roof, they faced away from me. Each had a door flanked by two small windows on the back side. My vantage point on the wall was closer to the left end of the semi-circle. Far down the row to my right where the semi-circle curved around, I could see the fronts were all glass with sliding doors and patios. Light glowed behind semi-opaque blinds in the windows of villa number two, counting from the left. The rest were dark.

I lay there for a time, watching the grounds for any activity. The wall was warm on my chest and legs. I breathed in the pungent perfume of some night blooming flower. My patience was rewarded about ten minutes later by the sound of a door opening. I looked toward the villa with the lighted window. The door stood open and the unmistakable, bear-like bulk of Devlin Fonseco was silhouetted there. A flame flicked to life, a cigarette glowed, and Fonseco exhaled a great cloud of smoke. My perch was becoming more uncomfortable with every passing minute but I held still, gritting my teeth, left arm full of pins and needles. He sat in the doorway, sucking hungrily on the cigarette. Finally he inhaled the last drag, filter smoldering and crackling as he ran out of tobacco, dropped the butt in the plantings by the door, stood, and lumbered back inside.

I considered going down and exploring the grounds but I knew I didn't have the energy or alertness just then. I needed to get back and sleep if possible. I shook my arm a few times to get the blood flowing, then hung and dropped back down into the tall grass, rolling to a backward somersault to absorb the shock of the fall. I came up to my feet out of the roll, turned away from the wall, and was immediately knocked back down by a hard shove. Sitting in the damp grass, I brought my gaze up, confused. Noah looked down at me, face a rigid mask of disdain in the dim light.

"Thought you were being sneaky? I was watching you the whole time. You're not supposed to be here."

"No." Adrenaline shot through my body, waking me to danger. "I guess not." I scrambled back and stood, a hand on the wall behind my back.

"I've been waiting for this opportunity." He took a step forward, hands clenching into fists. "Fonseco's going to be pretty annoyed when you turn up dead. He won't know I did it though."

"Dead?"

"Most definitely," he said, pulling an arm back and swinging.

I ducked sideways and fell, rolling, got to my feet and scrambled back again. We circled each other.

"Why dead?"

"Faster than you look, aren't you? Because you deserve it."

"For what?"

"You lied to me. You invaded my home. You slept with my wife. Take your pick."

"Slept with…you sent her to me. Anyway, you're

divorced."

"No such thing as divorced in the Community. You should know that. Anyway, doesn't matter. I'm still going to kill you." He lunged on the last word, reaching to grapple me.

I sidestepped, ducking again and hit him in the throat with the heel of my hand. He staggered back but I could tell I hadn't made enough contact to really hurt him. Without thought, I turned and ran. I was in no shape to go ten rounds with Noah. If I could lose him I could make my way back to my cell. Brother Saul and Sister Serah wouldn't let him kill me. At least I hoped they wouldn't.

I crashed through the grass and onto the path. Tree trunks flashed by. Noah's feet pounded the path behind me. I was gaining distance. He wasn't a fast runner. I knew I wouldn't last long though. Exhausted from days of no sleep and hard manual labor, I could feel my energy flagging. The larger path opened out ahead of me. I turned left, skidding on the damp earth and kept going. A hundred yards on, I realized my mistake. I had turned the wrong way. My addled brain had me retracing my steps instead of heading back toward the ranch house. I burst out of the trees into the clearing. The pyramid loomed up before me, harsh lines dim in the moonless night.

Veering right, I headed for the tool shed. Maybe I could find a weapon. Noah was gaining on me now. Ten yards from the shed, he dove and caught my foot. I went down hard and rolled sideways, breath ripped from my lungs, gasping. Recovering first, he knelt over me, a hunting knife in his hand, raised to strike. My fingers scrabbled in the grass and found a chunk of rock, one of the many I or Brother Samuel had struck off with our chisels. I whipped it at Noah's face and it hit him over the eye, leaving a nasty gash. For a moment he reeled, stunned. I scooted back, jumped up, and found the hammer I had left on my workbench earlier. Noah rushed toward me. I turned, arm moving through a deadly arc and releasing the hammer. It caught him full on the left shoulder and caromed off his forehead, spinning. He cried out, falling, dropping the knife. I darted forward and aimed a kick at his face, bowling him over backward. I followed it with two more to his midsection, then one to his temple. He fell, thudding on the turf, eyes rolled back, out cold.

I allowed myself thirty seconds of deep gasps to catch my breath, then dragged him to the tool shed. Inside, I found rope and used it to tie his hands and feet, pulling the knots tight with shaking hands. Above me in the trees, a howler monkey whooped. Another answered from farther off in the forest. Someone had left a bandana hanging on a nail inside the shed. I tore a piece off and shoved it in Noah's mouth, then tied it around to stop him from yelling. Reconsidering, I took it back off. He looked bad. It was hard to see in the dark but one of his eyes seemed droopy. Did I kick him too hard? I felt panic rising in my chest. What if he was hemorrhaging? He was trying to kill me but I didn't want his death on my hands. He took erratic, shallow but gasping breaths, chest rising and falling.

I stood and stepped back, looking up toward the sky, into the forest, anywhere but at Noah. He drew another rattling breath and I looked down at him. I counted one, two, three seconds. One more gasp. I counted to five. To ten. To fifteen. He was done. His body, a dark form on the dark earth, seemed to sink and settle into the ground. I stood for a long time, staring down at him while the howler monkeys moved off, rustling through the canopy.

It had been self-defense, I told myself as I crouched and searched his pockets. He would have killed me. I found a keyring, a little penlight, an electronic keycard, another knife, a snack-size plastic baggie with several tiny pills in it, a wad of cash in a money clip, and a phone. The phone was locked with a six digit passcode. No chance of hacking that. I held down the power button until it shut off. I didn't want anyone finding Noah's body by pinging the phone. I kept the keys, keycard, and flashlight. Everything else, I put back. Shining the flashlight on his face, I saw a purpling dent in his forehead, the pupil below it blown. The hammer. He was a goner before I ever kicked him. That made me feel slightly better. I could have chosen not to kick him but if I hadn't thrown the hammer, I would be the one laid out on the ground. CPR wouldn't have helped either, or running for help. Nothing would have saved him. *Play stupid games, win stupid prizes*, I mumbled, feeling panic rising in my chest and fighting it back down.

I dragged his body into the forest, bushwhacking in as far as I could manage and dropping him at the base of a fallen tree. With a shovel from the tool shed, I buried him in dead leaves and dirt, sticks and stones. His body might be found in a day or a week. Or it might never be found. Bodies decay and decompose quickly in the tropics and the worker drones didn't seem to venture into the forest much. Anyway, I wasn't planning to stick around to find out. I had a strong feeling that the walled village I had discovered was where I would find Malena, if she was in Costa Rica at all. I would have seen her among the work crews if she was staying in the ranch house or the dormitories. I just needed to get in there, by invitation if possible. I knew Fonseco hadn't brought me all the way from Utah just to do manual labor on his pyramid. I was there for some greater purpose. He had said it to me himself only hours before. He was just waiting for my psyche to break down enough to acquiesce, to accept whatever destiny he had planned. I could act that role. Starting the next day, I decided, I would be the greatest zealot in Community history— greater even than dead Noah. I would take up his mantle.

I stood for a moment longer, surrounded by small sounds of creatures moving in the undergrowth. An owl hooted somewhere off to my left. The Romans considered owls harbingers of death. *Too late, owl. He's already dead.* Something else the Romans believed—an owl feather placed on a sleeper's pillow would make them speak, telling their deepest secrets as if from a trance. I was the owl feather and Fonseco the sleeper. It was time for the Community's secrets to be told.

Starting back, I felt pressed down by alien gravity, every step a plodding effort. A long walk in the dark later, shaking with fatigue, I emerged from the trees and crossed the open field. The outside door was still unlocked. I eased it open. Hallway clear, I crept to my door, picked up the Bluetooth speaker outside it, and turned it off.

What to do with the items I had taken from Noah? They had already found my secret pocket. Maybe they wouldn't search it again. I had no option really so I dug down, unzipped it, and stowed the keys and keycard and flashlight.

The Justin dummy still dozed beneath my sheet. I

wished I could swap with my doppelganger, go back in time and spend the last three hours sleeping while it bumbled through my life like one of the animated dolls of Oz. No such luck. I pushed the clothes off the bed and eased my sore body down. As soon as my eyes closed that spinning hammer glancing off Noah's shoulder then smashing his skull began to play in my mind's eye like a video on repeat. Even that couldn't keep me awake.

Chapter 14

Refiner's Fire
12/15: Costa Rica, Alajuela Province

I woke feeling feverish, my throat parched. Sister Serah was shaking me. I tried to sit up but thought better of it and lay back. My body was sore and bruised, my muscles like knots in old rope.

"Breakfast time. Get up."

"No," I croaked, and turned away to face the wall. Memories from the night before—still images, dim and fuzzy like waterlogged photos after a flood. The missile silo inside the pyramid. The walled compound. Noah's face as he fell, hammer spinning away into the night. My breath caught.

"You have to get up now."

"Why are you here, Sister Serah?" I asked the question without thinking, turning over and easing up to sitting.

"I'm here to wake you up." She stepped back, wary, taking a ready stance.

"No, sorry. I meant why are you in the Community? How did you become a member?"

"How?" she hesitated, lifting a hand through a shaft of morning sun, smoothing her hair. "I was born near here. My father was a stone mason. He worked on the house. Sister Eleanor spoke to him one day, from the TV,

168

but straight into his heart. He felt the light, the golden light, coming down and resting on his head. We joined. My whole family. I was only four. I've been here ever since."

"Have you felt that light? Like your father did?"

"Yes, every day. Every time I hear her speak. When I read her words. She's a great prophet." Her eyes went distant.

I watched her in her silent reverie, reliving the feeling. I couldn't quite get it. I didn't understand what it was that brought people flocking to this so-called prophet. Any prophet or guru, really. Jim Jones, David Koresh, Marshall Applewhite, Shoko Asahara, the Bhagwan Shree Rajneesh. Something about them intersected with a particular mind, drew those minds to them, locked them in, fed them what they needed. From the outside it seemed absurd, the cult leaders themselves repugnant. To the initiate, the believer, they were shining, saint-like, unimpeachable. But I had to pretend if I wanted to get free. I would do my best.

Brother Saul banged through the door with plates of food. Neither of them had mentioned the door being unlocked or the speaker. They were tired too. I could see it in their eyes. Maybe they didn't notice? Or assumed they had forgotten? I sat on the edge of the bed and took bites, chewed, swallowed, thinking about Sister Serah's story. I could have been eating boiled potatoes or filet mignon. It was all tasteless, without savor or texture. My mind was elsewhere, moving on to what I had discovered in the night. I had to show them that I had been converted, that their mind tricks were working. Honestly, I wasn't so sure their mind tricks weren't working. I felt unmoored, confused, shattered.

"I'm ready to work," I said, looking up from my plate. "It's a sacred job, isn't it? Building a temple."

Brother Saul nodded, peering into my eyes. "Yes, an honor. Let's go. Much work to do today."

Brother Samuel was there before me. As we emerged from the forest, he waved us over.

"Found this on the ground right over there," he pointed to a spot a few feet from the stone carving station. Noah's knife. The one he tried to gut me with. I had missed it when I tidied up. "One of our hammers is missing too," Brother Samuel complained with a laconic drawl. The hammer was with Noah's body.

"I recognize that knife." Sister Serah stepped forward, took it from Samuel and held it up. "It's Brother Noah's. He must have dropped it when he was on patrol last night. I'll give it back to him." She tucked it into her belt.

So they hadn't noticed his absence yet. Noah, Serah, and Saul were guards. I had seen at least three others on the pyramid or patrolling the grounds. One of them stood up on the pyramid already, guarding the door I had gone through the night before—a tall, skinny guy with an assault rifle. How many were there altogether? Only Serah and Saul slept in the building where they were holding me. The others must be mixed in or have their own quarters. They should have noticed he was missing. The anomaly told me their organization and discipline were lacking. That could come in handy.

Serah and Saul drifted off to patrol. I dedicated myself to the work that day, turning out perfect stones, nodding and smiling, calling everyone brother and sister. I did not look toward the woods where Noah's body lay only seventy yards from where I worked.

That evening, I sat on the edge of my cot, sore, head spinning from a fresh dose of the drug they were giving me, pretending to read Eleanor Jane Sibyl's The Odyssey of the Self. I had refused to eat earlier but they must have slipped the drug in my water. I felt hollowed out, empty, weightless like I might float up and press my back to the ceiling. My stomach grumbled. I could feel the blood shooting through my veins. I focused on a word in the book. Misinformation. My eyes skipped down the page. Healing. Another skip. Grace.

My door opened and Brother Saul stood just outside in the hallway.

"Justin, come. We are gathering."

I looked up, confused. "What?"

"We are gathering for a message from the prophet."

"A video?" I asked. "One of Eleanor Jane Sibyl's videos?"

"Yes but live. She is speaking to us from her sanctuary. Come."

He led me out, along a gravel path that curved around the old ranch house to a broad, grassy clearing surrounded by trees. In the long twilight, close to a hundred devotees were assembled on folding chairs facing a screen, silently waiting.

Fonseco stood at the back. Next to him, Dr. Vernier from the plane looking aggrieved. I hadn't seen him since we arrived.

"Justin. Brother Saul." Fonseco's voice stopped us. "Glad to see you here. You remember my friend, Dr. Vernier."

The man held out a hand and I shook it. His face was sour, eyes darting back and forth.

Leaving them, Brother Saul and I took seats in the

back row. A projector and laptop were set up on a folding table, extension cord snaking back under our feet and into the house through a rear entrance. The crowd buzzed with contained excitement. A bird called in the forest, sad sounding in the damp air. The woman in front of me turned around, smiled and nodded. Somebody fiddled with the laptop and then Eleanor Jane Sibyl appeared on screen.

She was in the same place as always—wood paneling behind her with the gold lace tacked up, artificial lighting giving her a flat, contourless appearance. She looked older, more tired.

"Good evening, my children," she began. "Tonight I am speaking only to you, my most loyal followers. Those who have gathered in this place to do the holiest work of the Community. In the power of the ineluctable diamond crystal of shining truth, I invoke the ancients. I invoke those from beyond the void of space. I invoke the cleansing fire upon those agents of ignorance and secularism and popular culture who defile thought. It is almost time for us to ascend. It is almost time for us to show our mettle. We will climb to the soaring heights of our temples, join hands in the holy circle, and float together on the uplift of pure being…"

She droned on and on while my mind wandered. I could only think of the missiles in their silos, Brother Noah's body in the forest, the weird, walled compound. I slumped forward with a hand over my eyes, pretending to listen. I may have drifted off. A timeless interval later, Eleanor Jane Sibyl's voice rose and my eyes opened. She was reciting the final prayer.

"The wise and holy beings, those who have ascended and those who come to us from far away, masters of the ancient wisdom, great builders, they see us gathered in this place. With our gaze set upon their wisdom and our hearts open to their words, we make our vow to uphold truth and the cleansing fire of pure spirit."

All the silent holy warriors sat with their heads bowed, basking in the moment. Eleanor Jane Sibyl bowed her head and the video feed went black. After a minute people began to rise, stretch, and wander off alone or in small groups. Brother Saul stood and I followed.

"A very inspiring sermon," he said.

"Yes, and an honor to be addressed live. Is she here on the ranch somewhere?"

"Perhaps," his eyes were distant. "I don't know her location, of course. It's a closely guarded secret. Come. Elder Fonseco wants to see you."

Threading our way through the crowd, people came forward and greeted Saul and me both, touched us on the shoulder, the waist, gazed into our eyes, blissful. Through the crowd, ten feet away, I saw red hair, long, a tall woman. She turned and with a start I realized it was Beth, the agent from Red Butte commune. She had managed to get an invitation to the big celebration. She must have played her part well. She wouldn't be happy to see me but I had to speak with her.

"I'm going to quickly say hello to Beth," A tiny, crow-like woman had enveloped Brother Saul in a hug and didn't seem to want to let go. I darted away, grabbing my opportunity.

"Beth. It's great to see you."

She turned toward me and her face flickered anger for a moment, quickly controlled. "Justin, wonderful to see you, too." She stepped close and spoke into my ear, gripping my forearm. "What the hell are you doing here? I told you to get out."

"Not my choice," I whispered back. "They forced me to come. They've had me locked up. Listen. This is important. The pyramids are silos. R36 Soviet ICBMs inside. Ready to launch."

"Impossible."

"Very possible. I got out. Broke into one of the silos. Warn your friends." I stepped away, smiling, as Brother Saul appeared at my side. "I'm glad you're here. It's nice to see a face from Red Butte."

"Yes," she answered, peering at me, struggling to process the information I had given her and look blissed out at the same time. "Nice to run into you."

Brother Saul led me up onto the ranch house porch and then inside through the back door. The interior was what I had expected—high ceilings with exposed beams, honey colored wood floors and door frames, rough plastered walls. We passed a giant kitchen, a dining room with a table that looked like it could seat twenty, a great room full of old couches where a massive stone hearth and fireplace loomed majestically. Other Community members drifted by in a kind of bliss trance, tired from their day of work and filled with religious fervor by Eleanor Jane Sibyl's sermon calling for destruction by fire of all that was impure. I wondered again, as I had all my life, what it was that made some people susceptible to religion and others not.

I had been raised in the Community but rebelled against it from day one. Many of these people had, presumably, chosen to believe after being raised in other faiths or no faith at all. From my perspective, it was unimaginable. Were some people predisposed? Or was it just about catching them at the right moment in their lives? I felt the drug dumping depleted stores of serotonin into my brain, rolling waves of unwanted empathy for these zealots through me. I fought against it with the only thing I had left—my deeply contrarian nature that rose up in opposition to any imposition of another's will over my own.

Brother Saul turned down a hallway, knocked on a door.

"It's Saul. I have Justin with me."

"Come in," Fonseco's voice called from inside.

Saul turned the antique knob and pushed the door open, standing aside for me to enter. I took two halting steps and stopped on the threshold. Fonseco sat in an armchair by an open window overlooking the field behind the house and forest beyond. Beside his chair was a little table, on it a Tiffany style lamp that glowed jewel-like, the only light in the room. Opposite Fonseco, an identical chair, occupied by a woman. She raised her head as I entered, brushing aside a fall of dark hair, and turning her face toward me. The light brushed across familiar planes and curves of her features. The old photo, the one of Malena and I outside the meeting hall, rose up in my mind's eye, superimposed itself over the woman's face. Softer than I remembered, older, but surely Malena's face.

I had found her at last.

Chapter 15

Engine Nine
12/15-16: Costa Rica, Alajuela Province

"Justin," she murmured. "I'm glad you came."

"Malena?" I was frozen in the doorway.

"It's been a long time. How did you like Sister Eleanor's sermon tonight?"

"It was…inspiring."

"Come in," Fonseco gestured. "Sit."

Brother Saul gave me a little push and I stumbled into the room. A chair bumped and scudded across floorboards and I was sitting, facing Fonseco and Malena.

"Nothing in the past matters," Malena said and I felt like her eyes were spiraling. Or the room was. Or I was falling, turning. Distances made no sense. "We're here now, brother and sister."

My face prickled, damp with perspiration. Cold and hot. I ran the back of my hand across my forehead. Seething darkness crept in at the edges of my vision. I was at the end of my rope. They had succeeded. They had worn me down.

"Yes," I mumbled. "Nothing matters. We're here now."

"Bother Saul," Fonseco's voice, far away seeming. "I believe Brother Justin is going to pass out." The floor rushed up toward me but strong hands caught my arms. A blur of jewel light, people standing. I closed my eyes and surrendered to the dark.

A sheet wrapped me, cool fabric on my arm and shoulder. A soft mattress underneath. Not the cot in my cell. Not the musty blanket. My head throbbed. I jerked up, opening my eyes. A dark room, dim shapes, sliver of light where curtains met. I stood, shaky, terra cotta tile under my bare feet, took a few steps and pulled a curtain aside. Harsh sunlight burned my retinas. I squeezed my eyes shut, then slowly opened them, just enough to see blurry plants and walkways, buildings in the distance. Inside the wall? I had to be—in one of the little villas I had seen from my perch. Someone was walking across the athletic field, small as an ant from my perspective. It was the same view from a different angle. My headache was calming into a dull twinge each time my heart beat. I opened the curtains just enough to illuminate the room, then turned from the window and explored.

A queen size bed, sheet twisted across it, filled the back half. Closer to the wall of windows, a simple desk and straight-backed chair were pushed up against one wall. A low, blocky couch and chair combo upholstered in orange corduroy straight out of the seventies, oblong coffee table separating them, occupied the rest of the space. Facing the bed, a big closet with louvered doors stretched across the wall. Above, the ceiling was high where it met the wall of windows at the front and sloped down toward the back of the room. In the shadows beyond the bed were two doorways. I walked back and pulled the closet doors open. My duffle bag was there on the floor of the closet. Above it hung several shirts and pairs of pants, all white and loose looking, made of linen or cotton. Noah's keys! The thought throbbed through my headache. I had hidden them in the secret compartment in the duffle along with my improvised lock picks. I pulled the bag out and dug down through it, feeling for the hidden zipper. Everything was still there. Having found my stash, they must have decided they didn't need to search it again. My gamble had paid off. Or was this more psychological warfare? I stood and my head swam. I needed water.

Through one of the doorways at the back I found a bathroom with a sage green tiled shower stall, nondescript sink and toilet. Through the other, a small kitchenette with a mini fridge and microwave, butcher block countertop and sink. Altogether, the place had the feeling of graduate student housing at a state university with time capsule decor thirty years or more out of date. Off the kitchen was an exterior door. I opened it a crack and looked out. Twenty feet away the wall loomed. Assuming the villas all had the same layout, this had to be the door I had seen Fonseco emerge from when he went out for a smoke. I pulled it closed.

Above the sink was an open shelf holding two cups, a bowl, a plate. I filled one of the cups with cool water from the tap and drank it down. Another. I stopped halfway through the third cup, feeling nauseous suddenly, and took deep breaths. I needed a shower, coffee, and ibuprofen. A shower, at least, was available. Undressing, I surveyed my battered body. The fight with Noah had left a deep bruise on my left side, and abrasions on my hands and forearms to join the minor cuts and scrapes from days of hard labor. I had lost a few pounds too. My cheekbones stood out. Dark rings smudged the flesh beneath my eyes.

When I emerged twenty minutes later, hair dripping, feeling a bit more alive, I dressed in the white clothes from the closet and wandered up to the front of the little villa. Someone had entered while I was in the shower and left a tray on the desk. It held a basket of dark bran muffins, a plastic wrap covered bowl of cut fruit, and a thermos of coffee. I reached for the coffee but stopped mid gesture. What if the food or coffee was drugged? Were they done dosing me? Either way, I had to eat and drink and I couldn't resist the pull of coffee. I shrugged, got one of the cups from the kitchen, and filled it.

Sitting on the musty orange couch, curtains fully open, I gazed stupidly out the window wall, drinking coffee and eating bran muffins. My Dustin Cruz watch said 6:53. The sun was well over the horizon, climbing the sky off to my right, throwing shadows and warming the air. I knew which way was east anyway.

A maintenance worker groomed the field, trawling back and forth on a riding mower, the sound a low hum. The two large buildings in the center of this side of the compound were dark. What were they for? What was on the other side of the wall that bisected the compound? Why had they brought me here at last? I was nearing the heart of the mystery but my brain was too addled from days of drugging and no sleep to work through the clues. The food and coffee seemed to be drug free at least. I felt no effects other than a pleasant caffeine buzz.

From the left, a person came into view. A woman— slightly built with long brown hair in a pony tail, dressed in the same loose white garments as me. I watched her wend her way among the ponds and fountains and palms, until she reached the front entrance of the larger of the two buildings where she swiped a card, pulled a glass door open, and disappeared inside.

After that, more people appeared, crossing over to the buildings, meeting and chatting, walking together. There were guards, dressed like Sister Serah and Brother Saul, people in all white like me, and what appeared to be maintenance, service, and landscape workers in gray work pants, polo shirts, and wearing large straw hats to ward off the sun.

A group gathered on the field and set to work on a half-built platform or stage of some sort. The site of the upcoming celebration?

It was an efficient little republic they had going with its producers, warriors, and guardians. I had no doubt Fonseco thought of himself as the philosopher-king, grasping the forms, truly understanding the world and interpreting the words of his seeress for the masses, turning them into action, or missiles.

I fell into a kind of daze, watching the comings and goings outside. Finally, at 8:00 a.m. sharp, a woman in the uniform of the workers appeared outside the sliding door of my villa. She knocked lightly, peering in. Shaking off my daze, I rose and opened the door.

"Good morning," she bobbed her head, speaking heavily accented English. "Please come. Senor Fonseco wants to see you. This way."

I followed her out into the warm sun. She led me past two villas. At the third, Fonseco was sitting outside at a wooden patio table, breakfast dishes pushed to the side, a book open.

"Ah, Justin. Good." He stood up. "Thank you, Marisol."

The woman bobbed her head again and walked off briskly.

"What is this place?" I asked.

"It's the center, Justin. This is where all the layers are peeled back and we arrive at what is real."

"I'd like to speak with Malena please."

"All in good time," Fonseco pushed at the air with both hands, deflecting my request. "Right now, you have a great honor in store. Let's go." He stood and stepped onto a path between a bed of ferns and drooping palm leaves. I followed.

"What happened to the other founders of the Community? Mark Sibyl? Samuel Miller? Are they here?"

"No, they have both been called to join the ancient masters. Mark passed away twelve years ago. He's buried nearby. Sam was drawn back into the world and abandoned us. We lost contact but I know that he passed a few years ago."

"So you and Eleanor Jane Sibyl are the only ones left of the original crew?" We turned onto another path, headed toward one of the buildings at the center of the compound.

"Yes, except for Harmony, Sam's widow."

"Harmony?"

"Not her real name, of course. A lot of us chose new names back then, to break away from the past and forge new identities. She is still alive and living in Vermont."

We had reached the building—a two story ridged concrete block with mirrored windows. Tiny black pebbles glinted dully in the cement. If we were on a community college campus, this building would have held the administrative offices. The other, looming up next door, would be the athletic complex. Fonseco swiped a card and pulled one of the double doors open.

"Please," he gestured me in.

A blast of AC hit me as I entered, chilling the perspiration on my forehead.

"This is our office space," Fonseco said, leading me through a dim, double height lobby, darkly furnished with plants and heavy textile wall hangings. "Worldwide headquarters of the Community. Not many of the faithful have seen this place." We entered an elevator and Fonseco pushed the 3 button.

"I didn't notice a third floor from outside."

"Penthouse. Difficult to see from below."

The elevator doors opened into a kind of sitting room. The walls were hung with the same banners I had seen at the commune in Utah—saints and holy people of all cultures framed by blue sky, rays of divine light bursting from their enlightened brains. Fonseco waved me toward a loveseat like the one in my villa.

"Wait there a minute. I'll be right back." He went to a tall wooden door opposite the elevator, knocked loudly three times, waited a moment, then pushed in. The door swung closed on its own, pulled shut by a hydraulic mechanism that emitted a ghostly whisper as it worked.

Five minutes later, the door swung open and Fonseco waved for me to enter.

"She's ready now. Hurry."

I rose and walked over warily, peering through. Fonseco grabbed my arm and pulled impatiently. Through the door, I felt like I had stepped back in time into a Polaroid photo. The room was windowless like a suburban basement, the walls lined with wood paneling. Green shag carpet covered the floor. Beneath a low ceiling crusted with popcorn texture, a table, a bed, a brown couch, and a recliner upholstered in jade velvet were arrayed. Arranged in one corner I saw that familiar piece of lacy gold cloth tacked to the wall, a stool, a camera on a tripod, and a couple of lights with diffusers. It was Eleanor Jane Sibyl's studio. And maybe her living quarters too? A faint hospital smell hung in the air— disinfectant, medicine, human body in decline. They had recreated a seventies era suburban American basement in Costa Rica.

The lady herself was seated on the recliner, tiny and frail looking, adorned in the same kind of prairie dress her followers wore. She clutched a remote control in her skeletal hand and faced a bulky old TV on a cart. The sound was off. On the screen, people picked through the rubble of decimated houses. It looked like the aftermath following the earthquake in Haiti. I stood and watched for a minute. Two minutes. Waiting for something to happen. The scene changed to a post-apocalyptic plain, strewn with rusting heaps of metal and circuit boards under a burnt umber sky. People squatted over open fires, desoldering electrical components.

"The end days." She said, not looking away from the screen, voice clear, still strong despite her frail body.

Fonseco guided me toward the couch with a hand on my shoulder. I sat.

"The apocalypse," Sibyl went on, light from the screen shifting and crawling across her features. "The turmoil heralding the end time. Sacred fire will burn away earthly fire. Fire of suffering. Fire of those who toil in the field of broken machines. The rubble of decadence. Sacred fire clears the way before. We invoke the holy warrior in his form of the triple hero. He goes before us. With his sword of flame, he will cut us free. Pollution, toxins, poisons, drugs, money, internal combustion engines, satellites, space stations. All types of decadent devices that battle the divine plan, all swept up, all burned by the fire."

Fonseco held a little tape recorder out, capturing her words. He clicked it off and nodded, satisfied. The scene on the TV changed to footage of people outside a government building, chanting, crowd surging, pushing down a chain link fence.

"Do you ever leave this room?" I asked.

Eleanor Jane Sibyl glanced at me, giving me a look like one might give a child who interrupted a lecture. "The physical body is an instrument for the work of the ascended masters. The location of the body is unimportant. I dwell in confinement. I speak their words. You have come here to join us in this place." She turned to me now, smiling. "One of the children of the Community. One of the special children. Sent to us for a great purpose. But where are my manners? Would you like tea? Devlin, please have Luciana bring tea."

Fonseco heaved himself up off the couch and picked up the handset of an old fashioned rotary dial phone. He dialed zero and waited.

"What do you mean when you say I am one of the special children of the Community?" I asked while Fonseco mumbled into the receiver, presumably ordering tea. "I was a foster child. My foster parents were Community members but I wasn't born into the Community and I left when I was seventeen."

"No, no. You have been with us since the beginning and you never left us. Whether you realize it or not. Begat in the wilderness to dismantle the machine."

"But I did leave."

"You never left us, Justin." She gripped my arm,

leaning forward, bringing her face close to mine. There was fervor in her eyes and the television screen reflected in her pupils showed an airplane, stark against a white sky. "You never left us in spirit. That's why you have come back. We've been expecting you."

"You had Malena call me."

"Maybe," she waved a hand impatiently. "The details don't matter. We're happy you came. Now we have all of you. All nine. Three threes begetting three. Sacred numbers. Divine numbers. The fulfillment of the promise. Strength comes from patterns completed." Her eyes drifted back to the television screen. I glanced over. The twin towers, burning.

"What do you mean? All nine?"

"All nine," she repeated, sing song. "Engine, engine number nine. Going down Chicago line. Running east, running west, running through the cuckoo's nest. O-U-T spells out and out she goes..." Her voice trailed off as she turned her attention back to the screen.

"She's tired now. We'll leave her."

Fonseco led the way. I looked back once. Sibyl watched the TV intently, watched the buildings burn. Her bony hands, skin so thin the blue veins stood out like highways on a roadmap, rubbed together, dry sounding, fingers circling in a washing motion.

A woman was just exiting the elevator when we emerged, carrying a tray of tea things.

"Please just serve Ms. Sibyl," Fonseco said brusquely, stepping aside. "We're on our way out." He seemed annoyed. Was it because his prophetess went off script? I couldn't escape the feeling that I had just glimpsed a modern day Delphic oracle. But instead of psychoactive vapors from a chasm, she breathed death, destruction, and upheaval from a television screen. Did they have a DVR hidden somewhere? A never ending loop of footage fed to her windowless sanctuary? A greatest hits of the worst of the news from the past seventy years? Did she even know she was in Costa Rica? Or did she think she was still in the compound in Montana?

"What did she mean by all nine?" I asked as the doors slid closed and we began trundling downward.

"Don't worry about that. She says cryptic things sometimes. We have to think and meditate to come to understanding. Reality is just a story we tell Justin. You know that. I'll have a guard take you back to your villa."

In the lobby, a guard stood behind a small reception desk. Fonseco called him over.

"Any sign of Brother Noah?" He asked, back to me, voice low.

"No, sir. You know how he sometimes goes off hunting though, when he is here on his visits. He should be back today."

"He'd better be. Please take Justin back to his villa. I have some work to do."

The guard nodded and started toward the doors at the far end of the lobby. "This way please."

I followed. Glancing back, I saw Fonseco swipe a key card through a reader near the elevator and pull open a wood paneled door. Inside, I caught a glimpse of glowing LEDs, a desk, a shelf of books. If that was his office, I needed to get in and search it.

Later. First I needed rest.

Chapter 16

Dinner and a Discovery
12/16-17: Costa Rica, Alajuela Province

They left me in the villa for the rest of the day. I spent most of it sleeping, catching up from my days of deprivation, despite the sound of hammers in the background from the crew building the stage. When I finally woke up around 5:00 p.m. my eyes were focused and my body responsive for the first time in days. Someone had slipped in and left a fresh tray of food on my desk. I sat cross-legged on the bed, eating fruit and staring at the wall, thinking through my predicament. I had no doubt that I could escape whenever I wanted to. They did not seem intent on holding me by force. Instead, they were playing mind games, trying hard to convert me as if they believed something depended on it. I had convinced them enough to be admitted to the secret compound. What was next? And when was the big event? How long did I have to disrupt their plans?

Around six o'clock, as the last bit of daylight was fading from the sky, two figures strode onto my patio.

"Justin?" A woman's voice. Malena?

They stood just outside the open patio door. I realized it was completely dark inside the villa. I had been sitting and thinking while the sun set and hadn't turned on any lights. Rising from the bed, I found a dimmer switch then crossed to the door under the glow of several recessed ceiling lamps.

"Justin. Can we come in? We brought wine. And dinner."

Malena and a man I hadn't met stood outside. He was taller than me by a couple of inches but thinner—Dark hair pulled back and gathered in a top knot, wiry and fit, very tan but probably naturally dark even in a less sunny climate. He held a tray on one arm. My stomach grumbled. Dinner sounded good.

"This is Oak. He's one of us."

"Nice to meet you." I clasped his offered hand then stepped aside as they entered. "One of us?"

"One of the castaways, orphans, foster children. Raised by the Community. Here for the anniversary jubilee."

Malena hovered in front of me for an awkward moment, standing very close. Then she stepped forward and I wrapped her in a hug. She squeezed me tightly then broke away and held up a wine bottle.

"Care for a drink?"

"That's unlike the Community, to have wine."

"It's a special time and we are the chosen." She smiled at me and brushed hair away from her face and I was struck by an intuition that made the hairs stand up on my arms—the person in front of me wasn't Malena. It made no sense. Of course, this was Malena. She had changed. It had been years. She looked just like my lost sister. An older version, but undoubtedly her face. Still, I couldn't shake the feeling. It was eerie, an atavistic impulse—danger of the imposter. Something trying to look like something else can be harmless but it can also be deadly. Camouflage works both ways. Good for the prey but also the predator.

"We have food, too," Oak said, setting the tray on the coffee table.

"I'll get cups for the wine." I escaped toward the kitchen. "I think I only have two."

"That's okay, we brought an extra." Malena/not Malena's voice called after me.

I kept looking at her, stealing glances, as we sat and talked. The feeling never went away. Every time the conversation turned toward the past, she would find a way to throw it to Oak. He was an easy talker, gregarious, spinning out stories of the various Community outposts he had inhabited in Southern California, Oregon, Louisiana, Mexico, Northern Canada. He'd moved around a lot, restless, but he had an entertaining, drawling way of speaking about it. I tried to go light on the wine, sipping slowly but it affected me, muddying my thoughts. Had they drugged me again? No, it was just alcohol and my defenses were weakened. At some point I noticed a small scar on Malena's hand, twisted like a burn mark.

"Where'd you get that?" I asked without thinking, pointing to the scar.

"Oh, that's old," she said, looking down and running a finger along it. "Touched the handle of a pan in the oven while I was pulling something else out."

As she spoke, I remembered a childhood incident—shivering cold, trudging through the barn early in the morning on the way to some chore, Malena in front. A sudden cry and she fell back, knocking me over. We both fell in a heap on the dirty floor. A cut above her eye, right on the eyebrow and bleeding profusely. She had run right into a horse pen gate, left open, and cut herself on the latch. It had left a scar when it healed—a thin white line in her black eyebrow. I studied the face of the woman sitting next to me, looking for the scar. It wasn't there. Who was this doppelganger, I wondered again? How did she look like Malena? Have the same voice? What kind of bizarre new trick was this?

"Are there others here?" I asked, shaken, trying not to show it. "Like us? Chosen, I guess. Although I don't really know what that means. Fonseco keeps telling me I'm here for some purpose. He took me to see Eleanor Jane Sibyl today and she said something about all nine. Three threes…"

Oak and Malena looked at me blankly.

"It's a great honor to meet her," Oak said after a moment. "You and I and Malena, we're the only ones here. Three of us chosen ones. We'll learn about our mission soon. We have great work to do. Elder Fonseco told me too. He said we will have the most important role in the jubilee. Our actions will help move us into the next era of mankind."

"When is it happening?" I asked. "The jubilee celebration."

"Solstice Eve. Only a few days to go." Oak smiled and nodded.

Finally, after a couple of hours of wine and food and conversation, they left.

I sat on the couch, thinking through what I had learned. It was December 16th according to my watch. Only five days until whatever they were planning was going to take place. ICBMs? A screaming across the sky? World War III? What role were the chosen ones supposed to play? Would Eleanor Jane Sibyl be standing on a stage, face raised to the sky triumphantly as the ground rumbled and the rockets lifted off? Were these maniacs even capable of what they were planning? It was, in fact, rocket science—legendarily difficult to get right.

I needed to get out and find a way to warn someone in authority. I had warned Beth but what if she was cut off like me? I couldn't trust that she would get word out. First, though, I needed to see Fonseco's office. Another nocturnal ramble was in store for me but I would have to wait until people were asleep. I set the alarm on my watch, turned off the light, and found a comfortable position on the couch, sipping the last of the wine left in my cup. It was acrid, too sweet, overwhelmingly cheap. Still, I drank it, hoping it would calm my nerves. I had a bad feeling smoldering in my chest. Wicked deeds and madness were in the air.

A shadow, barely seen, skulked outside my villa. A guard? Someone was watching. In the dark, eyes unfocused, I could feel their presence. Finally, around 1:00 a.m., tired of wearing out my eyes staring into the night, I got up, closed the curtains, and turned on a bedside lamp.

I waited another hour. Going out the back seemed like the best plan. They were short staffed with Noah gone. If they were watching still, I would have a better chance of slipping into the shadows near the wall. I changed back into the fatigues and t-shirt I had been wearing when brought to the compound, wrinkling my nose at the stale sweat and grime on them. Stinky as they were, the dark colors made them more functional for creeping around and breaking into things. I stowed Noah's keys, his flashlight, and my lock picks in the cargo pockets, then, leaving the light on, went to the back door off the kitchen, opening it a crack.

Outside, I saw only the gravel no-man's land between the plantings and the wall. I looked left and right, then crouched low and crept out, pulling the door closed behind me. Keeping to the planted area along the backs of the villas, I made my way around. I wanted to circle all the way until I could approach the office building from the far side, crossing between the pool area and the field. If the ghost guard watching my villa had noticed my exit and was following me, I couldn't detect it. Continuing around, I hoped my senses were recovered enough to warn me of any danger.

A dampness not quite fog hung in the air, parting before me and swirling behind. The other villas, dark and silent, receded as I rounded the curve, moving toward the pool. I wondered how many were occupied. Mine and Fonseco's, not-Malena's, and Oak's. Unless they were housed on the other side, the mystery half I hadn't seen yet. I had seen a few other people from a distance, dressed in the white garments that seemed to indicate they were not guards and not drones. Were they also chosen ones, whatever that meant, like me and my dinner companions? Or people who worked in the office building, managing the business end of the Community?

I hugged the wall, staying in the shadows as I made my way past the pool and keeping an eye turned toward my villa. I could just see the glimmer behind the curtains from the light I had left on. If a guard was posted outside, they were very good at hiding. Maybe I had imagined it.

Across from the office building, I stopped for a moment, breathing deeply and calming my mind. I could see Eleanor Jane Sibyl's weird penthouse limned against the sky now that I knew it was there. Below, the interior of the lobby that had seemed dim during the day now glowed through the big floor to ceiling windows. A guard sat at the reception desk, kicked back with legs up, arms behind his head. I would have to find a different way to enter.

Standing in the dark, looking in, the weirdness of the place struck me and I felt disassociated. What bizarre series of events led to the existence of this building, this whole compound, on top of a mountain in the cloud forest of Costa Rica? I knew part of the story but what I knew didn't sufficiently explain how it all came to be. I hadn't expected anything even remotely like this when I left my home and became, for a little while, Dustin Cruz. I had imagined myself spending maybe a week undercover, finding Malena, convincing her to leave with me. I should have taken her warning more seriously.

Moving silently from cover to cover, I approached the building, keeping clear of the lobby windows. The back side, facing the field and nearly completed stage, had an emergency exit but it did not have a card reader like the lobby doors and it could easily be alarmed. Above, on the second floor, was a balcony stretching half the width of the building, recessed and lined with plantings. The ridged exterior made for easy finger and toe holds. Boots off and hung around my neck by the laces, I began climbing. Rough but also slick with dew, the concrete was not as easy to grip as I had imagined. Still, I made progress. Halfway up, some kind of burly insect buzzed by and smacked into my forehead, careening off into the night. I almost lost my grip but managed to rebalance, scale the last few feet of wall, and scramble over the edge.

Crouched low on the floor of the balcony, I checked

out my surroundings—a patio table with four chairs, sand filled ashtray with several butts poking up, wall of windows, closed blinds, a glass door with a card reader. Maybe this was where Fonseco went for his smoke breaks in between scientific experiments? Now was my chance to see if Brother Noah's key card still worked. I dug it from a cargo pocket, crept over to the door, and swiped it through the slot. A soft beep sounded, followed by a green LED and a click.

Inside, a corridor passed straight through the building. Industrial gray carpeting with a double burgundy vertical stripe led me past closed office suite doors, a break room, a photocopier alcove. At the end, a glowing red EXIT sign illuminated an elevator lobby. It had to be the elevator we had ridden on our way up to Eleanor Jane Sibyl's weird cave. Was she up there right now? She must be. The thought sent a shiver down my spine. There was something uncanny about the Community's guru. If I was right, the elevator would take me down to the lobby near where the guard was stationed, undoubtedly making enough noise to waken him from his torpor. There was also a door with a red sign on it that said *En caso de incendio, use las escalera* in bold white letters. My Spanish wasn't great but I knew what that meant.

A big window nook full of potted bird of paradise plants looked out over the grounds, the wall, and the forest beyond. Moonlight shone on leaves swaying in a soft breeze. Everything about this place was weird, subtly torqued and twisted like a machine part that appeared straight but wouldn't fit no matter how you tried it. I stood for a moment, gathering my energy, calming my mind, then pulled the emergency exit door open to reveal a brightly lit staircase, and started down.

At the bottom, I stopped, thinking, calling up my visual memory of the lobby. The elevator was in a sort of nook, facing away from the desk where the guard probably still sat. The door from the stairs let out on the back wall of the nook, also out of sight from the guard. Fonseco's office door was on the wall facing the elevator. I couldn't quite picture whether or not it would be hidden or visible from the desk.

I pulled the door latch down and pushed, slowly easing it open, slipped out and guided it closed. Soundlessly, I eased along the wall, passing the elevator, and came to the corner. Fonseco's door was across from me now, definitely within sight of the guard if he was still at the desk. I peeked around. He was still there, facing away from me and staring fixedly into the night beyond the windows. A transistor radio on his desk murmured softly–some kind of sporting event, a crowd cheering. Still, I didn't like my chances. I needed a distraction. I found glass beads the size of marbles covering the humus in a potted palm nearby, picked one up and peered around the corner again.

Finding a target in the plantings near the door, I tossed the bead overhand and watched it arc across the lobby. Plonk! It hit a broad leaf and slid noiselessly into the dirt below. The guard's head shot up. He stood and marched over to inspect. Seizing the opportunity, I crept to Fonseco's door, pressed my body against the scanner to muffle it, and swiped the card. The lock disengaged and I slipped through, glancing back to see the guard, back to me, one hand on top of his head, looking up in confusion.

Turning away from the door, I was immediately

reminded of Fonseco's office at the Red Butte Commune. Approximately the same size, full of glowing LEDs, the lab hummed menacingly. One wall was all windows, venetian blinds closed and reflecting distorted colors from the equipment indicator lights. A sharp, acid-chemical smell like chlorine but sweeter pricked my nose. I turned and saw a desk to my right, piled with papers and file folders. Flicking on the desk lamp, I sat on Fonseco's chair and surveyed the stacks.

One of the stacks was composed of file folders like the ones I had seen on Fonseco's desk back in Utah—maybe even the same ones. They bore the same curious circle bounded by an equilateral triangle design on the front. I flipped through them, scanning the names, and stopped at J. Martin. Was it really a file on me? My hand hovered over it for several long seconds while my blood went cold in my veins. I flipped it open and found a printout from the database system, just like the one I had looked at in Fonseco's other lab—the paper old, slightly brittle, beginning to yellow. Justin Martin. A photo of me, probably fifteen years old, printed in monochrome in the corner. My date of birth. Place of birth: Community Ranch, Montana. A buzzing began in my ears and my vision narrowed, surrounded by black. Full Siblings: Sage Miller, Michael Fletcher.

I dropped into Fonseco's chair and sat for a moment, mind blank, then jumped up and dug through the folders. Finding S. Miller, I flipped it open. Place of birth: Community Ranch, Montana. Date of birth: about a year before mine. I found M. Fletcher and opened it on top of the others. Place of birth: Community Ranch, Montana. Date of birth: about a year after mine. Siblings? All born at the Community's ranch in Montana. Two brothers I had never met? It couldn't be possible but I heard Eleanor Jane Sibyl's voice in my head—*Now we have all of you. All nine. Three threes. Sacred numbers. Divine numbers. The fulfillment of the promise.*

I opened the rest of the file folders. Two more sets of siblings. Two sisters for Malena, one of whom I had presumably met already, pretending to be her. Not twins but alike enough to fool me for a little while. I hadn't seen Malena for years after all. A sister, similar enough in appearance, could be her but older. If not for the scar and my intuition I might still be fooled. Their names were Hazel and Mariposa. Two brothers for Oak. Everything began to fall into place—the missing women and children when the ranch was raided, the laboratory, children like me absorbed into outposts of the Community. My mind was racing and I felt an irresistible compulsion to flee, get out, away from Fonseco and his mad experiments, lose myself in the forest, find a safe place and hide.

I ripped the top pages from my file, folded and shoved them into a cargo pocket, then walked the periphery of the lab, agitated. Another door, opposite the one I had entered, had to lead back toward the rear of the building where I had seen the exit earlier. Abandoning caution, I pushed it open and found a dark office suite. Hurrying through, I exited into a corridor that matched the position of the one upstairs. At the end I found the exterior door and pushed through.

Damp night air cooled my face as I jogged toward the wall. I saw some kind of transformer or equipment box ahead, metal top reflecting moonlight. Without pausing, using it as a giant step, I vaulted myself up, grasped the top of the wall, and swung over. For an instant, dropping down on the other side, I realized I should have looked down first to check the ground for obstacles. Too late. My right foot hit first and my ankle rolled as a loose rock tipped under me. My left leg collapsed and I landed hard on one shoulder in tall grass. Dazed for a moment, I heard footsteps–someone running toward me. I jumped up, twisted ankle barely supporting my weight.

"Justin. I'm sorry but I have to take you back inside." Sister Serah faced me, her back to the trees. "You are not allowed to leave."

Chapter 17

Swiss Family Mosquito Coast
12/17-18: Costa Rica, Alajuela Province

"I can't go back," I said, testing my ankle. "Do you have any idea what Fonseco is planning? He's got Eleanor Jane Sibyl locked up on the roof." I gestured toward the building behind me. "Feeding her doomsday videos twenty-four seven."

"Sister Eleanor is a prophet," Sister Serah answered flatly. "She is chosen to reveal the truth."

"She's crazy."

"We can't stand here talking. Please walk that way. I'll take you back to your villa."

"Sorry, I won't. I don't want to fight you Sister Serah. But I will if I have to."

I barely had time to react. She came spinning toward me with awesome speed. I tried to duck to the side but my ankle gave out. Her hook kick, aimed at my head, caught me on the shoulder, knocking me to the ground. She was on top of me instantly, pinning my arms with her thighs, drawing a fist back. With a convulsive heave, I tipped her off. Her punch went wide. I had mass and raw strength on my side if not quickness and training. We both scrambled up. Back on our feet, we circled, her cat-like, me limping and trying not to show it.

"Remember when you asked me how I got here?"

She said through gritted teeth.

"Yes."

"That's just the kind of question an asshole outsider like you would ask."

"I don't underst…"

"Of course you don't. You have no faith." Her face twisted into a mask of hatred. "I would kill you if Elder Fonseco didn't forbid it."

"You're not the first person to say th…" I broke off as she came for me again, aiming a side kick at my chest. I didn't try to sidestep or duck this time, knowing it was futile with my ankle temporarily out of commission. Like most fighters who are well-trained, she was expecting me to take some evasive action. I saw confusion in her eyes for an instant, a momentary hesitation, and grabbed her leg in the middle of her kick. She reacted with blinding speed, using the leg I was holding as leverage to step up into the air and aim a back kick at my face. This time I did duck. Her boot caught my forehead and grazed the top of my head as I lifted up, tossing her into the air. She spun, tucking into a barrel roll and nearly pulled it off, landing solidly on her feet, but slipped in the wet grass and went down, breath knocked out and temporarily stunned.

Seizing the moment, I hobbled forward, fell to my knees over her, and punched her once on the jaw. I held back, thinking of Noah and squeamish about punching a woman. It was hard enough though and my aim was good. Her eyes rolled back.

"Sorry," I mumbled, rolling her on her side. I secured her hands with her belt, then whipped my own belt off, and wrapped it around her shins pulling it tight. It wouldn't hold her long and she only had to start yelling to rouse her comrades. I took one of her boots off, removed her sock, and worked it into her mouth. She was starting to come around. Using my teeth, I tore a strip from the hem of her shirt and tied it around, holding the sock in place. Her eyes cleared and she stared at me with hatred, struggling against the belts. I looked back toward the compound, then toward the woods. I had to get as far away as I could in the time I had.

"Sorry," I mumbled again. "Gotta go. Somebody will come along and find you." Standing, I limped to the edge of the trees and plunged in.

Branches whipped my face and hands. My shoulder caromed off a tree trunk. Damp fern fronds pulled at my legs. I fell, several times, rolling through decaying leaves and dirt. I was leaving an obvious trail. After ten minutes of struggle I came across what looked like a deer track— just the hint of a pathway. I went past it, kept going for thirty feet, then doubled back hoping it would throw off any pursuers.

The deer track meandered through the trees, crossed a small stream where I stopped to splash my face, and then steadily up, paralleling the stream at a mild grade for a quarter mile before dead ending at an escarpment that rose above the trees and mist, rock face glowing in the moonlight. To my left I saw a deep shadow. A cave or hollow? I scrambled up the damp, pebbly slope and felt my way in. It was shallow, formed by a massive boulder embedded diagonally in the hillside and resting on another forming a hollowed out triangle. I scooted back as far as I could and found a more or less dry patch of rock. Leaning against the boulder, I closed my eyes, calmed my breathing, and listened. Water trickling. Leaves lightly rustling. A motor running in the far distance, revving. A voice calling? My thoughts swirled, slowing. Fatigue grabbed me like a wave, my pulse slowed, and I slumped, borne down into the deep.

I woke to the sound of birds chirping and screeching in the trees. My body aching, throat dry, I struggled up to sitting. For a few minutes I just sat there, blinking my eyes. After a while, I straightened my legs and bent over, stretching. I tried moving my foot in different ways to test the extent of my ankle sprain. It had stiffened and swollen but it wasn't as bad as I had feared. I would be able to walk but not long distances and not quickly. A howler monkey hooted in the distance and its troop answered. I remembered the stream I had passed and the sound of trickling water I'd heard the night before. Scooting from the shadows to the mouth of the cave, I gazed out over the treetops. The sun, just risen, cast a golden light on the leaves. To my left, maybe three quarters of a mile away, I could see the compound with its high round wall. Beyond that, one of the pyramids poked up from its clearing. It seemed to be one of the other two—the completed ones I hadn't seen yet. Either that or my sense of direction was confused. If it was the one I had broken into I should have been able to see the ranch house somewhere nearby.

Not far from the cave I found a small rivulet that flowed down the cliff face in an ancient channel, forming a small waterfall near the bottom, then running off to join the larger stream I had crossed. I had no idea what microscopic dangers might be found in the water but I was thirsty enough to not care. I drank then put my head under the water and let it cascade over me.

Somewhat revived, I made my way back to the cave, scooted back into the shadowy interior, and sat, thinking about my next move. I wasn't keen on trying to hike out. I had no idea how far it was to the closest town and I would have to find and follow a road which might be monitored. On the other hand, staying was not an option. I needed to warn someone about Fonseco's plans. Who though? The CIA? The Costa Rican equivalent? I could figure that out but I needed to get to a phone. I didn't like the idea of leaving without Malena but it didn't seem like I had a choice.

Closing my eyes, I pictured the layout of the ranch as best I could, based on my spotty knowledge, and tried to draw a mind map. The sun was rising on my left as I sat facing the cave mouth so that had to be east. I couldn't see the peak of Arenal from where I sat so it had to be behind me, to the north. My brain spun its wheels for a moment, confused. Sun on my left meant I was looking south. I had been able to see Arenal from the clearing where I had worked on the pyramid. It had risen up over the trees in the far distance to my right as I came out of the woods. So, the ranch house and building that had been my prison had to be somewhat north and east of where I sat and the pyramid west from there, or nearly right behind me maybe a mile away in a straight line. The main road out, which had dead ended at the garage, had led west, away from the ranch house and downhill. So, if I walked north I should run into it. Following the road out was my only chance, really. I didn't have any choice. I would find plenty of water along the way and could hide in the forest if I heard vehicles or people.

It didn't take long to find a path up to the top of the cliff. My sprain made climbing difficult but there was an offset crack near the little stream that I could walk up like a ramp using vines and tree roots as hand holds. At the top, I took one look back, then plunged into the trees. The undergrowth coiled dense around my ankles but the stream flowed north-south and I was able to follow it, keeping the sun on my right. As I walked, though, I found myself losing focus, stumbling, waking from blank moments of lost time just standing over the trickling water. My forehead was hot and my lower back ached. Insects buzzed my face and I swatted at them ineffectually. My brain was working slowly, my body lethargic. Was this some kind of side effect from the drugs they gave me? Working out of my system? Or a tropical disease or parasite? I couldn't deny that I was sick. The forest rippled in my vision and waves of fever rolled over me.

Somehow, I kept blundering forward, one foot in front of another, stopping every twenty paces to splash cool water on my face, until I stumbled right into a clearing. I didn't even notice until a barrier of cargo netting loomed into focus directly in front of my face. I stopped, confused. Looking back, I saw a path disappearing into the woods. Had I been walking on the path without realizing it? For how long? I turned back to the net and through it saw, dappled in sunlight filtered through the leaves, a small building nearly subsumed by the forest around it.

I stood there, hands tangled in the netting, for a long time. I might have fallen asleep on my feet. A sharp cough woke me and I focused my eyes. An old man stood outside the cabin—tall and lean with long white hair tied back and an unkept beard. He wore cut off fatigues and a t-shirt so worn it looked like it might disintegrate into scraps at any moment. He gazed at me across the clearing and I stared back, straining to focus my eyes and stay on my feet.

A moment later, he was standing next to me, peering into my eyes and nodding. Then he lifted my arm over his shoulder and half dragged me to the doorway of his cabin.

"Sigue adelante. Unos pasos más."

"No hablo español," I croaked.

"English? You're sick. Need to lie down."

Light entered the cabin through a couple of small window openings hung with mosquito netting. I stumbled over old cement, cracked and crumbling in places, as the man led me to a mattress in the corner and helped me collapse onto it. A moment later he was crouching next to me with a canteen. I drank hungrily, water running in rivulets down my cheeks, then collapsed back.

"Let's see," he said, squinting at me. "Sage?"

I shook my head, confused.

"Michael or Justin, then. You're not Oak or one of his brothers."

I remembered the papers in my pocket as a wave of fever washed over me.

"Justin," I croaked.

"Ah, Justin. I was there. I was there when you were born."

"Who?" I asked.

"Me? Sam. Sam Miller."

"Fonseco said you were dead."

"He would. Of course he would. He wishes I was dead. But he's afraid to kill me."

"Feel like I'm going to die."

"No. I'll keep you alive. Don't you worry. I have drugs. Good antibiotics. Good pain killers. I'm well stocked." He rose and I heard him shuffling around, digging through a box or chest. I drifted out of consciousness for a while, woke long enough to swallow something with another gulp from the canteen, then fell into dreamless sleep.

It was night when I woke again. I jolted up, fear and confusion straightening my spine like an electric current. My face was slick with sweat. A chill ran down my arms and I shivered. Moonlight filtered through the windows bathing the floor in silver. I saw the old man laid out on a sleeping bag nearby, snoring. I had taken his bed. Uncouth of me but nothing I could do about it right then. I lay back and closed my eyes.

I woke again and sunlight shone through my eyelashes, blinding, golden. I blinked and turned my head. A clinking sound. A whoosh of ignited gas.

"Coffee?" Asked Sam Miller.

"Yes," I tried to say but no sound came from my mouth. I swallowed and coughed. "Yes, please."

I sat up, looking around. The place was square, maybe fifteen by fifteen feet—a concrete cube with two window holes and a door hole but no door or windows. Instead, as I had noticed the night before, the openings were covered with mosquito nets. Sam stood in the kitchen area, back to me, facing a counter fashioned from an old door on legs of roughhewn logs. He had a propane stove going and water in a pan. My fever had broken but I felt exhausted, barely able to hold myself up on my elbows. Still, I was more mentally alert than I had been for days, maybe since before the planned accident back at the commune in Utah and the sedative that had been the first in a chain of drugged days.

I scanned the rest of the room. Not much to see—

just some shelves with clothes neatly folded, some books swollen from the humidity, a couple of large crates like the ones I had loaded onto Fonseco's plane, a generator of some kind in one corner, and a few other odds and ends in faded boxes and bins.

Sam brought the coffee over, pulled up a milk crate, and sat down companionably, back against the wall. I struggled up to sitting, the wall cool on my back, and sipped my coffee. Sam had made it strong and sweet with condensed milk.

"What are you doing out here?" I asked.

"Thrown out. I used to live in the compound over there of course. Got in an argument with Fonseco a few years ago and he convinced Eleanor to have a vision about me leaving."

"About?"

"The argument? Different ideas about the future of the Community. Fonseco's a holy warrior and he's got Eleanor on his side. Feeding her poison. I just wanted to keep building it up slow. Missionary work."

"How long have you been living…" I gestured at the walls around us.

"Here? Couple of years I guess. Outbuilding for the old ranch. It was full of vines and bugs when I found it. No idea what it was originally built for."

I nodded. "Long time to live in the woods by yourself."

"Don't mind it that much really. I don't know where else I'd go at this point. Always was a bit of a Thoreauvian. My daughter comes and visits. Brings me food."

"She still lives inside?"

"Yeah. Hard to give it up when you grew up in the

faith."

"I saw how Fonseco has Sibyl cooped up in the penthouse. He took me up there. Does she even know she's not in Montana?"

"Not always, no. She's not connected to reality anymore. She lives in the dreamtime."

"She's a prophet right?" I couldn't keep the bitterness out of my voice.

"Didn't say that. Never believed it myself. A lot of us don't. It's about the ideals. Communal living. Not being part of the machine. Dropping out and creating our own simpler life closer to the land." He ran a hand through his hair, pushing it back from a high, deeply lined forehead. "I always just tolerated the mystic part of it. So did Fonseco until recently. He has his own weird reasons for keeping the Community going."

"Genetic research? Test tube babies?" I asked turning to face Sam. "What was going on in the lab at that ranch? What did you mean you were there when I was born?"

He looked at me for a long moment. I could almost see his mental process externalized as his weathered face twitched through several configurations—the urge to keep a secret, doubt, the decision to get it off his chest.

"I was there. Fonseco and his wife Gwen had a daughter."

"Abigail."

"Yes. She had a rare genetic disease called Fanconi Anemia. Most people with it don't live past their teens or early twenties. They get cancer, bone marrow failure, organ failure. Fonseco went a little nuts, decided he was going to cure her. He needed what he called a pure donor. He was experimenting with IVF and creating embryos in the lab. I don't know if any of it was real science or if that was when he started taking Eleanor seriously. He created three sets of siblings. Carried by three different women at the commune. They all gave birth right there in the ranch house and all the babies survived. Of course there were other attempts, still births, miscarriages. Fonseco and Eleanor saw it as a miracle. Three threes. Nine pure children. They built a whole mythos around it."

I stopped listening and leaned back against the wall, eyes closed, blood pounding in my ears. He was talking about me, about where I came from. Some anonymous mother body. Born into Fonseco's hands. Who was the sperm donor? Fonseco himself? Who was the egg donor?

"And then the raid happened," I said, opening my eyes. "And the children were scattered."

"Yes. Scattered to the wind. No organization. Took us forever to track you all down."

"And that's when you came to Costa Rica? After the raid?"

"Mhmm. Yeah. Relocated here. We'd bought the land a few years before. Purchased through a third party of course. Untraceable to the Community or any of the founders."

I closed my mouth and stared at the wall for a while. Sam sipped his coffee.

"You know what he's doing, right? What he has in those temples?"

"In the temples? The pyramids? I've never been inside. But I've been watching them build those. I like to wander around and keep an eye on things."

"I broke into one of them. At night. I found a rocket inside. Those temples are missile silos."

"Rocket?" He looked at me, uncomprehending. "Sure you weren't dreaming?"

"No. It was real. A cold war era Soviet ICBM. R-36. They had crates of parts too. On the plane. We flew here from Utah."

Sam turned away, stood up. He went to the kitchen area and put his cup down on the counter. "Fonseco always did love flying," he said. "Time for my walk."

"You don't believe me?"

"Need to go for my walk."

"They're looking for me. Are you going to turn me in?"

"No. You have a right to leave. Everybody has the right to leave the Community if they choose. That's how it's always been. People come and go. We offer our way of life and they choose it or don't."

"Fonseco didn't give me a choice. He was keeping me there against my will."

"That's not right. I'm going out now. You're welcome to stay here. You need to rest. There's food here. And water." He pointed to more milk crates and a ceramic water barrel.

"I need to warn someone. Can you help me? I need to get to a telephone."

"Plenty more water in the cistern on the roof. Don't worry about running out. Rest. I'll be back in a couple of hours."

I stood with some effort and hobbled to the door just in time to see him disappear around a bend in the path, swallowed by trees, moving quicker than I would have expected given his age.

I went back inside, found a granola bar, and ate it while I searched the place. I was still weak but I couldn't sit around waiting to see what would happen. There wasn't a lot to search. Within a few minutes, I had gone through everything. The only item of interest was a metal lockbox with a three digit combination lock I found tucked into the bottom of one of the large crates.

It looked old, made of heavy sheet metal painted blue, big enough to be a cash or gun safe, filigreed with rust around the edges where the paint had worn away over years of use. Something big and heavy slid around inside when I lifted it. Easy to open though—I just tried every combination starting at 000. I knew it would only take twenty minutes maximum to get through them all. When I hit 547 and tried the latch the lid popped open. I lifted it. Inside I found a passport expired since 1990, a birth certificate showing that Samuel Jefferson Miller was born in Little Rock Arkansas in 1953, a couple of diaries, some old photos of a young girl in typical Community prairie dress—probably his daughter—and a device that looked like a boxy, old, cell phone from the nineties. I lifted the phone out. Black plastic, tiny screen, and an alphanumeric key pad—it didn't seem particularly old. The brand was Iridium. A satellite phone maybe? The antenna was far more robust than on a regular cell phone. I pressed the power button but nothing happened. A charging cable was coiled in the bottom of the box. I picked up both and shuffled over to what I had assumed was a generator on first inspection.

The bulky block of orange and black plastic sat in one corner on top of an upside down bucket. It had a little LCD display, a couple of outlets, and a barrel plug port with a cable plugged in. I followed the cable to where it snaked out one of the windows. Curious, I limped outside and saw, up on the roof, a solar panel. So, the device had to be a battery storing energy from the panel.

Back inside, I plugged the phone in. The LCD lit up, backlit green with a charging battery icon. I sat on the floor next to it, watching and thinking. I couldn't trust Sam. He was an honest person but still tied to the Community from what I could tell. Had he gone to see Fonseco? There was no way to know. I had to leave before he returned.

Apologizing silently, I went through his things again. I packed an old backpack with more granola bars, amoxicillin in blister packs, a two liter bottle of water, iodine tablets, and a sleeping bag. Next, I went back and checked on the phone. It had booted up and the screen showed what I supposed was the current date and time. I had lost track of days. Was it really only the sixteenth? It seemed longer. Either way, not much time left before the solstice. The screen showed four bars of signal. It had to be a satellite phone. I'd never used one but I assumed it was the same as making a call on a cell.

I picked it up, fingers poised over the keypad. Who to call? 911 wouldn't work in Costa Rica. Ashna's was the only phone number I had memorized. I dialed her number and hit the call by button.

"Who's this?" Her voice sounded distant and clipped.

"It's me. Justin."

"Justin! Where the fuck are you?"

Chapter 18

Lawn Party
12/18-19: Costa Rica, Alajuela Province

"Costa Rica. In the cloud forest somewhere. South of Arenal."

"I know that you asshole," Ashna answered. "I came to find you. What are your GPS coordinates? I'll come to you."

"Wait a second," I said, confused. "You're here? At the compound?"

"Yes. Maybe. There are a couple of compounds. Maybe more actually depending on how you define compound. I'm nearby."

"Okay. I need to get out of where I am right now though. I can meet you. I'll go back to the cave. I can send coordinates when I get there. If I can figure out how to do that."

"Are you on a sat phone? You must be. It's built in. Look in the menu. Send me your position now and then again when you get where you're going."

"Okay. I'm going to hang up, send it, then go. It'll probably take me an hour to get to the cave."

"Why the fuck are you going to a cave?" Exasperation lifted her voice into a higher register.

"Long story. I'll tell you when I see you."

I knew I'd been following a stream the day before

and then somehow ended up on a trail. If I backtracked, I should be able to find the stream and let it lead me back to the cave.

I scribbled a note of apology and left it inside the lockbox. Then, hefting the backpack, phone in my pocket with hopefully enough charge to contact Ashna, I headed back down the trail. It was only maybe two hundred yards before I came to a little rivulet cutting across the path. Was it my stream? I would just have to take a chance.

I went slowly, bushwhacking and staying with the trickling water, going with the direction of flow this time, trying to step where I wouldn't leave footprints. My stiff ankle hobbled me a bit but it was healing. I kept on.

Sandflies and mosquitos swarmed me. Giant black ants scurried underfoot. I batted insects away from my face while a group of capuchins, white faces mocking, jumped and chattered in the trees above me. A juvenile, curious, descended and hung from a branch off to my right, staring at me out of eyes like black marbles while it munched a fat green caterpillar clutched in its tiny hand.

"Looks tasty," I said and the monkey chattered back at me, noise dying out behind me as I continued on.

My estimate had been good. It was almost exactly an hour later that I emerged from the trees on the ridge above my cave. I took the same path down, scooting on my butt rather than trusting my ankle not to give out and send me tumbling down the rocky slope.

At the bottom, I splashed handfuls of cool water from the stream over my face and head, soothing my bug bites, drank until my stomach sloshed, then scrambled up into the cool shade.

Leaning back against the wall, I fumbled through the menus on the phone, found the command again, and sent my location to Ashna. It was difficult to believe she had somehow located my position in the mountains and come to find me. I could definitely use her help. The possibility that she would appear in the cave mouth seemed distant, unlikely. I leaned my head back against the rock and closed my eyes.

"Justin. Wake up."

Someone was shaking my shoulder. I opened my eyes and Ashna's face came into focus.

"You look terrible, dude."

"I feel terrible. Probably need another dose of Sam's antibiotics."

"Who's Sam?"

"I'll tell you later. Backpack." I pointed. "Drugs."

****

"So how did you figure it out and show up finally?"

"Ah, yes. Answers to questions." Ashna scooted over and lowered herself down next to me. The sun was down and I was feeling better. I sipped instant broth from Ashna's thermos and pulled her sleeping bag around my shoulders. She had brought a full camping and surveillance set up in a tricked-out backpack. We sat in the mouth of the cave, looking out over the trees. The compound was spread below us, distant and gleaming in the moonlight—wall, field and pool, buildings. "I got here two days ago. Your message in the forum told me you were in Costa Rica in the mountains. I downloaded a recent set of satellite images and wrote a little program to go through the data looking for triangle patterns in the pixels. It took about an hour to find the three pyramids.

Pretty easy to find based on your clues. Got on a plane. Rented a jeep. I've been creeping around, watching, trying to figure out what the hell is going on. I actually saw them taking you in there." She pointed to the compound. "Two big dudes carrying you. Pretty scary. Now *you* need to tell me what the hell is going on here. All the details."

I nodded, cleared my throat, and began. When I finished, she just sat there for a little while, staring at the big sky, tracing constellations with her eyes. Finally, she turned and looked at me.

"A fine mess you've gotten us into, Justin."

"I didn't make the mess. I just discovered it."

"So, the solstice. We only have, what? A couple of days?"

"Yes," I sighed. "We have to stop them somehow. But I want to get Malena out, too. She has to be here somewhere."

"I have an idea about that. But first, tell me what you found inside the building. You must have had a reason to sneak in there." She pointed back toward the compound.

"Oh, yeah. Fonseco's office or lab or whatever. It's in there. I wanted to search it."

"Find anything useful?"

"I don't know if you would call it useful." I pulled the pages from the file out of my cargo pocket—folded and damp and generally worse for wear but still legible.

Asha perused them by flashlight for a minute. "This is really weird Justin. It says you were born in Montana? On a ranch?"

"That's the original ranch where the Community started."

"And two siblings?"

"Mmmhmm."

"Who you've never met?"

"Yep." I nodded. "That's not even the weirdest part. There are two more sets of siblings. Malena is part of a set, too. Fonseco had files on all of us. He was making test tube babies in his weird laboratory. Probably implanting them in women from the Community. When the ranch was raided, they got tipped off and evacuated all the women and children beforehand. They must have sent the children out to various families and communes all over the place."

"So that's how you and Malena ended up on the farm?"

"Has to be."

"Weird. How does it feel to have siblings you've never met?"

"I don't know," I paused, thinking. How did it feel? I had no idea. "I haven't processed yet, I guess. I mean, they're only my siblings by strict definition. If you didn't grow up with someone, never even met them, how much of a bond can you have?"

"True."

"What did you mean you have an idea about where Malena might be?"

"Let me show you. We should get back farther into the cave. They could spot the light."

We crab walked back, Ashna leading the way. Against the cave wall, tucked into the shadows, she had unpacked a thermarest, a little camp stove, a laptop and satellite phone. Her backpack hung from a stick wedged into a crack in the wall. I sat down underneath it, leaning against the cool stone while she dropped down next to me and opened the laptop.

"Crappy bandwidth paired with this phone," she mumbled, pulling up a map. It was an overhead satellite image—basically a sea of trees with shadows showing where the land below dipped and rose, broken in a few places by clearings. I spotted the landing strip first, eyes drawn to the tan rectangle in all that green.

"That's where we landed." I pointed to it. "And here's the ranch house and outbuildings. That's where they held me at first. Here's one of the pyramids. And the two others." I traced an equilateral triangle with the pyramids at the points. Directly in the center of the triangle was the compound bisected down the middle by the dividing wall. From above it looked like a circle with a slash through it. A warning—no parking, no smoking, no free thought, no questioning Eleanor Jane Sibyl's mystic visions. On one side I saw the office buildings, the little villas. On the other—the side I hadn't visited yet—was one large building with gardens and ponds surrounding it in an arc.

"That's where they all are," Ashna said, pointing to the unfamiliar half of the circle. "I've seen them in there. Your brothers and sisters I guess."

"All together in there?"

"Yep. Like a happy little hippie commune. All wearing the same groovy outfits and saying om together."

"So I need to go back in to get Malena."

"What if she doesn't want to leave Justin? Have you thought of that?" Ashna put the laptop down and turned to face me. "It's not that hard to escape is it? You did it. You just walked out."

"Not quite. I had to fight Sister Serah. She just about kicked my ass."

"Yeah but you're a special case. Fonseco knew you were resisting it. He knew you were an unbeliever. It looks like the rest of them have all been living in this cult their whole lives. None of them left and struck out on their own like you."

"I guess it's possible." I looked down at my hands, clenched together.

"It's completely possible. Imagine being introduced to a bunch of brothers and sisters you never knew you had. I know you're a weirdo loaner misanthropist but think of how a normal person would react, especially one who grew up in this cult. Then imagine Fonseco and Eleanor Jane Sibyl are telling you you're the chosen ones or some shit like that. You have a destiny. You're special." Ashna broke off, exasperated, took a breath. "She could be totally wrapped up in it."

"But why did she warn me away?"

"I don't know."

"There's a chance. It might be small but I still need to make sure. If she wants to leave, I need to help her get out."

"Okay." Ashna said, thinking. "Okay. But you're in no shape for that right now. You need to sleep. Tomorrow we can watch them, figure out their patterns. Tomorrow night you can go in. I'm worried about the missiles though. What's the chance they actually work?"

"I don't know." I shook my head. I hadn't really considered whether or not they had the technical expertise to actually launch a rocket. "There's another guy. Dr. Vernier. He's a friend or associate of Fonseco's. We picked him up in Mexico on the way here. He must be involved somehow."

"I mean, people don't say 'it's not horse grooming'

or 'it's not literary criticism' when they're trying to say something isn't super difficult. They say 'it's not rocket science'. Building and launching rockets is sort of legendarily difficult." Ashna broke off and thought for a moment. "I still feel like we should warn the authorities. If they do manage to launch an ICBM or two it's going to be bad. Really bad."

"There was an agent of some kind in Utah," Beth's face jumped out of my muddled memory. "She was undercover at Red Butte commune. Then I saw her again here. The night they took me to the compound. I warned her. She must have reported it to whoever she's working for."

"That's good." Ashna nodded. "We need to be prepared though. Go to sleep. You need to rest. I'm going to do some work."

****

When I woke, Ashna had somehow wormed her way into the sleeping bag with me. Her warm back was against my chest and her breathing was deep. The first rays of daylight were shining on the cave opening. I eased out of the bag, careful not to wake her, scrambled down to the tree line and relieved myself against a twisted Ficus tree, then went to the stream and drank. My body felt stiff and sore, scratched and abraded in a hundred places. I needed a shower badly. And clean clothes. The best I could do was undress, dump handfuls of water over my head, and rinse my shirt and pants in the steam. I left them on a big rock near the cave mouth to dry, retrieved Ashna's binoculars, then sat in the sun watching the compound. I saw a couple of maintenance people out working on the landscaping but no other inhabitants stirring. I trained the lenses on Fonseco's villa. Nothing but dark windows, curtains drawn. The other half of the compound, beyond the dividing wall, where my weird siblings lived was hidden from my vantage. I put the binoculars down and closed my eyes, listening to the forest.

Ashna woke soon after. I heard her moving around in the cave, metal clinking, her stove lighting. She called to me from above, asking if I wanted coffee.

"Absolutely," I answered and crawled up into the cave. "I can't believe you brought coffee."

"Of course I did. I'm not uncivilized. Just uncivil."

We drank our coffee in silence, accompanied by instant oatmeal and granola bars, giving it our full attention, like a ritual. The dregs drained, I put down my collapsible cup. The day was warming up already. I wiped perspiration from my brow.

"So, surveillance?"

"Yes. Let's take a look. We'll have to go around to the other side. I found a good place over there yesterday."

Ashna's surveillance spot turned out to be the top of an old water tower—another part of the ranch that, like Sam's shack, had fallen into disuse. We climbed rusty rebar ladder rungs that had been molded right into the side of the concrete cylinder and stretched out flat on the top. From there, we could see the other side of the compound. The building sat back in the grounds, up against the dividing wall. Its style was a bizarre mashup of hippie ashram and Spanish colonial with some Cambodian temple arches and stacked towers thrown in. A broad patio shaded by pergolas ran across the front and a low wall extended out from there enclosing a rectangular lawn, perfectly groomed. Beyond that, palm trees and flowers, paths and water features filled the grounds, just as on the other side of the wall. Landscaping maintenance workers came and went, dressed in gray, with broad straw hats to keep the sun off, and carrying the tools of their trade. I watched them work, then pack away their tools in a shed of fitted stone near the center of the grounds.

We watched for an hour before anyone stirred from the ashram. The first one out was a woman, dressed in the white garments of the chosen. She had a young girl with her, maybe eight or nine years old. They both sat on lounge chairs, steam from the beverages they carried rising in lazy tendrils. The woman looked like fake Malena, but heavier, rounder, with longer hair. One of the three sisters, I guessed. Hazel or Mariposa? Or Malena herself? Did Malena have children? I had no idea but I guessed not or I would have heard about it back at the commune in Utah. She had been the teacher there, then transferred away. No one had mentioned a husband or children.

"Her daughter?" I whispered, handing Ashna the binoculars.

"Probably," Ashna answered. "Same face in miniature."

"I haven't seen any other children here."

"I guess it makes sense they would let the chosen ones bring their kids but not anyone else."

"Yeah. I just didn't even consider that any of them would have kids."

"They're your age, dude." Ashna passed the binoculars back.

A few minutes later another woman emerged with a boy maybe a year older, taller. The two kids ran off together, laughing, playing tag in a wild race across the grounds. More grown-ups came out, carrying plates and hot beverages. One more child accompanied them, younger than the first two by a couple of years. She ran off to find her playmates, long dark braids flying out behind, while the adults took seats around a large table under the pergola and finished their breakfast. After another twenty minutes or so, they started to rise, one by one, picking up mats from a basket, and convened on the lawn where they began a yoga routine. No one was leading but they were all more or less in sync, as if they had done it a hundred times.

"Eight," Ashna said. "That's all of them. Looks like a nice life down there. Better than sleeping in a cave. You sure you don't want to go down and join them? Round it out to nine? One big happy family."

"I'm sure Fonseco would love that. It's all he ever wanted. Why only three kids though? Seems like they would have more. And what about spouses? Where are they?"

"No idea."

"The one closest to the patio is Malena. I'm sure of it." I could feel that it was her. I trained the binoculars on her face, squinting and trying to compare it to memory. It seemed like my eyes and brain had reached some kind of limit though, like a digital image zoomed in farther and farther, abstracted into giant pixels. Finally seeing her now felt weird, uncanny, after all I had been through trying to find her. Utah, drugs and captivity, dead Noah, missiles, Sam's shack in the woods. Too many emotions at once. I repressed the feeling, forcing myself to stay rational and examine the situation. "How am I going to get her out?"

"Go in after dark I guess. That building looks like it has a lot of rooms though. No way of knowing which is hers."

"I can't wander around, knocking on doors. They probably eat dinner together at that table under the pergola."

"Probably," Ashna agreed.

"I'll sneak in. Try to waylay her and talk to her when she's alone. Sometime before or after dinner."

"That sounds a little creepy," Ashna broke off and turned to her right. "What's happening over there?"

"Looks like a jeep."

Far off, near where the wall rounded out of site, a dirt road dead-ended at a big roll up door that would give access to the other side of the compound. A jeep had just pulled up. Two guards climbed out.

"That's where I saw them bring you into the compound. Let me see the binoculars." Ashna reached back and I handed them over. "They're unloading somebody. Unconscious just like you were. A woman."

"Let me see those." Ashna handed the binoculars back and I trained them on the scene below. "Shit. That's Beth. The agent."

"The one you warned?"

"Yeah."

"She might not have had a chance to get word out."

"Not good."

"No, not good at all."

I watched the guards roll up the gate and carry Beth in. Her arms swung limply and her mouth hung open. Was she even alive? I couldn't tell.

"This changes the calculation," Ashna whispered. "Now we definitely have to warn someone."

Chapter 19

The Ashram
12/19: Costa Rica, Alajuela Province

"Okay, I sent anonymous tips to the FBI and the U.S. embassy in San Jose."

"What if they don't take it seriously? Or get here too late?" I turned to where Ashna sat at the back of the cave, bent over her laptop.

"Real possibilities." She shook her head, not taking her eyes from the screen. "That's why you have to go monkey wrench the rockets."

"What?"

"Sneak in and damage them or disable them. You got in before."

"Yeah but that was only one silo and nobody was there. We're closer to the event now. They probably have them guarded all the time."

"You know I wouldn't normally suggest something like this. I value you whole and alive. You're my best friend and all that. But we're talking World War III here. You have the skills. You've been thieving for years. But let's make sure this doesn't happen."

I turned and looked out over the trees. The forest was alive with movement and bird sounds. I really didn't want to go back in. I'd get caught, trapped, drugged, and put in a cell again. Or maybe just killed. The thought made me shudder. It was hard to refute Ashna's logic though.

"They use three RD250 engines. They're from the late fifties, early sixties. Effective but not very complicated. Nitric acid and nitrogen tetroxide fuel. Even with the rocket fully stacked and sitting in the silo you should be able to reach the throttle actuator from underneath." She motioned me over and I crawled back. A technical diagram of an engine was open on her screen.

"Where did you find this?"

"Rocket nerd site. These people who are into rockets are deep nerds."

"As opposed to you?"

"Oh, I'm a deep nerd. But not rockets. Other stuff. My laptop's about to die though so take a look at this." She pointed to a part near the bottom of the diagram. "That's the throttle actuator. You'll have get underneath and reach up past those bell shaped parts."

"You mean the ones that will shoot super heated plasma into my face and turn me into a charred husk in a matter of seconds if the rocket ignites while I'm in there?"

"Definitely. Charred husk. Maybe nothing left at all. These are hot launch missiles."

"As opposed to cold launch?"

"Yeah. Hot launch, the engines ignite right in the silo. They have to have some kind of duct to exhaust the hot efflux. You'd be incinerated. Cold launch, they use pressurized gas to lift the rocket out of the silo before the engines ignite."

"I did see something that looked like openings for ducts. Around three sides of the pyramid."

"Good. Maybe you can get in that way. They're not going to launch while you're in there. The throttle control motor is right here." She pointed at a different part of the diagram. "You see that wire? Cut that and the throttle won't work. It'll be stuck closed so no possibility of flames burning your face off. The wire's protected by this sheath though so you'll have to cut through both. You'll need a torch or some really big bolt cutters or something."

"How do you know closed is the default position?"

"I'm not a rocket engineer and I don't read Russian so I'm going to call it an educated guess. See this?" She shifted to another open tab in her browser. "A Historical Systems Study of Liquid Rocket Engine Throttling Capabilities. I read that. Or skimmed it really. Pretty dry."

"Very reassuring."

"Anyway, if the throttle's not working it's going to make the rocket malfunction one way or another. Maybe it will shoot straight up at full power and explode from overheating or maybe it won't ignite at all. Either way, World War Three averted. Hopefully. If not, where better to be than Costa Rica, right? We can go sit on the beach while the world melts down."

We made it back to Sam's house around noon and crept silently up to the clearing. In the sunlight, three small deer stood near the front door, buff colored, white speckles like sun dapples across their backs. A twig snapped under my foot and they froze, turning their heads toward us. A moment later they all burst into a run and disappeared with a rustle of leaves into the trees on the far side of the clearing.

"You scared Bambi away," Ashna hissed in my ear.

"Yes," I whispered back. "I guess Sam isn't here or those three wouldn't have been hanging out in front of his door."

"Unless they're used to him feeding them maybe. We should check."

Ashna stayed in the shadows while I crept around the periphery and peeked in the windows. It looked just as it had when I left–coffee cups on the makeshift counter, bedding on the floor where Sam had slept. The place had a feeling of neglect. I motioned Ashna over.

"I don't think he's been back."

"Weird."

"I wonder if he decided to go confront Fonseco? They might have stuck him in a cell like they did to me. They definitely wouldn't want him messing up their big event or talking to anyone about what I told him."

"Was that how it seemed when he left? Like he might be heading off to do that?" Ashna asked, pushing the netting aside and peering into the dim interior.

"Yeah. He definitely didn't like it when I told him they locked me up. And the missiles. He wouldn't answer me when I told him that. Just said it was time for his walk. I got the impression he might have been heading that way to check it out."

"Well," Ashna pushed through the netting and stepped inside. "I guess we'll see if he shows back up. For now, we're requisitioning this dump."

I followed her in and we got settled. It was a relief to be inside out of the sun with a roof over our heads and a place to lie down, no matter how basic the accommodations. Ashna plugged in to the battery unit, booted her laptop, and bent over it cross-legged on the floor. She used her sat phone for internet access, probing and testing the Community's systems for weaknesses.

"Was that IP address I sent you useful at all?"

"Hmm? Oh, yeah. Sort of. It got me into the Community's database system. But that hasn't done me much good. It's some kind of homegrown software. No known vulnerabilities. I de-obfuscated the code and I've been crawling through it looking for anything that would let me elevate privileges."

"Try nfisher."

"What's nfisher?"

"Dead Noah's username. That's how I got into the restricted part of the system."

"Do you have to call him Dead Noah? It's creepy."

"I'm using it as a way to deflect and sublimate my guilt."

"He was going to kill you. It was self-defense. No guilt. What's Dead Noah's Password?"

"ejs13152. Eleanor Jane Sibyl's initials and birthdate."

"And I'm in. Just like that. Now I need to see if I can find something that connects me back to here. Maybe an access log with IP address. Maybe a username…"

Ashna's attention turned back to her screen and her consciousness of the outside world faded away as it always did when she was deep in some code. She did this thing where her mouth hung open a little and she ran her tongue along the tips of her incisors. I decided to nap while she worked. I had a long night ahead.

I woke several hours later to the sound of Ashna still tapping and clicking away on her machine. Sitting up, I noted that the sun had nearly set while I slept. My watch said it was after five.

"Hungry," I said, standing and stretching, then

headed for the pantry, such as it was. "Any sign of Sam?"

"Nope," Ashna rasped without looking up. "You'd better get going soon if you want to catch Malena. I put together a map and suggested route for you." She slid a piece of paper toward me. "Hopefully I'll get into the control systems before you try for the first pyramid. Almost there."

"Okay," I answered, cranking into a can of soup with a rusty opener I found in a crate of tumbled utensils. "Just need some sustenance first."

"Justin."

"Yeah?" I looked up from my cold soup.

"Don't get killed. Or seriously injured. Or captured."

"I'll do my best."

A little over an hour later, I was back at the water tower, watching 'the Ashram' as I had come to think of it. A couple of my brethren were setting the table and carrying out dishes of food. Their turn to cook tonight? They probably had a rotating duty. The rest drifted out in pairs or trios, bringing the children with them. I saw fake Malena and Oak. The food looked good–rice and curries in steaming bowls. I even imagined I could smell it. I hadn't had a real meal for days. For a moment, I closed my eyes, wishing I had never set out for Red Butte Commune. I couldn't wallow in self-pity, though. I needed to get into the grounds if I was going to ambush the real Malena. She was down there, back to me, sitting a bit apart from the others. I might have been reading into it, but she didn't seem as gung-ho. She held her body stiffly and didn't speak much unless directly addressed. It gave me hope that she might leave with me if I could just get to her.

I put the binoculars away, shouldered my pack, and headed down the ladder into the forest. I had scouted a good spot to get over the wall. It was a door with a ledge and light above, identical to the one I had used before. I felt confident I could make it over.

I got up on the first try, jumping from my good leg, and sprawled atop the wall on my stomach, listening for any sign that my scrabbling and gasping had been heard. For a couple of minutes I waited, breathing slowly, but nobody came. Directly below me, inside the wall, was a little manicured patch of lawn. It looked soft. I hoped it was. Easing over, I let myself down to hanging, took a breath, and let go. I leaned to the left to take the brunt of the landing on my healthy ankle. With an audible squish, my foot sank a good two inches into the turf and I rolled out of the fall, coming up with a damp back.

I crouched there, waiting again. Incense drifted on the air–Nag Champa. They weren't doing anything to dispel the Ashram vibe. I heard a creature scurry through the plantings nearby, the drone of a distant airplane engine, a fountain plashing softly. Cautiously, I crept through the grounds, staying low.

Halfway to the Ashram patio, I passed the gardeners' little storage shed built of big, round fitted stones, mortared roughly. The door was partially open so I peeked in. A straw sun hat on a hook, a shelf holding bags of dirt and pots, shovel and rake hanging on a rack, a clip board with a sheet of paper and pen on a string– nothing stood out as particularly useful so I continued on. The low wall around the periphery was just right for me to kneel behind and peer over. They were still at the table but seemed to be finishing. The children were already up and playing a game of soccer with two potted palms as the goal posts. Malena was about forty feet away, her back to me.

Squatting there, trying to figure out how to get close and speak to her, I realized I was dressed just like one of the guards. I was, in fact, wearing the exact uniform which had been supplied to me by Brother Saul and Sister Serah when I first arrived–probably just extra clothing they had in storage. I realized, too, that I had occasionally seen the guards wearing sun hats like the one I just passed up in the shed. Turning away from the dinner scene, I scooted back, bear crawled to the cover of a yuca plant, then stood and hurried back to the shed. Inside, I grabbed the hat and put it on. The clipboard held log sheets for tracking watering and maintenance. I tore a piece off the top sheet and scrawled a note for Malena.

At the edge of the patio I stopped again, peering over the wall. The table was lit by lamps overhead on the pergola. The hat's wide brim would cast a shadow over my features. My plan was just weird enough to work. I scooted around to a place where steps led up to the patio, stood, and walked purposefully up. Without pausing, trying to look both bored and officious, I strode across, stopped next to Malena and held out the note.

"Message from Brother Fonseco."

She glanced up, brow creasing, and took the note. In my peripheral vision I saw a couple of the others glance my way. Turning quickly, I walked off and rounded the house, moving out of their sight.

The note told Malena to meet me at the gardener's shed. I had signed it and added 'the barn door is open' at the bottom. Now I just had to get back there and wait. If she wanted out, she would come meet me. If she didn't she might turn me in. I chose to trust her, across the years, on the basis of our old connection. Just standing next to her on the patio I had felt it still—a current that connected us. A bond of love, trust, and shared purpose. Maybe it wasn't real. Maybe I was delusional. I would find out soon.

Still, I almost gave up. After an hour in the shed I was getting anxious. Had she been caught trying to sneak out? Had she decided to ignore my note? I resolved to wait another thirty minutes max. I couldn't spend all night there. My watch ticked away the minutes. I was just rising to leave when a dark form appeared, blocking the half open shed door.

"Justin?"

"Yes. It's me."

She slipped in and I felt myself wrapped in her arms. She squeezed me tightly. I felt her warmth, smelled the incense on her hair, but also felt that she was trembling with adrenaline.

"God. It's been a long time," she whispered, stepping back.

"Yes, it has been."

"What the hell are you doing here? I told you to stay away."

"I know. I couldn't leave you trapped though, maybe in danger."

"How did you even find me?"

"Long story. I'll tell you but right now I need to know if you want out? I'm here to get you out if that's what you want."

"Yes." She turned to show me the backpack she wore. "I'm ready to go. There's something weird going on. I don't know what it is but it's scary. I think they're planning something awful."

"You're right. They are. Once again, long story. Let's get out. I can fill you in later. I have a friend nearby."

"We have to be careful. They have guards watching us all the time. Patrolling."

"I know. We'll slip through their net."

I led Malena back through the grounds to the door in the wall where I had gone over. From the inside, it had a keyed lever style handle. I turned the handle and pushed. It was locked as I had suspected. I motioned for Malena to crouch down in the shadows and got my homemade pick set out. Years of exposure had corroded the metal and the pins inside were sticky. I raked them with the pick then lightly tapped each pin, feeling them give and push back. It took several tries but the lock turned under the pressure of my tension wrench and I pulled the handle down, exerting steady pressure with my shoulder. With a solid thump as it escaped the frame, the door swung out. I winced. The sound had to have been loud enough to be heard back at the Ashram.

"Let's hurry," I whispered.

We scrambled out and I eased the door closed behind us. I got us into the woods as soon as I could, heading toward the stream that led back to the cave and from there the path to Sam's house. Malena followed as I pushed through the vegetation. I had a flashlight but I didn't want to use it in case anyone was watching the woods. Malena had said they were watched by guards at all times but I had only seen occasional patrols when observing the Ashram from the water tower earlier that day. It was possible she felt their presence more than actually saw them. Fonseco had worked to create a kind of self-fulfilling jail. From what I had seen, the guards were sloppy and understaffed. Maybe Noah had been the one who kept them in line when he wasn't back in Utah. Still, I went carefully, trying to be as quiet as possible and leaving the light off.

Walking in silence with Malena was comfortable but also deeply weird. When we were kids we used to go for walks around the countryside just to get out of the house and away. Long, slow, meandering conversations would unfold–visions of future plans, fantasies of life away from the farm. After all this time, we had so much to discuss and clear up. I wanted to burst out with questions. She felt familiar but also like a stranger. I wanted to put her in focus, dispel the awkwardness. There would be time for that later though.

I heard the stream before we reached it–a gentle trickling sound up ahead–then stepped in it without warning as I rounded a giant clump of ferns. I stopped and Malena bumped against me.

"This is the stream," I said, turning. "I need you to follow it until you come to a trail. It's about a mile…"

"Without you?" She broke in. "I don't understand."

"There's no time to explain. I have some stuff I need to do back at those pyramids. I need to stop their plan."

"You can't go back. You'll get caught."

"I have some special skills. I'm good at this. Sorry I can't fill you in right now. But I'm not the awkward kid you knew. Not any more than you are. We've both grown up. My life took some twists and turns. I'm really good at sneaking into places and getting out undetected. It's what I do. You'll have to trust me."

"Okay." She nodded. "But you'll come back and meet me?"

"Yes. But right now you need to go to where my

friend Ashna is. She's waiting for you. If you follow the steam you'll come to a path. It's…"

"About a mile. You said that part already." It was classic Malena. She used to interrupt me with that same tone all the time–teasing but not mean.

I smiled. "Right. Turn right at the trail. Go a little bit farther and you'll come to a clearing with a small building. Ashna's inside."

"Sam's house?"

"Yeah. You've been there?"

"Once. Zelda, his daughter, took me there. Brother Fonseco was not happy."

"Good. Call to her from outside and tell her who you are. She can fill you in. I'll meet you back there as soon as I can. Or at the road. Ashna and I both have satellite phones. We'll keep in touch."

"Got it." She hugged me then stepped back. "Be careful." Something strange in her eyes? Was I just seeing things in the dark of the woods? I looked again but it was gone.

"I will. You, too." I turned and headed back down the steam. I glanced back after twenty paces but she was already gone, swallowed by the forest.

Chapter 20

Burning Steel
12/19-20: Costa Rica, Alajuela Province

The first pyramid was guarded. Following Ashna's map, I arrived there about thirty minutes after parting ways with Malena. A network of trails connected the compound, the ranch house, and the three pyramid silos. Ashna had surveyed them all via satellite data and drawn a good approximation. I encountered two patrols on the way but hid among the trees while they passed. The guards patrolled in pairs. It looked like they had drafted some of the workers for guard duty. I recognized their faces from my days of stone cutting labor. They walked silently, unspeaking and alert, sticking to the center of the path. I held absolutely still, watching them pass. Leading the second pair, Sister Serah plodded forward, a hulking, dark haired man behind her. It was too dark for me to see her face well but I thought she looked tired and I could see the bruise on her jaw.

I waited until they were well past, then crept out and continued. Not far now if my calculations were correct. Five minutes later, I saw the peak of the temple silo poking up above the trees and left the path, cutting through the woods. The ground rose as I circled around the back side and I wound up on a low ridge where I crouched and fixed the binoculars on the apex of the pyramid. The moon, a couple of days past full, had risen while I walked. In its clear light, I saw a guard standing on the top, an automatic weapon hanging from his shoulder.

Going in through the top didn't seem like a good option with the guard there. It never had anyway. There had to be some access to the silo from the control room area but that would be guarded and manned as well. I wanted to avoid human contact if possible. My other option was one of the openings at the base. They had to lead back to the silo. Ashna's information had convinced me they might be a sort of exhaust escape system for the hot gasses that would be produced by the rocket engines. But those were protected by steel bars. I pictured it–just above ground level, three vertical pieces of rebar set into a cement frame, mortared in place among the limestone blocks. The opening was large enough for me to crawl through if I could get rid of the bars. I had seen a portable oxy-acetylene torch rig in the tool shed at pyramid three. Did they have one here too? If so, I could use it to cut through.

Keeping to the edge of the woods, I made my way around the perimeter of the clearing until I found the tool shed. It was in more or less the same place relative to the pyramid as the one I was familiar with. For a few minutes, I watched the guard. He was restless, pacing from edge to edge on his lofty platform. I counted. Five seconds to go from one side to the other. I watched him march toward me, reach the edge, turn. I darted out and flattened myself against the shed, waited. He turned again and I crept inside.

Dark. Smell of oil and earth. Vertical lines of handles stacked in a corner. I touched a plastic utility

238

shelf. A stack of heavy tarps worn to an almost felt-like texture, chisels. I risked turning on Ashna's penlight at its lowest setting. The weak beam limned the form of two tanks on the upper shelf, strapped to a nylon harness. I lifted the apparatus down, shifted my backpack around so I was wearing it frontward, and shrugged on the straps. The torch rig rode high on my back. I grabbed a couple of the tarps, too, and stuffed them into my backpack.

Peering around the door frame, I saw the guard still pacing, waited for him to turn, and dashed back to the forest edge. Moving through the underbrush wasn't easy with my new load. I had to go slow, testing each step before I lowered my weight and meandering in whichever direction was clear. But I made it back around and only fell once when I stepped on the uneven roots of a fern.

The guard seemed to be sticking toward the front of the pyramid's plateau, eschewing the area where the silo doors opened and not worried about anyone approaching from behind the clearing. Three openings led from the base of the pyramid to the interior. One at the rear, two on either side. The rear was my best option.

I made my way to the edge of the trees again and waited a minute, watching and listening. The forest behind me murmured with breeze through the leaves, animal sounds, dripping water, rustle of insects. A jet engine droned, high above. The ranch seemed to be on the flight path from San José to some destination. I had heard the jets off and on since I arrived. This one seemed to be getting louder, growing closer. I grabbed the chance, darted out, and crouched near the wall of stone that formed the temple's base.

Dark, inky shadow filled the opening beyond the rebar grill. A steady whisper of air flowed out, cool and dryer than the humid night. I bent and sniffed the current. Metallic and chemical–like the air inside the control room of the other pyramid. Pulling out the tarps, I draped them over me in a makeshift tent to block the light and some of the sound. With a spark from the igniter, the torch glowed to life. I had it turned down low to limit the hiss and blast of sound when it lit. Slowly, I turned it up until a two-inch flare of plasma jetted from the nozzle. It cut through the rebar like the proverbial knife through butter. I severed the steel at top and bottom, catching the pieces before they fell and jamming the glowing ends down into the earth at my feet.

My entry clear, I folded the tarps, slipped out of the torch rig harness, and wriggled feet first into the opening. The tunnel was square, maybe three feet by three. I pulled the tanks and tarps inside, placing the rig on top so that I could pull it along behind me.

Trying not to think about what would happen if the rocket in the silo ignited while I was in the tunnel, I turned and began crawling forward, dragging the equipment with my booted toes, moving downward at a gentle angle that increased the farther I went. The R-36 missiles, I knew, were 106 feet tall. Fonseco's pyramids were about twenty feet shy of that. The silos would need space below the rocket as well. So, I would have to go down quite a bit below ground level to get to the bottom. Visualizing the control room and the video feeds from the inside of the silo I had seen on the screens, I tried to convince myself for the hundredth time that I would not be seen. My memory told me there had been a camera showing a view looking up toward the top of the silo, one looking down along the length of the rocket to the bottom, and a couple focused on the nose cone. The video was low quality, black and white, with very little grayscale. The bottom of the silo had been a dark well of shadow, unlit. I could only hope this silo was the same.

Near the end, I had to turn around again and scoot feet first down the steepening slope, using the friction of my boots on the rough floor and walls to keep from sliding. Cool air blowing up from the depths chilled the sweat on my face and arms. Absolute darkness enveloped me. Worried, I dug Ashna's pen light out and turned it on low, holding it in my mouth as I descended. Fifteen feet farther on, the tunnel flattened out and ended at a wire screen. Clearly not meant to survive the blast, the flimsy wood frame pulled out easily under a little pressure and the wire mesh–no sturdier than you would find in an average window screen–crumpled. They had probably placed it there as an afterthought to keep out rodents and insects. I set it aside, turned and scooted forward until I could see into the silo.

From a light far above, a small amount of illumination filtered down to the bottom of the well, glinting on the tops of tubes and cables and a massive ring that the missile itself sat on. The thrust mount, I guessed, which itself sat on giant shock absorber-like dampers. I slid down through the opening, grasping a strut and lowering my feet to a sort of ledge. The lethal cylinder of the missile loomed above me, rising through the silo, tipped with a black final stage that curved to a stubby point. Was there a nuclear warhead contained inside? Some cold war artifact obtained on the international black market and transported to Costa Rica? Was Fonseco that insane?

I pointed the pen light up at the six bell shaped thrust chambers, looking for the throttle control and the wire Ashna had shown me in the diagram. Right where it should be, dull metal shielding surrounding it, it flowed around the other components and entered the throttle actuator housing.

Dull silence filled the silo, broken only by a steady drip of water somewhere below me and my own rustling movements. I bumped the handle of the light against the thrust mount ring accidentally and the report pinged through the silo like a flock of chattering birds. There was no chance I would be able to cut the wire without being discovered if anyone was listening. I didn't think they were. I was more worried about the light from the torch. If someone was in the control room actively monitoring the video feed, they might see the little bloom of luminescent flame in the depths, although it would be mostly shielded by the rocket and mount. I could just make out a steel door below, presumably connecting the silo to a warren of tunnels and stairways. They would come that way if they spotted me. To be safe, I put the harness back on then pulled one of the tarps around me like a cape. I could use it to block most of the ambient light from the torch.

Weighted down and bulky with the equipment on my back, praying that the rocket wasn't fueled up and I wouldn't slip and cut though one of the fuel chamber walls, I climbed up under the engines, bracing my feet on one of the dampers and a strut that crossed below. Awkwardly, I struck the spark and lit the torch, threaded the nozzle up between the thrust chambers, and focused the flame on the wire housing. It glowed orange, then red to white, then melted away, the wire inside crisping, sundered almost immediately. I cut the torch and the metal cooled, glow dying out like a burning cinder flying up from a camp fire into the night.

I hoped Ashna was right and it would be enough to keep the missile from reaching its intended target, wherever that was. For a moment, I stood below the engine looking up at the pure forms of the components, almost wishing it would ignite. Sticky with sweat and grime, body and mind aching with exhaustion, the rocket seemed ideal in comparison to my imperfect carcass–a machine with one purpose, perfectly, lethally tuned to its task.

Getting back up the tunnel with the oxy-acetylene tanks was harder than getting down. I wormed my way up, pushing them in front. After a Sisyphean eternity, I emerged and gulped fresh air. Crouching in the margin of the forest again, I kept an eye on the top of the pyramid, looking for any sign that I had been spotted, while I checked Sam's sat phone. No messages. That meant I needed to head for pyramid number two. My conundrum was whether to carry the bulky tanks with me or abandon them, move faster, and get the set from the storage shed at the next site. Moving through the forest and evading any patrols I ran into would be nearly impossible with the tanks on my back. I tore fern fronds, covering the tanks with them and stood, leaving them behind.

Half an hour later, with Sister Serah and her bear-like companion pointing automatic weapons at me outside the tool shed at pyramid two, I reconsidered.

"Put down the tanks and raise your hands." Sister Serah jabbed her rifle at me. They must have seen me and followed me to the shed. I had messed up somewhere along the way.

"Okay," I lowered the rig to the ground, let it drop, and held my arms up. "Sorry about the bruise there…"

"Shut up. Frisk him."

The bear man took my backpack and frisked me, patting me down with his massive paws. He found everything I was carrying. I cursed myself for not having tucked the lock picks into my waist band. He might have found them anyway.

"Walk that way," Sister Serah gestured with the gun again. "Take the path. Don't try to run or turn around. We *will* shoot. Don't speak."

I stumbled up the dark trail, the sound of their footsteps behind me.

"Target acquired, bringing him in to base," Serah said into her walkie.

"Copy that. Take him to the utility block." A man's voice I didn't recognize.

They brought me back to the building by the ranch house, marched me up the hallway, and locked me in my old cell. I had almost forgotten how much I hated that room. My old friend the gecko was still there, clinging to the wall by the window. I greeted him and dropped onto the bed. The blanket was fresh but the cell stank of old sweat and damp and desperation. It galled me to be so easily caught. I knew I wasn't in good enough shape either physically or mentally to be doing what I was trying to do.

Footsteps approached in the hallway. I stretched out, trying to look even more exhausted and spent than I was.

Sister Serah entered first, gun trained on me. Fonseco came in next, darkening the doorway with his bulk, followed by Dr. Vernier. He looked nervous. His face contorted like he'd smelled something unpleasant. He probably had. How many days since I'd showered?

"Sorry about my aroma," I said, not rising from the bed. "It's been a while since I bathed."

"Justin," Fonseco said. "I'm disappointed. Was it you who broke into my office? Where have you been?"

"Just hanging out in the forest. Met some nice sloths."

"Don't lie please. I know you found Sam. We hoped to find you there but you had already cleared out. Apparently you told him some fantasy about rockets in silos."

"Not a fantasy Fonseco."

"What did you do?" The doctor broke in. "Did you do anything to my missiles? Were you in a silo? Or a control room?" His voice rose, high and shrill.

"Dr. Vernier, please. Let me handle this." Fonseco turned to face him.

"Your missiles?" I sat up on my elbows, watching Vernier's face. "Interesting. What kind of doctor are you? A rocket scientist?"

"Aerospace engineer, not rocket scientist, please."

"I didn't do anything to your missiles," I said, lying back down.

"How do you know about them?" Fonseco asked, turning back to face me.

"Just guesswork," I said, an arm draped over my eyes, trying to sound bored. "I peeked into those crates on the plane. Rocket parts. Soviet. Clearly for an R36. I happen to be very interested in rockets," I lied. "Have been since I was a kid. You might call it obsessive. Kind of like you with airplanes. The R36 is hot launched from a silo. Those pyramids look like a great way to hide a silo."

"Impressive, Justin. Unfortunately, we will need to keep you here for a while. We have work to do and we can't have you running around in the forest. I had hoped you would be able to join your family at the compound. My attempts to help you fit in have clearly failed."

"Square peg in a round hole," I mumbled.

"Yes. It's a pity you will have to miss the celebration tomorrow night. The guards will bring you food and water, and fresh clothes. I'm afraid we won't be able to let you leave this room." Fonseco turned to go, motioning the others out ahead of him.

"No philosophical musings this time Fonseco? No lectures?"

"No, Justin. It's too late for that."

They brought me clothes, a meal, and a washcloth and towel. I stripped down and gave myself a sink bath. My skin looked livid in the bright light of the overhead bulb, covered in bug bites, rash, small cuts, marbled purple, black and green with various bruises. I dressed and sat cross-legged on the cot, eating cold dinner. So they knew I had been to Sam's house in the woods. They had gone there looking for me but found it empty. That probably meant Ashna and Malena, assuming she had made it there, were safe for now. One missile was disabled, two to go. I had a day to figure out how to escape and take them out, unless Ashna managed to hack the control systems first.

As I sat thinking through my predicament, a rhythmic sound began to emerge from the background hum of forest and AC unit and water in pipes. Clank. Clank. Clank. Spaced two seconds apart. A metal cup on concrete maybe? Or a spoon on a water pipe? Some new form of psychological torture? I got up and moved around the room, trying to figure out where it was coming from. A small vent up near the ceiling over my bed seemed to be the culprit. I stood on the cot and put my ear to it. Definitely coming through the ducts. Maybe a wobbly fan? Or a person trying to communicate. As an experiment I got the spoon they had given me with my dinner and answered clank for clank. The rhythm changed and I matched it.

"Justin?" A faint, questioning voice.

"Sam?"

"Yes. Two doors down from you. I saw them bring you in."

"So they locked you up, too."

"Yes."

"I'm going to find a way out. I'll get you out, too."

Chapter 21

Sacrificial Lamb
12/20: Costa Rica, Alajuela Province

I paced my cell, searching fruitlessly for some way out. I decided at last that my only chance would be to overpower a guard next time they entered. They always came in twos though. Wary of me, they kept their weapons up, one of them covering me from the hallway. It would probably be suicide. I had no idea whether or not I would actually try it. It would be a decision made in the moment. Lying down at last, I slept fitfully, waking throughout the night.

The next day I found breakfast on a tray just inside the door when I woke. I crouched on my cot, brooding for hours while I waited for them to come again. I had resolved to try jumping a guard—but they didn't come. Outside the window I saw people hurrying back and forth carrying things, heard car engines, walkies barking orders. The final preparations for the evening's event were underway.

By late afternoon, they still had not come. They were going to leave me to rot while they held their event. After that, what? They wouldn't just let me go. Trapped, furious, I stood and kicked the bed hard. The flimsy cot jumped and skittered across the floor, bouncing with a hollow bang off the wall. Something dropped to the floor beneath it, clattering metallically. Great, I thought–probably a bolt. If I broke my bed I'd be sleeping on the floor. I got down and looked under it. Something metal glinted. I reached blindly and closed my fingers around a long, thin piece of steel. I dragged it out and held it up to the light–the extra length of spring steel I had hidden under the mattress days ago. I stared at it, confused, remembering. I'd been drugged, sleep deprived. The memory was like a dream. I saw myself shaping the picks I had used to break out. The file! Was it still there? I lifted the mattress. Yes, still there–woven between three of the nylon straps that made up the undercarriage of the cot.

I got to work immediately, breaking the ribbon of steel in half, filing, bending. By the time I was done I estimated the time to be about five o'clock. They had taken my watch but I could tell from the quality of light outside my window and from the activity. The people I saw hummed and glowed with repressed excitement as they went about their final tasks. I felt like I knew the Community enough by then to guess accurately what the plan was. They would all gather for a meal, then they would all stream to the event site at the compound. Eleanor Jane Sibyl's big speech would happen after dinner, on the stage I had seen them building, live streamed to the whole world. Did they plan to launch the missiles at the crescendo? I imagined it. Sibyl on stage, floodlit, raises her arms. The ground shakes. A crackling, rumbling sound fills the night. Then, in a triangle around the compound, flames rising, arcing across the sky. I had to get out and contact Ashna, get to the other launch sites if she hadn't already disabled them.

Having already worked that lock, I knew its

idiosyncrasies and opened it in a few seconds. I eased the door open and peeked out. No guards in the hallway but they had to be nearby. Or, they might be busy with preparations, confident I was locked safely away with no chance of escape. I scooted down the hall and unlocked Sam's door. He sat up from the cot when he heard the door open, lethargic and bleary eyed.

"Justin?" He rasped.

"Shh." I put a finger to my lips and waved him over.

He rose stiffly and came to the door. "How did you get out?"

"Doesn't matter. Go now while the guards are busy," I whispered. "I have to find a phone. Head for the woods. My friend Ashna is at your house. Tell her what happened. The missile in the north silo is disabled. I'm heading to the others. Southeast first unless I get a hold of her and she says she already hacked the control system."

"Good luck," he said, grasping my arm and holding my eye for a moment, then slipped out and hurried down the hallway. At the end he gave me a thumbs up, then opened the door and walked off, heading toward the woods as I had advised. I had no idea whether he had understood or retained what I told him. I could only hope.

The night I broke out, discovered the compound, and killed Noah, I had circled the building, looking into the rooms from outside. I remembered seeing an office with a phone. How many days ago? I had lost any sense of time. This weird, ahistorical place existed in a kind of eternal present. I turned to the right and crept down the corridor to the T intersection. If my mental map was correct, the office I had seen was located to the right again and then the second or third door down.

The yellow bucket and mop were still there, handle leaned against a wall. I passed one door and listened at the next. No sounds from inside. The knob turned and I eased it open, revealing a small room–fake wood grain Formica desk, light from the window above it pooling on the scuffed surface, pile of papers to one side and a landline office phone on the other. It looked like the office of a janitorial supervisor. Maybe it was. I hurried in and closed the door. The phone had a dial tone. I guessed nine would give me an outside line. I pressed the filthy button, listened for the tone change, then dialed Ashna's number with the country code. Weird clicks and ghostly bloops came down the line, then a ring, two rings.

"Yeah?" she sounded suspicious.

"Ashna."

"Holy shit, Justin! Where the hell are you?"

"Got caught. Just broke out. In an office near the ranch house. Did Malena make it there?"

"Yes, she's here."

"Missiles disabled?"

"The one at temple three is. That's southwest. I got in and fucked up their code. No way they're going to be able to launch. I programmed it to play Peggy Lee singing *is that all there is* when the rocket fails to launch. I wish I could get a live video feed when that happens. I can't get into temples one or two though," she snapped, exasperated. "It looks they cut the internet connection. Maybe they were suspicious or maybe it's just part of their protocol for the day of the event."

Footsteps thundered in the hallway, coming my way. "Just a second." I crouched, ready to spring if the door opened. The steps grew louder, passed, turned and died away. "Okay," I said, thinking hard. "I got to the one at the north silo before they captured me. So we have southeast left. I'm headed there. Then we'll rendezvous at your jeep." The footsteps approached again, receded.

"Be careful. I don't like this getting captured BS. No more of that."

"As always, I will do my best."

I went through the desk drawers before I left, looking for anything that might be useful, and found an ivory handled pocketknife, a small pair of greasy pliers, and a handful of paperclips. To the left of the desk, a wire shelving unit held battered boxes full of cleaning supplies and engine parts. A wide brimmed straw sun hat like the one I had stolen at the compound hung from a corner of the shelf. I put it on, pulling it low to hide my face. The clean clothes they had given me were more of the same–cargo pants, a dark gray t-shirt. I could pass as a guard. An ear to the door told me nobody was in the hall. I slipped out and headed straight for the exit.

Outside, a few stragglers were heading toward the woods, moving in the direction of the path that would take them to the temples and the compound. I guessed the compound. It would make sense for them to gather there. I fell in behind a pair of young women, keeping a distance and hiding my face with the hat. They were happy, chattering and touching each other on the shoulder or arm as they spoke, excited for the event. I wondered how they would react if the missiles launched. Would they gaze up at the fiery trails with horror? Or jubilation?

They had taken Ashna's hand drawn map but it was burned into my memory–the three pyramids forming a triangle around the compound at the center, ranch house complex at the midpoint of a line drawn between the two southerly pyramids, the paths in the forest that connected them all, and the streams that cut through, failing to respect Fonseco's sacred geometry. At the branching path that led to the compound, the two women turned. I kept going, hearing their chattering voices slowly die away into the mix of forest sounds. I considered going off-path to avoid meeting anyone, but my suspicion was that everybody would be either at the compound or one of the temple silos. Probably a skeleton crew at the silos— one or two operators in the control room, doors locked, maybe a guard there but I doubted it. Fonseco thought he had me in a cell, Sam in a cell, the mystery agent Beth either locked up or dead. The likelihood of running into anyone seemed low. I stayed on the path, choosing speed over caution.

At the edge of the clearing, I stopped and observed. The pyramid looked unreal in the rapidly dwindling light, flat and foreboding. I watched for a few minutes but saw no guards. In through the exhaust vent again? Or through the main door? I had seen a door in the silo giving access to the bottom of the well. I didn't know much about missile silos but I guessed there had to be one up at the top, too, so that the business end of the missile could be accessed if needed.

My first stop was the shed. I knew that shed well. Crossing the clearing, I remembered my fight with Noah. I thought of his body not far away in the woods. Guilt overwhelmed me for a moment. I hoped he hadn't died in vain. If I could stop the missiles, maybe the lives I saved would pay for the life I had taken.

Inside the shed I found the oxy-acetylene rig right

where I expected. Shouldering it on in the dark, I took a moment to calm my breathing and center my mind. This was the endgame. No room for mistakes. Searching the rest of the shed for anything that might be useful, I found a pair of work gloves, a coil of the polyester rope they sometimes used to lift carved stones into place, and a hammer. I shoved it all into a burlap bag, added a couple of tarps, then tucked it in between my back and the tanks. If I entered the silo from the top I would have to rappel down.

Creeping across the meadow, I felt as exposed as a fish caught in a tide pool. Getting up the steps, sized for gods, not humans, with the tanks on my back was no cakewalk. I nearly tipped over backward at one point, overbalanced by the weight, but managed to hop down a step and shift my mass forward. Like the door to my cell, I had picked the pyramid's lock once before. It was no challenge. My weird brain worked like that, remembering every detail of locks I had previously bypassed. I would forget to check in with friends for months on end, procrastinate paying my bills until the final disconnect notices arrived, but never forget the idiosyncrasies of a particular lock.

Inside, door closed behind me, I felt the cool, dry air again carrying its acrid aroma. The floor seemed to thrum and vibrate below my feet. I remembered that, too, but this time my thick brain realized what it meant. There had to be a massive generator running somewhere in the depths of the pyramid. How else were they getting power to their control room and silo? They certainly hadn't run buried power lines all the way out from the ranch house complex and I hadn't seen any above ground cables. If I could get down there and disable the generator it would give me the time I needed to vandalize the missile and get out. Their cameras and lights and controls would be off and they would be scrambling to restore power, not looking for an intruder.

This time, instead of going straight to the control room, I turned and started down the steps I had bypassed before, careful not to bang the tanks on my back against the walls of the narrow stairwell. The air grew cooler as I descended. The steps turned twice, then ended at a landing and a dank corridor. Two oval, hatch-like doors faced each other at the midpoint. At the end, steps continued down. The noise and vibration came from behind the hatch on the left. I pushed and it swung inward, heavy steel groaning on its hinges. A concrete room, maybe ten by twelve lay beyond, bathed in stark, cold light from a caged bulb on the ceiling. Taking up half the space was a big box constructed from riveted panels of army green sheet metal, raised off the floor by a couple of pallets. Next to it were several drums—probably fuel. The sound was deafening, filling the room with a physically nauseating intensity. I stepped forward and touched a door panel with circular latches. It hummed under my touch. Stenciled block letters read CAUTION HEARING PROTECTION REQUIRED WHEN DOORS ARE OPEN. A thick pipe led from the top of the box, up through the ceiling. Probably exhaust. I was pretty sure it was a diesel generator.

Several shiny metal conduits exited the rear and fed into an electrical panel on the wall. Next to the panel, a piece of plywood was bolted into the concrete. A couple of pairs of ear defenders, a flashlight, and two hard hats hung from nails pounded into the wood. I lifted the flashlight off its hook and tested it. The beam was weak in the bright room but it worked. I put on a pair of ear defenders and drew the pliers I had pilfered earlier from my pocket.

Inside the door panel was a bank of knobs, toggle switches, and gauges. One big button was labeled EMERGENCY STOP. A toggle switch said AC CIRCUIT INTERRUPT. Around the side, another smaller access door hid a tangle of wires and fuel lines. A rash plan came to me and I put it into action immediately. Flashlight on, I slapped the emergency stop button. The generator coughed. The light above me dimmed. The generator sputtered twice more and died, the light going with it. I tore the bulky ear protectors off, scooted around the side, and, using the pliers, yanked a couple of wires out of their contacts.

Out in the corridor, I headed for the stairs at the end. They had to lead to the silo. The flashlight beam shone on damp steps. I heard dripping and remembered I had heard it before when I was in the silo. At the bottom, I found another corridor sunk in foul smelling water an inch deep. I splashed through, coming up against another steel door like the hatch to the generator room. This one had a handwheel that probably activated rods or some kind of mechanical device inside that would wedge the door securely closed, making it air and water tight. I spun it until it clunked and the door sagged open. I was becoming less and less impressed with the Community's building skills. They had slapped this place together. Beyond the door was inky shadow. I pointed the flashlight beam in and saw what I was hoping for. The bottom of the silo. Stepping through into another puddle, I yanked the door closed behind me but it creaked open again, pulled open by its own weight in the crooked doorframe.

Their cameras were off and I had no time to waste so I jammed the flashlight handle into a space between a strut and the wall, angling it so I could see, and climbed up, getting my feet onto the ledge inside the thrust ring. A squeeze of the flint sparker on the rig harness and the torch bloomed to life. I used its light to find my target then applied it to the wire housing which resisted for a moment, glowing hot white, then burned away. For a moment then, I rested, watching the metal cool, afterglow in my eyes dying out.

Eager to be gone, I went too fast, missed a hold, and landed on my butt in the puddle below, tanks banging the hard floor with a sound like a shot. Wincing, I sat there, listening to the echoes die away and searching my body for injuries. Weirdly though, the echoes kept going. Thump. Thump. Thump-thump. Dull and on the edge of hearing. Where was it coming from? Thump. Thump. It sounded like someone pounding on a door far away. Unless my ears were playing tricks on me, I thought I could also hear a voice, muffled, high pitched and yelling out. I stood, shrugged off the cutting rig, and walked a circle around the perimeter of the silo, stopping and listening. The sound came from above.

My stomach dropped when it hit me. My mind went black. Somehow, before I knew what I was doing, I was halfway up, feet against the wall, back to the cool shell of the missile, rope coil draped over my shoulders. Step, step, slide–I inched my way up, the pounding growing louder. I was almost there.

At the place where the nose cone connected to the body of the rocket, a door like the one below was set into the silo wall, a hinged catwalk folded up over it. I could feel the thumping now. It thrummed against my back. But I was pressed against the hatch in the nose cone and couldn't open it without falling.

A hook above the door held the catwalk in place. My legs trembling with the effort of holding me there, I tucked the flashlight in my belt, pointed up, pulled the rope over my head, tied a lasso in the end, and tossed it at the tip of the rocket. On my first try it almost caught but came tumbling back, landing on my lap. My right foot slipped an inch. Thighs burning, I threw the rope again. It hooked over the nub of the cone. I pulled it taut.

The work gloves were in my cargo pocket. I pulled them on, grasped the rope, and hung while I spun a half turn and got my feet on the missile with a clang that echoed down to the bottom of the silo and back up, dopplering as it passed.

The thumping increased and I heard the voice again, calling, wailing. Hand over hand, I climbed higher. Then, holding on with one hand, feet braced against the curve of the nose cone, I leaned and reached back, laying out almost flat. My fingers just reached the catwalk. Two legs folded out to make a triangle that would hold it up against the silo. I pushed it toward the wall, releasing the latch, and lowered it as gently as I could.

When it was flat and solid, I jumped down, landing in a crouch on the diamond plate platform, the impact jarring through my body. The hatch in the nose cone had a small, thick window, fogged on the inside. A small hand struck against it. The latch was recessed—a handle inside. I tore at it, turned it, pulled it. The hatch came open with a sigh of air whooshing out. A terrified face gazed out at me, squinting against the flashlight beam, the youngest of the three children from the compound.

"Come on," I said, holding out my arms, fighting back a wave of emotion. "Come on. I'm here to help. I'm Justin. I'm your uncle. I'm going to get you out of here."

Chapter 22

Night Flight
12/20: Costa Rica, Alajuela Province

"I don't know why I'm here. Where is this? I was asleep and woke up in there." Her trembling voice sounded thin, tired. She crawled out, face streaked with tears, and wrapped her arms around my neck.

"I don't know why either." She was squeezing me with every ounce of strength left in her small arms. "We have to get out though. Can you hold on tight?"

"Yes."

"Don't let go. I'm going to lower us down on a rope. You have to hold on around my neck and with your legs, too." I felt her head nod against my shoulder. "Here goes."

I stood and threaded the rope through my legs and back over my shoulder, closed the hatch, and swung out to the side, off the catwalk. The friction of the rope around my body gave me enough purchase to let go with one hand and lift the catwalk back into place. When the lights and cameras came back on, I wanted everything to look normal. The girl couldn't have weighed more than fifty pounds but it was not easy rappelling down that missile in the dark and eerie silence of the silo. Every fiber of my being wanted to hurry, to run, to get out, but I forced myself to go slow, be calm. Expecting the flood lights to come on with every cautious foot of progress, I kept at it, crawling like a bug down the missile surface. The girl's tears wet my collar and she held on with a strength that gave me strength.

At the bottom, I sat her on one of the dampers, keeping her bare feet clear of the water, and whipped the rope, sending a wave up. The loop jumped off the nose cone and the full length came piling down into my arms. Just as the lasso hit my hands, the lights turned on. We both looked up, frozen.

"Okay, I whispered. That's our signal to get out. See that opening?" I pointed to the exhaust vent tunnel. "We have to go through there. It's not far but we'll have to crawl. Can you do it?"

She nodded, holding back a fresh wave of tears, shivering in a thin dress of ruby colored double gauze that shone like fire where the light touched it.

"Good. I'll boost you up."

She went ahead on hands and knees and I followed, dragging the oxy-acetylene tanks behind. As we climbed, I tried to decide what I was going to do. I couldn't abandon the child and I couldn't put her back in Fonseco's hands. It was insane, almost impossible to process. Children in the missiles. Sacrificial victims. A line from one of Eleanor Jane Sibyl's sermons came back to me--the flames that propel the trinity, the ancient three on their journey to the stars. Not a metaphor. She meant it literally. They had even dressed the kid in Sibyl's beloved jewel tones. I could take her back to the compound and her mom or dad. Did they have any idea what was happening? Or had Fonseco simply told them their kids were going to be watched by someone while they participated in Eleanor Jane Sibyl's ritual. I imagined them waving cheerful goodbyes, thinking they would tuck them into bed that night after the event. If I took her back, explained to them what was happening, would they protect her? I had no choice. I couldn't make it to Sam's cabin and back in the time I had left. I needed to get to the other children–north pyramid first. Ashna had disabled the launch system for the southwest pyramid but the missile in the north silo could still launch. It wouldn't fly right. It might explode. But that wouldn't be a better outcome for the child locked in its nose cone. There was no time to lose.

At the end of the tunnel, the girl tumbled out and I followed her, leaving the oxy-acetylene tanks inside. She looked up at me and I put a finger to my lips. She nodded.

"What's your name?" I whispered.

"Summer."

"Okay Summer. We're in danger here. I need to get you back to the compound. Is your mom there? Or your dad?"

"My mom."

"Good. We're going now. You need to follow me close, okay? If anyone tries to stop us I want you to run into the woods and hide, understand?"

She took a deep, shaky breath. "Yes," she whispered.

The attacker hit me from the side. She was behind a big tree just off the path and came at me without warning. We both hit the ground and rolled. I felt something crunch painfully in my shoulder, radiating lines bursting like fireworks behind my closed lids, but bucked her off and managed to scramble back on my elbows as she rose into a fighting crouch.

"Beth?"

"Justin? Shit! You asshole!"

"Me? I'm an asshole? I'm sick of this! You attacked me." I sat up, poking my shoulder, testing the joint. "I think you dislocated something."

"Uncle Justin?" I turned and saw Summer standing just off the path.

"It's okay, you can come out."

"Who the hell is this?" Beth almost shouted.

"You need to chill out. This kid is traumatized." I gave a quick rundown of the situation. Beth's face lost its hard edge as I spoke, her chin dropping and eyes opening wide with horror. She crouched down and put an arm around Summer's shoulders.

"In the missiles? He put them in there?"

"Yes, I need to get the others out. How did you get away? I saw them carry you into the compound."

"Escaped." She shrugged. "These people are amateurs. Dangerous amateurs. Listen, Justin? Not Dustin?"

"Justin." I nodded.

"An army of US and Costa Rican agents is about to descend on this place. Transport copters. I can hear them now."

I cocked an ear. A low hum, just audible, thrumming the air.

"What time is it?"

"6:27."

"Too late," I replied, shaking my head. "They won't get here in time. Take care of Summer. I'm going to the north pyramid. Tell them to go to the southwest one. Get the kid out over there. That missile won't launch. My friend disabled it."

"Wait," she called after me.

"Keep her safe," I yelled over my shoulder, and kept going.

The fastest way was around the compound and straight north from there. There was a chance of guards patrolling the perimeter but I doubted it. Fonseco would want everyone watching and listening when Eleanor Jane Sibyl spoke. They would be inside, stationed at the edges. These people were zealots.

Limping along as fast as I could, I rolled my shoulder and swung my arm around in a circle. Not dislocated, just bruised. The wall loomed up in front of me. The Ashram half of the compound lay to the right– less chance of guards that direction. I turned right and skirted the wall, moving through the cleared area along the periphery. One of the doors was coming up. A hundred feet short of it I stopped. Something white lay crumpled at the base of the wall up ahead. I crept forward. A body? The door was open and a person sprawled across the opening. A woman. Panic shot through me. Malena? No, it was the one who looked like Malena. She lay there in her white garments, head resting on her arm as if she had crawled half way out, then, overcome with fatigue, decided to have a nap. I crouched down, felt her throat. No pulse. No warmth. I could see no sign of violence. But she was dead, irrevocably, unquestionably.

Stepping over her, I entered the compound. The grounds were silent, eerie. A bird called in the forest, long and plaintive. Lights shone on the Ashram patio– glistening halos around them in the humid night air. Keeping to the shadows, I crept forward. They were all there, some in lounge chairs, some curled up on the cold flagstones, cups clenched in hands turned to claws by rigor mortis or shattered where they fell. On the table I saw two ceramic jugs, brown and roughhewn. Poisoned? I sniffed the top of one. Red wine. I turned back and looked at the wreckage of human life scattered around me. It reminded me of images I had seen from Jonestown–all the bodies strewn where they had fallen or stretched out in the dirt for their final sleep. Fighting the urge to run, I looked at each face, some peaceful, some twisted. They were my siblings. All of them. Two of them my full brothers.

Finally, before the horror of it paralyzed me, I melted back into the shadows, hurried away, banishing the image to some locked room of my mind. I didn't have time to process it. I needed to save the child who was still alive.

A cheer rose from the other side of the compound. I imagined the Community members over there, gathering around the stage, waiting for their prophet. I imagined the members all around the world, gathering in their meeting halls, watching the live stream. The scene I had just fled would make it to them eventually. What would they think then? Would their belief be shaken?

I slammed through the door at the north end of the compound, jumped across the margin and into the trees. The forest around me was a tunnel of leaves, endlessly scrolling by. Abruptly, it opened up. I kept going, dashing across the clearing. At the pyramid, I scrambled up the steps, climbing with hands and feet, and stopped at the door, breathing hard, lungs burning. Forcing myself to take deep breaths, I pulled the picks out of my cargo pocket and inserted the tension wrench, focused my brain on the mechanical problem before me–rake the pins. Tap each one. Rake again. Tap carefully. Feel the haptic feedback. A bit more tension and the lock turned.

Inside, door closed behind me, silence reigned. I moved slowly down the corridor, plotting. There was no time for the trick I pulled at the other silo. I needed to go straight through. If there were people in the control room, they wouldn't be expecting me. That was in my favor. Against me was the possibility there were two or more of them. I remembered the office, the kitchen area. They all seemed to be laid out the same. A chair would be my best weapon, unless they had something better.

I stopped at the door and listened. Footsteps approached then stopped.

"What?" A man's voice, inside.

Someone else spoke, unintelligible.

"Yeah. Door code is red. I'm going to check. Probably just another malfunction."

There must have been a magnetic sensor on the front door. Stupid of me not to check. Still, a good opportunity. The door opened outward into the hallway. I listened, tracking the footsteps until he was just on the other side, hand on the latch, then yanked it open. His eyes went wide and I hit him with the heel of my hand, doing my best to smash his nose right into his brain. He fell back, bouncing his head off the office door frame. As he fell, I reached for the side arm holstered at his hip and, pulling it free, jumped over him.

The other operator was reaching for his own gun as I burst into the control room.

"Drop it or I'll shoot," I yelled.

He hesitated for a moment. I fired at the meat of his thigh and he cried out, falling back over his chair and dropping the gun. I glanced back down the hallway. The first guy was still down. Kicking the gun back out of reach, I stepped forward, aiming at the man's chest and sizing him up–a small, lean guy with a black buzz cut, face lined with pain.

"How long until launch?"

"Countdown's there," he gestured to the monitor at my elbow, wincing and sliding back to the wall.

I glanced over. In the corner of the video feed from the silo, blocky red numbers were counting down. 12:32. 12:31. 12:30. Twelve and a half minutes.

"How do I stop it?"

"You can't. Not without Fonseco's code. If there's a problem we call him or Vernier. They give us the code to stop it."

"Get up. Walk back to the office."

"Can't walk. My leg."

"Crawl, then. And drag your friend in. Throw your keys over here. Which one is for the office door?"

"Small silver one," he said, taking the keys off his belt and sliding them across the floor. He crawled, leaving a smear of blood behind but not a fatal amount. I followed him and watched as he dragged his much larger companion into the office. Blood had flowed freely from big guy's nose, leaving a puddle on the floor, but it was only a trickle now. He groaned and half opened his eyes.

"Give me his keys, too. And your phones and a watch." Small guy slid them over. "Stay there," I said and closed the door, locking it with his keys. It was a keyed bolt lock on both sides. They would have to break the door down or break through the wall to get out– neither of them was in shape to do that right now. I strapped the watch on, glanced at the countdown clock in the control room, then started a timer. Only about ten minutes left.

I bolted out and up the stairs I had seen. They had to lead to the upper silo hatch. At the top I followed a hallway to a small room, empty, hatch in the opposite wall. The wheel turned easily and the hatch released. Just outside was a catwalk identical to the one I had used at the other silo. I unlatched and lowered it, dropping it into place with a resounding clang, echoes chirping and chittering.

The aperture at the top of the silo gaped open, stars shining above. I hurried to the missile. The hatch resisted. I leaned back and pulled with all my weight, fatigued muscles straining until it released all at once and I fell back sprawling on the diamond plate. Inside, curled into a ball, was the other, older girl, in a dress like Summer's but sapphire colored. There wasn't even a seat–just an empty cone of space, barely big enough for a child—made to hold a nuclear warhead. I reached in and shook her shoulder. Nothing. She was breathing but deep asleep–drugged probably. I got my hands under her arms and dragged her out, across the catwalk and into the room.

Another glance at the operator's watch showed less than five minutes left. I slammed the hatch closed, spun the wheel, then bent down and hefted the girl up over my shoulder in a fireman carry.

Somehow I made it out and down the steps of the pyramid. When I hit the ground, I ran stiffly. The girl was dead weight, her arms bouncing against my back. They had sedated her with something powerful. Summer must have gotten a lighter dose. All the way across the clearing I was expecting to feel the rumble, hear the crackling roar but I made it to the tree line and collapsed behind a big cypress wrapped in strangler fig. I laid the girl down in the soft duff and leaned around the tree. The rumble started then, just a vibration in the air at first, growing louder. Smoke and steam erupted from the vents at the base of the pyramid. The ground shook. A crackling, ripping sound filled my ears and the missile lifted out of the silo, bright fiery tail, shooting up, up, then a thundering boom as it exploded. I ducked behind the tree, covering my ears. Chunks of hot metal rained down. I covered the girl, hunched over her. Finally, I looked up, ears ringing. Smoking debris littered the clearing, smoldering on the damp ground.

The girl snorted and sucked in a deep breath. Her eyes opened but didn't focus, closed again. I picked her up in my arms and she held on instinctually, wrapping her arms around my neck.

"Let's got out of here," I said, eyes burning from the cloud of smoke rolling out from the blast, legs shaking as I stumbled toward the trail.

Five Sikorsky troop transport helicopters crouched raptor-like on the lawn in front of the ranch house. Agents in royal blue FBI labeled jackets stood in small clusters conferring and speaking into radios. I hung back in the shadow of the trees, still carrying the girl. A truck rumbled up the road, pulled to a stop, and disgorged a group of men and woman in riot gear. They milled around for a moment, then, led by one of the agents, jogged off in formation toward the compound.

I spotted Beth's red hair among the agents, then through the open door of a van nearby, I saw Summer with the boy, Elijah. They both sat hunched against the far wall of the van, parked near the edge of the trees. I was pretty sure I could get to them without being observed.

Darting out in a crouch, I scurried to the open door. Summer looked up, confused when I appeared.

"Uncle Justin?"

"Hi, Summer. I have your cousin here. Can you take care of her for me?"

Summer nodded sleepily and I laid the other girl down.

"Okay. Gotta go. Keep her warm and safe."

"I will," she said, snuggling up against the older child.

I darted back to the woods using the van as cover, and plunged in just as a distant sound of automatic weapons firing reached my ears, followed by the dull whump of an explosion. I gave up on moving silently, crashing through the undergrowth like a panicked prey animal, wanting to be as far away as possible from the agents and the shooting. A couple hundred yards in, I stopped at the base of a big old banyan, fitted my back into a fold of its trunk, drew my legs up, and closed my eyes.

I sat like that for a full minute, just breathing and trying to calm down. What now? I had saved two children. The last one was safe. What was the plan again? Rendezvous at the jeep? My ears still rang from the explosion. My lungs still burned. I could smell acrid smoke in the air. Was something else on fire? I needed to contact Ashna. I was supposed to meet her and Malena. I patted my cargo pockets absentmindedly, feeling for her map, remembered it was long gone, but felt something else and drew it out. A phone! One of the phones I took from the silo operators. I dialed Ashna's number on the chunky, ruggedized keypad and hit the green button.

"Justin?"

"Yeah. I'm in the woods. Where are you?"

"Also in the woods. Near where I left the jeep. It's no good. They have the road closed off. Cops and military everywhere patrolling. Searching."

"Shit. What now?"

"Didn't you say there was a plane?"

"Yeah, we flew in on a plane."

"What kind? Where?"

"Airstrip. South of the ranch house maybe a mile. On a kind of plateau. It's a DC3. Antique."

"Okay, meet us there."

"Who's going to fly it?"

"I am. Never flown a DC3 before but I think I can handle it."

"I know you were taking lessons but did you ever actually get licensed?"

"Of course not. You know I don't want my name attached to anything official. No papers. No licenses. No bank accounts. Do you really think a representative from the FAA is going to be standing next to the airstrip demanding to see my fucking pilot license before they clear me to steal an unmarked smuggler plane and fly it out of Costa Rica?"

"Okay. How far away are you?"

"Already south of the ranch house. Not far."

"Me, too. I'll see you there soon." More gunfire pounded through the night.

"Shit, the cult members must be fighting."

"They're pretty well armed."

"Let's get the hell out of here."

I headed southwest through the forest, crossed a

stream, and eventually came out on the trail we had walked the night I arrived. The grade was steep, climbing, and the trees grew sparser as I went, the ground rockier. A small animal scurried away into the shadows. An owl hooted.

"Too late," I whispered to the owl as I climbed. "You're supposed to be a harbinger of death. The death already happened. Still happening I guess..." I broke off, realizing my whisper was taking on a borderline hysterical tone.

The trail ended, the terrain leveled, and I scrambled up onto the plateau. At the far end of the airstrip, the plane sat, upper parts glowing with a patina of dust and moonlight. A light shone from the cockpit. The cargo door was open. I headed across at a limping jog, my body protesting. Something flickered in my peripheral vision and I looked left. Another figure loped forward, also heading toward the plane. Malena or Ashna? No, too big. A man. I picked up my pace. He also sped up, aware of me. He was ahead. His trajectory would get him there first but he was slowing again, running out of steam. Giving up on beating me to the plane, he turned to head me off. Ten feet apart, thirty feet short of the plane, we both stopped.

"Justin," Fonseco gasped, breathing hard. "Congratulations. It was you, wasn't it? You disabled the missiles." He held a briefcase in one hand and a hand gun in the other—a lethal looking automatic.

"Yes. It was me."

"You fucked everything up," he spat. "Did you call in the police as well? Or was it that bitch with the red hair?" He broke off and looked back over his shoulder. Someone else was approaching now. We both waited as he jogged forward, clearly struggling, gasping. Dr. Vernier stopped near Fonseco, bent over and heaving.

"Devlin. You have to take me with you."

With a casual violence, Fonseco swung the briefcase, catching Vernier full on the side of the head and knocking him to the ground.

"You're no use to me now," he said, looking down at the prone scientist.

I sprang, going for Fonseco's legs, locking arms around his knees and putting my shoulder in his midsection. He fired the gun, missing me and falling hard on his back. I slammed my fist down on his gun hand, smashing it against the tarmac. The gun fired again as his trigger finger convulsed and the bullet went skittering harmlessly across the airstrip. I smashed his hand again and he let go of the gun, grunting with pain. His body spasmed and he bucked me off. On my feet first, I aimed a kick at his face and sent him sprawling.

"Justin," he said, wiping at a stream of blood from his nose. "Stop. I'm your father. We can work together."

"What is this, Star Wars? You're not anyone's father. You're a sperm donor. And a fucking psychopath."

He tried to rise and I kicked him again. He fell on his back and groaned. I reached down and took the briefcase, picked up the gun. The DC3's engines whined to life behind me.

"Have fun explaining everything to the FBI," I said, and turned away, hurling the gun into the brush at the edge of the airstrip.

Malena was there at the cargo door. She reached a hand out for me and I took it. Somehow, she pulled me up. Ashna had the plane moving before the door was closed. With a sickening rush of G force, the plane sped up and lifted away, leaving the compound, the pyramids, the ranch, Fonseco, and everything else behind. I closed my eyes. Malena, seated next to me, rested her head on my shoulder.

"Thank God," she whispered. "Thank God we're out. I didn't think we would get out."

Chapter 23

Coda
1/23-3/20: San Francisco, and Helem, UT

"Here. You should have this." Ashna slid a piece of paper across the table, pushing aside an empty platter that had been stacked with sushi not long before.

"What is this?" I picked it up. Frayed and crumpled, dirty and water stained, it looked like it had been through some hard times. "Something you found in the gutter?"

I unfolded it. The sheet I had torn from Fonseco's file.

"I kept it."

"I thought I lost it."

"No. You left it with the rest of your stuff at Sam's shack in the woods when you went off to be a hero."

"Thanks." I began to fold it back up.

"Wait. I think there's something on there you might not have noticed."

"Where?" I laid it out flat on the table.

"There," Ashna pointed.

At the bottom of the page it said 'Parents:'. How did I not notice it before? I had been agitated, sleep deprived, in a state of near collapse. I read the line. Devlin Fonseco, father. So he hadn't been lying. Next to his name: Linda Hathale, mother.

"Linda," I said, looking up, remembering Linda's

market and the woman named Linda behind the counter. *I was one of the originals out there at the school,* she had said. One of the originals at the ranch too? She hadn't told me. Her age was right.

"What?" Ashna asked.

"Nothing. It's just…I met someone named Linda. In Utah."

"At the commune?"

"No. An ex-member. She ran a store in town. I stayed in a little rental cabin she had out back when I first got there."

"Unusual name. Probably not hard to check."

****

"The children are in short-term foster care, waiting for a placement."

"We're their closest living relatives," Malena said.

"I know but it's not that simple." Agent Beth Fields leaned back in her chair, arms crossed. She looked different in a pants suit and blouse, makeup, hair carefully controlled in a pony tail. Still no-nonsense but professional grade. "How are you going to support them?"

"I'm getting my teaching credential," Malena said, looking down at her hands which were nervously twisting a napkin into knots. "And Justin will help. He already bought this house. It's enough space for me and the kids."

"And what will your role be in their lives," Beth asked, turning her gaze to me.

"Uncle Justin," I answered. "I'll make sure they have what they need. I'm not really cut out to be a father but I think I can be the fun uncle who takes them camping and skydiving and teaches them how to pick locks."

"Very funny. Well, I'll see what I can do. It certainly makes sense for them to be with a relative instead of strangers. I'm sure I can arrange it. Do you intend to adopt them formally?"

"Of course," Malena answered. "They need stability and good home after what they've been through."

"Good," Beth nodded.

"What about Fonseco?" I asked. "And Eleanor Jane Sibyl? And Dr. Vernier? Can you tell me anything now? Did you get them?"

"Wait," Beth said, thinking. "Information for information. Where's the plane?"

"What plane?"

"I'm not stupid, Justin. You didn't walk out of there. And you didn't drive. Fonseco and Vernier were captured at the airstrip. Only a few minutes before, a plane took off. Two agents saw it. They were on their way up the hill. That plane is evidence. We need to retrieve it."

"Okay, yes, we flew. It was Fonseco's plane. He was smuggling the rocket parts in it. A DC3."

"Where did you leave it?"

"I can give you the GPS coordinates. I made a note. I'll email you later. It's in Nicaragua. An abandoned airstrip we found in the jungle. Pretty overgrown. Probably a smuggler operation."

"Who flew the plane? You?"

"No, that's not one of my skills."

"I wouldn't be surprised."

"Someone else. I can't tell you who."

"You were both on the plane, then? Plus a pilot?"

"Yes," Malena murmured.

"We had two fighter jets on standby at Solo Cano you know? If we hadn't found Fonseco they probably would have intercepted you. Lucky you didn't get shot down. I wanted to scramble them anyway but I got overruled. Apparently it costs about thirty thousand dollars an hour to have one of those fighters in the air." She looked at me, exasperated. "Fine. You don't have to tell me who flew it. They're all in custody in Costa Rica," she said. "Fonseco. Vernier. Sibyl. I can't give you any more details. They will not be going free any time soon though. I promise you that."

After Agent Beth left, Malena and I sat in the kitchen of the house we had purchased in Oakland for her and the kids, sipping coffee and thinking our own thoughts. The briefcase I took from Fonseco before getting on the plane had contained $2.4 million in hundred dollar bills–just enough to buy a four bedroom Victorian fixer in Oakland's Temescal neighborhood after my old fence Domenico helped me launder it and took his sizable cut.

It felt comfortable to sit there with Malena. We were getting to know each other again after so long apart. The old closeness was still there but we were different people now. In my closet, an old leather biker jacket hung that I used to wear every day when I was in college. I hadn't worn it for years. If I put it on now, I would remember the feel of it, the weight, the way the zippers sounded, the smell of the mink oil I used to rub into it but it would take time for the jacket to reshape and conform to my changed body, the way I moved now, the way I held myself, and for me to readapt to the way the shoulder seam rubbed and the right pocket had a hole in the lining where things got lost. Our relationship was like that–an old jacket, abandoned for years. We were wearing it together though, rediscovering it together.

"I can't wait for them to be here," Malena said, looking up, imagining the children in her kitchen. Summer, Yarrow, and Elijah.

"They are going to be hurt," I said. "They'll need a lot of care. We should find a counselor."

"I know," Malena nodded. "It will take time. What are you going to do?" She asked, changing the subject. "Are you going to go see her?"

"Yes, I think so. In a little while. I'm not ready to go back there yet."

"Neither am I. That town." She shuddered. "And the commune. Cold. An unhappy place. What do you think they're doing now? Do they know what happened in Costa Rica?"

"I don't know. I hope they're just carrying on."

****

On March 20th, the first day of spring, I pulled into Helem, Utah, my mind calmed and nearly hypnotized by hours on the road, red rock canyons and bluffs scrolling by, blue, cloudless sky, Bach violin sonatas on the stereo.

I passed the same long, low steel building beside the highway, one lone pickup still parked next to it, dark afternoon shadows stretching out from both. The butte rose up behind it, afternoon light golden red, picking out every detail.

I passed Lucky's Grill and saw the staff readying for the dinner rush, mopping floors, putting out place settings, behind the big plate glass windows.

LINDA'S MARKET came up on my right. I pulled up in front and stopped the engine. For a while I just sat there in the car, mind blank, listening to the echoes of the music in my head, dying into silence. I opened the console and pulled out the tattered piece of paper, looked at it once more, looked up. I could see Linda inside, seated behind the counter, facing away. She turned when I closed the car door and peered at me through the window, then her face changed and she smiled, recognizing me.

I waved and walked toward her.

A word about the author...

I am a writer, teacher, and educational technology professional. I was born in the Midwest and grew up in Seattle but have been slowly migrating southward with stops in Portland, Eugene, San Francisco, and now Los Angeles where I live with my wife, son, and JiJi the cat. I studied Dance and English Literature as an undergraduate and Anthropology in grad school. Before embarking on my current career, I worked as a professional ballet dancer.

http://bradleywwright.com

Thank you for purchasing
this publication of The Wild Rose Press, Inc.
For questions or more information
contact us at
info@thewildrosepress.com.
The Wild Rose Press, Inc.
www.thewildrosepress.com